C000147834

OTHER AUTHOR HOUSE BOOKS BY JACK DOLD

Crosshairs

You Don't Stop Living

Boris

Eva

Canada — The World Next Door

Family on the Move

And the Swan Died

THE MAN IN A VACUUM

JACK DOLD

authorHOUSE®

AuthorHouse™
1663 Liberty Drive
Bloomington, IN 47403
www.authorhouse.com
Phone: 1 (800) 839-8640

Published by AuthorHouse 10/28/2019

Front Cover Design: Kasey de Caussin

ISBN: 978-1-7283-3346-5 (sc)
ISBN: 978-1-7283-3345-8 (hc)
ISBN: 978-1-7283-3344-1 (e)

Library of Congress Control Number: 2019917134

Print information available on the last page.

This book is printed on acid-free paper.

ARTEMUS WEBB

Artemus Webb was a depression baby, born on a winter night in 1934 to Darius and Melinda Webb in Hingham, Massachusetts in the shadow of the venerable Old Ship Church. There he was baptized into the Congregational practice, where from an early age he was imbued with the Protestant Ethic. Darius Webb was prominent in the burgeoning ship building industry in nearby Quincy. He ascribed to the belief that life had only one goal—to make money through hard work. Anything that distracted a person from that goal was to be eliminated, a philosophy that Artemus heard from the first moment he could remember. Toys were not permitted in the Webb house unless they had a function—small lawn mowers, carpet sweepers, flash cards for reading and math. The book supply was extremely limited. As soon as Artemus discovered that he didn't know anything his classmates were talking about where toys were concerned, he stopped talking to them, becoming a loner, and consequently, a deep concern of all his teachers. His father, however, brushed off those concerns as the ravings of people who didn't have a serious approach to living.

Artemis attended Derby Academy in Hingham, the best of the town's private elementary schools. He was easily the tallest boy in his class, by the 6th grade almost 5'10", and skeleton thin. He was a very fine student, usually at the top of his class in just about every subject. He didn't participate in any of the extra-curricular activities offered by the school, all of which were proscribed by his father's strict precepts. If it bothered him, he never showed it.

After school he often biked to Quincy to visit his father's shipyard. Serious from the start, he wandered almost unnoticed around the plant, absorbing the interactions of workers, bosses and office staff. Carefully he catalogued the things he would change when he came of age. At twelve years old, Darius Webb gave him a job on the factory floor, sweeping up metal shavings, oiling some of the smaller machines, running errands. He soon became obnoxiously vocal in pointing out the misdeeds and malingering of the workers and was quickly shunned by most of them. One bright morning in late winter, he was riding his bike to the beach on Walton Cove, when he found himself surrounded by older school boys, mostly from Quincy High.

"Where do you think you're going, snitch?" one of them asked sarcastically.

"Get out of my way," Artemus said, jumping off his bike, tossing it to the ground, confronting the largest of the boys.

"Not on your life, you little turd. We're here to convince you that you ought to keep your mouth shut."

The boy took a swing at Artemus' head, barely missing its mark. Artemis connected with an uppercut beneath the bully's ribs which doubled him over. In that moment, Artemus learned a valuable lesson about people. He saw the hint of fear replace hatred in the boy's eyes. The others in the gang quickly jumped him and he was pummeled into unconsciousness. They battered his bike, and left it bent and broken alongside his inert body. A neighbor, hearing the commotion outside, found Artemis lying on the sidewalk. The boy was taken to the emergency room at Hingham Hospital.

"Who did this?" Darius Webb asked when he arrived at the hospital and saw his battered son.

"I don't know, father. I never saw any of them before," Artemus lied. "I think they were from Southie. One of them had an Irish accent."

He was released the next morning, sporting a badly cut mouth, a couple of black eyes and a cracked rib. The following day he was back on a new bike, heading for the shore, something he repeated every day after school, defying the bullies to confront him again.

"Can I buy some weights?" he asked his father the week after he was released from the hospital. The Webb house in Hingham occupied almost five acres along the shore. One of the outbuildings covered a large coal-burning boiler that sent steam through pipes to keep the garages and cellars warm in winter. Above ground the building had once served as a workshop for the property but was now filled haphazardly with old wicker furniture and random house castoffs. Artemus cleared out the debris and converted the shed into his weight room, where every morning before school, and every night after dinner, he tested his body with ever-increasing weights. By summer that year, the effects of the strenuous workouts were starting to show. He was benching 200 pounds and his tall, slender frame began noticeably to bulk out with new muscle.

Artemus had imprinted in his memory the face of every one of his attackers. He watched them after school to determine their habits, and after a month of stalking he was ready for action. He began with the leader, in whose eyes he had first detected fear.

"Where are you going punk?" he asked after he had stopped the boy on a back street. "Remember me?"

"What do you want, Webb? Get out of my way or I'll beat the shit out of you again."

"I want you to try. I don't see any of your friends around this time. Let's go over to that vacant lot, shall we?"

He bestowed a terrible beating on the boy that afternoon, leaving him bleeding and crying in the dirt. If anyone had been around, they would have seen Artemis with a vicious grin on his face as he left the battlefield. One by one, he avenged himself on the entire gang who had put him in the hospital, until finally he figured the debt had been repaid. Word of Artemus' reprisals spread quickly in the student grapevine at both Derby Academy and Quincy High School. By the end of summer, he could discern fear in the face of every boy he encountered. He would never again be challenged. The girls were generally intrigued, but they too kept their distance.

"Have you noticed, Darius, that our son doesn't seem to have any friends?" Melinda asked her husband one evening as Artemus was nearing the end of his elementary schooling. "I don't think he has ever brought a classmate home with him, and I don't think he has attended a single dance or school rally. Do you think we should have Doctor Samuels look at him? Perhaps there is something physically wrong."

"That's nonsense, my dear," her husband responded. "Artemus is just a serious boy, not attracted by all of the tomfoolery his classmates seem to enjoy. He'll be fine when he gets into high school."

"Where are we going to send him? Most of his classmates are going to Andover. He'll be the same loner there, I'm afraid."

"Then we'll send him somewhere else. Maybe that fight he got into a year ago made him afraid of the boys in school, although he doesn't seem afraid of anything. I'll ask around about the other schools."

They sent him off to Deerfield Academy in Western Massachusetts, a venerable old school nestled in a second-generation village in the northern part of the Pioneer Valley. By this time he was a muscular 6'2", nearly 200 pounds. The football coach got very excited when he saw Artemus get out of his parent's car. His excitement was short-lived.

"No, I don't want to go out for football," Artemus told him laconically. "I guess I've never been much of a team player."

"But you have the size to be a great player, son."

"I said I didn't want to play football. And I'm not your son."

The basketball and wrestling coaches never even approached him.

❧

"Don't you ever relax, Artemus?" Jason Burr, his roommate at Deerfield asked one night in the spring of the first year. "You've been in the books since the day you got here. You skipped all the dances and didn't go to any of the football or basketball games. Don't you want to have any fun?"

"I'm having fun, Jason," Artemus responded, leaning back in his chair with something close to a smile. "I'm learning how to make a fortune. Why are we in school? To learn how to make money. I don't give a rat's ass about football games and sock hops. I'll do that later, after I have made my fortune."

"And by that time, you'll be so full of yourself, you won't have time for anyone else. Good luck to that!"

Jason stomped out of the room, completely exasperated. He had been egged on to confront Artemus by some of their classmates, who regarded his roommate as something of a freak. To say that Artemus had been antisocial was giving him the benefit of the doubt.

He got straight "A" in every course that involved math, business, literature and history. He flunked fine arts, not turning in a single paper or answering any of the test questions. This was a great concern for both the faculty and administration. Deerfield Academy sat in the middle of the village, known as Historic Deerfield. Nearly every house, most of them from the 18th century, some even dating back to the Deerfield Massacre of 1704, maintained an art collection of national repute. Decorative Arts was at the very heart of Deerfield, and the Academy had made a reputation by exposing the students to the best in American decorative and fine arts. Artemus exhibited the complete contradiction of the school's fundamental mission statement. In addition, he absolutely refused to participate in any athletic activities, not even showing up for his classes in physical education. Personally, he followed a rigorous training schedule that included long sprints, literally around the entire village, and hours of work with the dead weights at the gymnasium. Without question, he was the most physically fit student in the entire Academy. The coach of every sport the school offered drooled at the thought of somehow enticing him to their team.

The conundrum of Artemus Webb filled the discussions in the faculty rooms as well as the administration. And in the student body, sarcasm began to make itself public.

"What's our mascot this year?

"A muscle-bound sociopath!"

"Does it have a name?"

"Art Emus. He's a menace!"

Finally, James Friary, Deerfield's headmaster, put in a phone call to Darius and Melinda Webb.

"Mr. Webb, we would like to have a conference with you about your son."

"Artemus? Is he in trouble?"

"Frankly, Mr. Webb, we're not at all sure. Can you please come to the school?"

"Of course, when do you want us there?"

"As soon as possible. Is tomorrow too soon?"

"It's a four-hour ride. We can be there in the afternoon."

Darius Webb immediately phoned his son at the dorm.

"Artemus, we have been called to a meeting with Headmaster Friary. What is this all about?"

"I have no idea, father," Artemus responded in his usual monotone. "Maybe they're upset with my art grades. I can't stand those classes. But all of my other grades are fine."

"There's a reason they phoned, and I think you know what it is. We will be there at noon tomorrow. I want you to meet us in front of the Brick Church. We'll get lunch at the Inn and talk. This is serious, Artemus, or they wouldn't want us to come there so quickly. I will want the truth tomorrow. That gives you the night to consider your answers."

Artemus was sitting on the steps of the Brick Church when his parents arrived. They parked behind the Hall Tavern across the street, and with a fair amount of trepidation, walked over to greet their son. During the long drive from Hingham, it occurred to them that this was perhaps the first time they had ever had a serious conversation with Artemus. Artemus gave his mother a perfunctory kiss and nodded to his father.

"Let's get a table at the Inn. We can talk there," Darius declared. He turned and walked away, his wife and son trailing behind.

Once seated, he wasted no time in broaching the subject.

"Now, what is all of this about, Artemus? I want a brief and precise answer."

"They think I'm too antisocial."

"What exactly does that mean?"

"They are upset because I don't go to any of the games or dances. I don't socialize with the other students. I just go to class, work out by myself, and go my own way."

"Don't you want any social life, Artemus?" Melinda Webb asked, concern in her voice. "It's the same as the Derby School, Darius," she continued, turning to her husband. "Artemus didn't have any friends there either."

"Is that all, Artemus?" his father demanded, ignoring his wife. "You aren't a cheerleader and they aren't pleased?"

"That's it exactly. I have been called in half a dozen times. They say it's not normal to be a loner. I keep telling them that I am here to learn and to become a rich man. They want all of that other bullshit."

"Artemus!" his mother gasped.

"Leave the boy alone, Melinda. He's right. If that's their problem, this will be a short meeting. Now, what do you want for lunch? The Deerfield Inn is famous for the chicken pot pie. That long ride has made me hungry."

Headmaster Friary had always postulated to whomever would listen that a son is a younger version of the father. He was not at all comfortable in calling Darius Webb to this meeting, but his sense of duty overcame his trepidation. He was dreading what he was certain would be a highly uncomfortable conversation. He was sitting behind his desk when his secretary escorted the Webb family into his office. He didn't have time even to stand and greet his visitors.

"All right, Headmaster. Here we are. What is the great urgency that calls me away from my shipyard in the middle of a busy week? Is my son failing in his classes?"

"No, he is doing very well, with the exception of fine arts, but we can make some adjustments in that area. In fact, Artemus is a fine student."

"Has he been caught in a felony? Or been involved with alcohol or drugs?"

"No, nothing of that sort."

"Then what the hell am I doing here?"

Headmaster Friary had been searching for an opening.

"Mr. Webb, your son does not fit in with the philosophy of this school. He is antisocial in the extreme, and his education is not filling out as we expect it should."

"What on earth is that supposed to mean, sir? 'Not filling out?' What kind of gibberish is that?"

"It is no sort of gibberish, as you put it, sir." The headmaster retorted, with an edge to his voice. "A Deerfield graduate is not only a careful thinker, and a developed athlete; he has also been educated to fit in as a productive member of the social world. Thus far, your son has totally avoided any opportunity to participate in anything remotely social. He does not so much as converse with his school mates outside of classroom intercourse. I would think that this would be of concern to you and Mrs. Webb, as much as it is to us."

Darius Webb could barely control himself. He clenched both fists which were resting on his lap, then relaxed them, rubbed both hands across his thighs and let out a long sigh.

"Sir," he began, clipping his words as though they were weapons. "We are paying a great deal of money to send our son to this school, with the goal of preparing him for his rightful place in the world of business. All that concerns Mrs. Webb and me is that he excels in the classroom. I don't give a tinker's dam about his social life. What he chooses to do when his studies are done each day is his to decide. When he leaves this school, he will go to a world where they don't have badminton games or sock hops after the work is done. In our world, we take our work home with us. We don't fritter away our free time with meaningless trivia."

"Prep school athletics are hardly meaningless. They teach the student..."

"Spare me the sermon, sir. You want my son to play football because he's the biggest and strongest athlete in your school. Winning a football game teaches the athlete nothing. Winning a football game makes your alumni want to donate more to your bank account. Don't give me all that baloney about life lessons. Do your job headmaster. Teach my son mathematics and business models and whatever it is that history has to teach him."

Melinda Webb put her hand on her husband's arm to try to calm him a bit. He had grown beet red in the face. Artemus, for his part, studied Headmaster Friary, carefully observing the emotions that played out in his face and body language, clearly showing the strain of the verbal onslaught directed at him.

"What are your intentions with my son, headmaster? Is he under probation for not dancing to your tune?"

Mr. Friary shifted slightly in his chair, interlocking his fingers, his chin resting on his upraised thumbs, considering his response.

"Mr. Webb, your son's lack of social and athletic participation is almost unheard of in any prep school, much less Deerfield Academy. I would think that it would be of grave importance to you and Mrs. Webb, that Artemus develops fully as a human being. If it is not of concern to you then this meeting has wasted your time and mine. I apologize for asking you to drive this long distance for no reason."

"Leave Mrs. Webb out of this. You didn't answer my question. What are your intentions where my son is concerned?"

"I have no intentions, sir. As long as his classroom grades are up to our standards, he is a welcome member of Deerfield Academy."

Headmaster Friary rose.

"Thank you for coming in, Mr. Webb, Mrs. Webb. I hope you have a pleasant journey home."

Mid-way through his sophomore year, Artemus turned sixteen, got his driver's license and asked his father for a car.

"Why do you need a car?" his father demanded. "It will just distract you from your duties."

Artemus was fully prepared for the objection.

"Father, Deerfield is in the middle of the Mohawk Trail, and that crosses the Connecticut Valley. There are hundreds of miles of mills and factories that produce everything from power tools to Windsor chairs and plastic combs. I want to start studying how they work."

"What do you mean, 'studying'?" his father asked, somewhat surprised by the argument.

"They are all dying, Father. I have been reading about those mills. I want to know why they are dying. Maybe there is an opportunity there."

"Those owners won't let a kid just walk in and start snooping around. I wouldn't. You wouldn't get as far as the front gate of my shipyard."

"I would if I told you I was working on a school research project, and Webb Shipyards was sponsoring me."

Darius Webb smiled and pushed back in his chair.

"Okay, Artemus. We'll go up to Good Chevrolet in Boston next weekend. But you are getting nothing fancy."

He drove back to Deerfield in a brand-new royal blue '47 Chevy, a coupe that would make him the envy of every boy at Deerfield Academy. From that day on, every spare minute found him somewhere along Highway 20 in Western Massachusetts, or down in Springfield or Hartford, visiting towns that were perched along the many rivers, where water powered some of the first mills in America. Each town seemed to have a specialty. Gardner was the Chair City. Leominster was the pioneer in plastics, filled with factories that spewed out combs, brushes and mirrors, even pink flamingos and Foster Grants, the first plastic sunglasses in America. Millers Falls manufactured small power tools, its huge plant spreading from Greenfield south to Deerfield. Sawmills in Erving supplied two chair factories as well as a million telephone poles a year. Half of the towns around Springfield manufactured some sort of firearm—Enfield, Southwick, West Springfield, Hartford. From colonial days on, Connecticut was rightfully regarded as the center of American industry—almost all of it, water-powered.

One day toward the end of his sophomore year, his history teacher, Mr. Phelps, singled him out in class.

"Mr. Webb, would you be so kind as to meet me here after school today?"

Sydney Phelps was new to Deerfield Academy that year, engaged to teach American history and Civics. He had attended nearby Amherst College, where he finished near the top of his class. He was a small man with a long, waspish nose, a skinny voice, a full head of thinning hair and acne. A quiet man by nature, he struggled with class discipline during this first year, and his future as a high school teacher was considered by the administration to be dubious at best. Without question, he was highly qualified in his subject, but seldom was he able to communicate his knowledge in his rowdy classroom. His students quickly came to regard his American history class as playtime. The one exception was Artemus Webb, whose fearsome scowl was the only moderating factor in the room.

"Mr. Webb, I understand that you have been visiting many of the factory towns in the region," Sydney Phelps opened their discussion one afternoon after school had let out. "I would like to make you a proposal. If you would be willing to put your explorations into a term paper, I think I can assist you in opening doors, and perhaps give you a bit of background on some of these companies."

"I'm not interested in writing any report," Artemus responded quietly.

"Why are you doing this then?"

"I want to know how these factories operate. Before long I will have one of my own to run."

Phelps looked into his student's eyes. "Really?"

"My father owns a shipyard in Quincy. I am his only son."

"So you have a goal in mind for your explorations."

Artemus responded as though this were an infantile idea.

"Of course I have a goal. Why would I do it otherwise?"

Taken back by the young man's curt reaction, Phelps turned the subject.

"Have you made any observations thus far?"

"They are all dying, or dead."

"And that is precisely why I would like to assist you, Mr. Webb."

"I don't need help."

"Have you been to Plymouth?"

"No."

"Go take a look at the Plymouth Cordage Factory."

"Why?"

"It has lessons to teach. I'll have a letter of introduction for you in class tomorrow."

With that, Sydney Phelps stacked up his books and walked out of the room, leaving Artemus with a bemused look on his face.

❧

It was the biggest rope factory in the world, an enormous complex that rambled along the shore of Cape Cod Bay, just north of Plymouth in the town of Kingston. Most of the citizens of those towns were employed at the place, to produce the lifelines of the sailing and shipping industry. Founded when the sailing ship ruled the commerce of the seas, it had prospered especially during the recent war, buoyed up by defense contracts which supplied the largest navy in U.S. history.

Artemus was met at the office beneath the Cordage Tower by a middle age man wearing a rather threadbare, blue suit and bow tie.

"Mr. Webb? I am Charles Pedri. Mr. Caldicott, the superintendent, asked me to give you a tour of the plant. I understand you are doing a report on Massachusetts industries. I must admit, I was expecting someone older. They said you were from Amherst College."

"I am doing a term paper sponsored by Amherst, Mr. Pedri. I appreciate your time and help."

"Well then, shall we proceed?"

Artemus was led along what seemed an endless series of ropewalks, where fine hemp was wound into the classic ropes of the maritime industry. The building hummed with activity, well-trained workers monitoring the engines that slowly twisted the rope.

"Are all of the ropes made with hemp?" Artemus inquired when they had entered a relatively quiet area.

"Yes, it makes far and away the strongest, finest quality lines."

"I read that there were other fibers appearing on the market."

"Those synthetic ropes?" Mr. Pedri snapped out the word "synthetic," with obvious scorn. "They won't stand up to the needs of the industry. There will never be an adequate substitute for hemp."

❧

"What did you learn?" was Sydney Phelps' curt question when he met with Artemus a few days later.

"That healthy bodies often hide a fatal disease."

"Very good, Mr. Webb. Very good. Anything else?"

"Nothing that I didn't already know."

"Give me two things you already knew."

"I already knew that if you don't change, you die."

"And?"

"That labor is a luxury."

Phelps tried not to raise an eyebrow but failed. He succeeded in suppressing a smile.

"So even though Plymouth Cordage just announced one of its biggest profits, you would not invest in it?"

"No."

"Where would you put your money then?"

"In nylon."

The teacher wanted desperately to hug this enigmatic and brilliant boy, but knew that if he did, all chance of a teacher-student breakthrough would be lost. Phelps stood and walked behind his desk, where he shuffled through some papers. Finding the one he sought, he handed it to Artemis.

"You will need two days for this one. I'll get you excused from school."

It was a letter of introduction to the Amoskeag Industries, in Manchester, New Hampshire.

❧

Amoskeag Manufacturing Company had once been the largest textile plant in the world, far outstripping those of the city's namesake, Manchester, England. Almost 25,000 looms were capable of churning out a quarter of a billion yards of material in a single year, employing an army of 75,000 employees.

Artemus drove into a picture of abandonment. Manchester no longer had to endure the cacophony of machine thunder that had assaulted the ears of its worker-citizens, because the mills had shut down more than a decade before. He stopped at the Amoskeag Bank in the center of town, at ten stories once the "skyscraper" of Northern New England. There he was directed to the office of Harvey Milbury, the vice president of Amoskeag Industries.

"I have a busy schedule for you, Mr. Webb. Your teacher, Mr. Phelps said you were interested in what happened to the textile industry here and what we are doing to replace it. I personally find it refreshing that a young man would be interested in such things," he said with a degree of condescension and slap on the back that Artemus managed to ignore. "I think you will find it illuminating."

He walked Artemus through blocks of abandoned brick buildings, most of them at least four stories in height. Inside were the remains of perhaps ten percent of the machinery that once operated there, churning out the material that had secured the wealth of New England during the industrial age. Artemus sat through a half-hour movie relating the history of the industry in America, ending before the fatal collapse a decade earlier. There was little sign of life along the river where once thousands of people had toiled.

"What are you going to do with all of these empty buildings, Mr. Milbury?" Artemus asked quietly.

"We intend to rehab them for modern uses—as senior housing, shopping malls, small industries."

"What will the people do who live here?" the boy asked.

"They will work in city services, and in small businesses they create."

Artemus was about to object, but held back, simply nodding.

❧

"I'll ask you the same question as I did for Plymouth, Mr. Webb. What did you learn?"

"They should dynamite that city and start over."

"Only that? I'll admit that the factories are closed, but wouldn't you rather rehabilitate them?"

"There was nothing along that river when they first built those factories. They managed to support a city for more than a hundred years with that first investment," Artemus said, surprising his teacher with the flow of words. "That's a very good return on their money. They should do it again. Those buildings were meant for a specific purpose, not for whatever someone can adapt them to."

"You mean demolish the plants and start over?"

"I just said that, Mr. Phelps."

"Yes, you did. Do you have a plan for finding someone willing to make that investment?"

"I do."

This declaration was followed by silence, that neither teacher nor student was willing to break.

"I have another assignment if you wish to take it," Sydney Phelps finally volunteered.

"Why?" was the monotone rejoinder.

"Why what?"

"Why are you doing this, Mr. Phelps? Why do you care what I do?"

"Because of all of my students, you are the only one who is really studying something useful, Mr. Webb."

"What is useful about visiting dead factories?"

"Thinking." He bestowed the tiniest of smiles on his hesitant student. "Something you might not do on a football field."

"I'll write the report, Mr. Phelps."

"Well, Artemus, have you learned anything from all of your factory visits?" Darius Webb asked when his son returned from school at the end of June.

"I've learned that our company won't survive very long unless you change it, father," Artemis responded laconically. "Our plant is getting old. Our workers are too expensive. Our ships are going to be outmoded before long. I'll send you my term paper when it's finished."

"Not a very optimistic report as it is," his father answered, looking up in curiosity at the stoic demeanor of his son. "I don't see our economy as very weak at all. In fact, many parts of New England are booming right now, including the ship works in Quincy."

"The shoe industry in Lynn and Brockton have moved to Europe. The textile plants are all in the south, or in Asia. The furniture factories are mostly closed, reopened in Carolina. All I have seen so far are the empty carcasses of brick and stone factories, spread along rivers with mills that no longer can be water powered. New England is dying. And Webb Ship Works will too if changes aren't made immediately."

Darius Webb lit a cigarette, took a deep drag and considered his response carefully.

"I don't know what they are teaching you in that damned prep school you are in, but I'm not going to write another check if those are the ideas they are putting in your head. Our company has just experienced the best five years in our history, and you stand there and announce we are going to die. Artemus, I've about had it with your 'I don't give a shit,' know-it-all attitude. You speak to nobody in your school. You won't join any of the clubs. You have no friends. Instead, you drive around the country looking at old factories and announce that the sky is falling. I should never have bought you that car."

He slammed his fist down on his desk, glaring at his son.

"You will report to work on Monday morning at 8:00. You're going to see just how decrepit Webb Shipyards really is."

Artemus discovered a new reality when he showed up for work that Monday. He no longer held the position of favorite son in his father's factory, and he was thrilled. Working as a welder's apprentice, he did double shifts except on Fridays on a large contract to repair military ships that had survived the war. They were being refitted for sale to Third-World countries. His uncomplaining effort gradually gained him a grudging respect from his follow workers, who were at first deeply suspicious of the "boss's son," the snitch during his grammar school days.

At the suggestion of Sydney Phelps, Artemus approached this summer job with the same detached attitude that he had accorded the many factories he visited during the school year, carefully observing the systems at work, the age of the equipment and the direction of the contracts his father was writing. By the end of the summer, he concluded that his earlier appraisal which had so aroused the wrath of his father was completely accurate. It would be the subject of the paper he had agreed to write.

Life settled in for Artemus during his junior year. Under the direction of Sydney Phelps, who somehow had retained his job after a tumultuous first year, Artemus expanded his investigations of American industry.

"You've seen the skeletons of the old factories, Artemus. Where did the businesses go? Or did they just cease to function?" And if they are gone, what is going to take their place?"

"They're gone, moved to places that have cheaper labor. There's nothing left but outmoded plants. I don't see what can possibly take their place."

"That's not an acceptable answer and you know it. There are ten million people living in New England. They can't live on yesterday. There has to be a tomorrow."

"New England is in a depression right now. People are out of work in virtually every town. There's nothing to do."

"Do depressions last forever?"

"I think it's possible."

"I think you are getting lazy. Start looking for the future. If Webb Shipyard's days are numbered, as you assert they are, what are you going to do with it? It's going to be yours you say. Are you saying that your inheritance is worthless and there is nothing you can do about it?"

"I would sell it before it goes under."

"Who would buy it? Other investors are looking at the same things that you are. Do you think you are smarter than everyone else?"

"Yes."

"Mr. Webb, that is the first mistake I have ever seen you make."

Sydney Phelps walked out of the room.

❧

"Mr. Phelps, here is the first draft of my term paper."

"Thank you, Mr. Webb. I will look forward to reading it. Does it have a title?"

"Of course, it does," Artemus snapped.

"I mean a *meaningful* title. But I think you know that."

"It's meaningful to me."

"Yes?"

"It's called, 'The Future of America's Shipbuilding Industry.'"

"I see. So you have decided it does have a future?"

"Not in America."

❧

"Webb, we're all going over to the Q after work. Want to join us?" Joe Callahan, one of the welders, asked late one afternoon.

"What's the Q?"

"Only the most authentic pub in America. You ever had a boilermaker?"

"What's that?"

"Something you have to get good at—whiskey and beer."

"I'm only seventeen. I can't drink."

"This is Massachusetts, man. Haven't you heard, the drinking age is eighteen? Or out of diapers, whichever comes first. You still wearing diapers?"

Artemus gave him one of his best stares.

"Lad, it's time you were initiated into the fine world of metal workers."

Half a dozen men piled into a couple of cars after work the following Friday, driving into Southie, where they settled in at the Quencher, a pub that no stranger would ever consider entering on his own. Callahan yelled out to the bartender, a huge man with arms as big as rafter beams.

"Paddy, we have a new man in our crew to be initiated. Let's start proper—Bushmills and Harp. We'll do the rotgut later. Paddy Joyce, this is Artemus. He doesn't take kindly to being called Artie, but he will by the end of the night."

The bartender drew a pint draft of Harp beer and poured a shot glass full of Irish whiskey."

"You drink a couple of gulps of the beer to make room for the whiskey," Callahan instructed. "Then you pour the Bushmills into the beer. That makes the boilermaker."

Artemus tentatively took a couple of swallows of beer and started to pour in the whiskey.

"No! No! You just drop the shot glass and all into the beer."

Artemus watched the glass descend to the bottom of the pint, and inwardly shuddered.

The night consisted of three boilermakers. Artemus, who had never had a drink in his life, assumed that he could hang in there with his fellow workers, but his training had come in a completely different form. Physically he could have stood up to any of these men, but they had learned the mysteries of alcohol and he was no match.

"Where'd you find this babe?" Paddy asked the rough men who were trying in vain to prop Artemus up on his stool.

"He's the boss's son, sent out to do a day's work."

"Old man Webb? You're shittin' me! You guys lost your brains? Get him the hell out of here and sober him up. Jesus Christ! Get the fuck gone."

They took him back to his Chevy that was parked in the shipyard lot, and left him there, mumbling and groaning and puking. The night watchman, Chuckie Carafoli, making his rounds, found him there, sound asleep. He considered phoning the boss and quickly discarded the idea as dangerous. Instead he woke Artemus with a douse of cold water and held out a cup of coffee he poured from his thermos.

"Better drink this Artemus. It's the first step in the cure for what's ailing you."

As his senior year began, Artemus decided on a new workout routine of cross country runs after his afternoon classes. He had visited most of the factories in the region and wanted something different as fall approached and the foliage started to change. He was breathing heavy, having just sprinted around the South Meadow and was walking along the Deerfield River path.

"I've seen you out running every night. Would you mind if I joined you? My name is Allison Fielding. I've watched your pace, which is faster than mine, and it would help me a lot if I could run with you. I didn't hear your name. Do you go to school here in the valley? You have a very nice running style."

The girl, who had been running in the opposite direction, had pulled up in front of him with her torrent of words.

"I run by myself. I don't need a partner."

"Nonsense. It is better to have someone to run with because you don't always feel like running, and you can encourage each other. I often have to force myself to start. Once I've been running for a mile or so I settle in, but it would be much easier if I had someone to run with. I'm going to make the cross-country team if it kills me. I go to Smith. I'm a freshman. Are you at U. Mass or Amherst?"

"I'm at Deerfield."

"You're still in high school? My God, I would never have guessed that. But it doesn't matter at all. I've never worried about age in people. Did I tell you my name was Allison? What's yours?"

"It doesn't matter, because we're not going to be running together."

Artemus sprinted away, leaving Allison Fielding standing there, caught in mid-sentence. She quickly recovered.

"Oh, of course we'll be running together!" she yelled at the departing boy. "I don't discourage easily, Mr. Deerfield."

Allison was there the next afternoon, and the next. As soon as Artemus began running, she hesitated a few seconds and then took off after him. Not a word was spoken. They appeared to be two unconnected joggers out for an afternoon run. Artemus' route generally took him from the green in Deerfield Village, and out to the Deerfield Road leading to Highway 5 that headed north toward Greenfield. A couple miles up he turned on River Road through East Deerfield, a relatively flat stretch of about five miles along the placid river. Finally he turned west on Pine Nook Road, through the low hills skirting Pokumtuck Rock and back to Old Deerfield. It was a run of about ten miles, something he generally did in about an hour.

For a week Allison followed him, breaking off just before he reached the grounds of Deerfield Academy. Then for another week she didn't appear, though Artemus ran as usual, not seeming to notice. Then one day she was there again.

"Did you miss me, Deerfield?" she yelled just after he had taken off from the green. "I was having my period and didn't feel like running."

Artemus came to a stop, turned and glared at the slim girl, who returned the stare with an amused smile.

"I told you I don't welcome your company," he spat. "Why don't you find someone else to bother?"

"Oh, nonsense, you big brute. You know you like me to run behind you. Otherwise you would have gone at a different time or taken your cute little Chevy to another place entirely. Just shut up and run. You are making me faster with your pace. Now go!"

"My Chevy? You know I have a Chevy? What are you, stalking me?"

"Of course I'm stalking you. You're going to make me a better runner. And you're awfully cute too. It's just that you either don't know it or don't care. I figure you are basically afraid of people. That's why you won't talk to anyone. I've read about cases like yours. You're afraid of people, really. Did you know that?"

Artemus stood there, mouth open, glaring at the outlandish girl, shocked by what he was hearing. Without responding to the deluge of words, he turned and sprinted away. Smiling, she pursued him, completely satisfied with herself.

"Look at you, running away!" she yelled after him.

By the time he reached Highway 5, Artemus was doing five-minute miles, a pace he kept up all the way to the river. Laboring heavily, Allison fought to keep up, but found herself falling back. Artemus took a quick glance back as he turned on River Road. The girl was nowhere in sight. He picked up the pace again, down the long stretch of river run.

For the first time since he began his long distance running, Artemus skipped the next day. And the day after. He was walking across the green on the following Saturday morning when he heard a car honk. It was Allison, driving a shiny red Ford pickup.

"Want to go for a run, Deerfield?"

"No, get out of my life," Artemus hissed. "Go run by yourself."

"Oh, stop that act right now. Go get your running gear. I'll wait. I have a great run that you will want to try. Go! I'll stay right here. Go!"

He found himself heading back to his dorm, where he stuffed his shorts and shoes into a gym bag. Still sullen, he walked back to the girl and got into her truck.

"That's more like it. You're going to love this run. It winds through all of the tobacco farms down in Southwick. Lots of rolling hills to get your stamina up. You know, watching you take off the other day and keep up that pace, you could qualify for Hopkinton. You only have to run about seven-minute miles to get admitted. You have a great running form, you know. I wish I could run like that. Why are you so angry all the time? I noticed you never talk to anyone around here. You should get out more, and ..."

"Don't you ever stop talking, Allison?"

"You remember my name? I don't believe it. Now, Deerfield, that makes my day. I figured you not only didn't talk; you probably didn't listen either. I'll be damned!"

"It's not Deerfield, it's Artemus."

"Artemis? Really?" Allison burst out laughing.

"What's so funny?"

"Did you know you are named after a Greek goddess? Artemis?"

"It's not a Greek god. I was named after Artemus Ward. It's spelled with a 'U'."

"Artemus Ward? He's no more a real person than Artemis, the goddess," Allison blurted. "There's no real Artemus Ward."

"What are you talking about?"

"I was just reading about Artemus Ward. That wasn't his real name. It was Charley Brown or something like that. He was a buddy of Mark Twain."

"I don't care. I was named after Artemus Ward, whether he was real or made up, not some Greek goddess. Are we going to run or not?"

"Okay, I'm sorry...Artemus. We're going to run around Congamond Lake. It's pretty and a fairly tough run. It'll take us about forty-five minutes to get there. There's a place we can change."

It was, as Allison had promised, a great run, with views of the many tobacco barns that were the economic mainstay of the region, producing a fine Sumatra leaf that was much prized in the cigar industry. With Allison talking almost non-stop, Artemus found himself enjoying the run. At the end, Allison produced a bag of sandwiches and cokes, driving to nearby Camp Berkshire, where there were tables in the shade.

"We can shower at my place," she said when their lunch was finished, "and I'll get you back to your school."

"Where do you live?"

"Amherst. You'll never guess who my next-door neighbor is. Well, I'll tell you, Emily Dickenson. Oh, you probably don't know who she is. She's one of America's great writers.

They pulled up to a small house on a tree-lined side street behind Amherst College.

"My folks are off in Florida, "Snowbirds" we call them, soaking up the sun while New England is freezing. Did you know that the Yankees all go to the west side of Florida and the New Yorkers to the east? I guess they never did like each other much, so they even stay apart on vacation. Isn't that interesting? Here's a towel. You shower first. The bathroom is right there."

Overwhelmed, and tired of listening, Artemus grabbed his clothes and went into the bathroom, happy to be away from the torrent of words at least for a few minutes. He was luxuriating in the warm stream of water when he heard the door open and close. Allison parted the shower curtain and stepped in with him.

"What are you doing," he stammered, instantly feeling himself rise. "Get the hell out of here."

"I figured if you didn't talk to anyone, you probably have never had sex before. This is as good a time to learn as any."

Before he could protest, she was in his arms, kissing him passionately, her tongue forcing its way toward his.

"Can you lift me?" she breathed heavily. "Take my waist. I'll do the rest."

He did as he was told, as Allison deftly led him into her and started moving rhythmically. It didn't last long before he exploded into her and she let out a scream of pleasure, holding on to his neck with all her strength. They stood there, locked together, breathing heavily, the shower flowing over their bodies, her tongue probing his ear, his hands massaging her back and buttocks. Finally, she pulled her head back to look into his eyes.

"We will continue this in the other room," she said, sliding to her feet, taking his hand and dragging him out of the shower. She didn't even turn the water off, as she pulled him into bed on top of her. Their love making filled the rest of the afternoon. It was nearly midnight when Allison dropped him off at the Deerfield green. Exhausted, strangely contented, confused, Artemus walked slowly back to his dorm, trying to come to grips with an experience that he had never anticipated. He found himself looking forward to his next after-school run. And Allison.

He never saw her again.

Every day for a week, he went off on his run expecting to see her, but she never appeared. Finally, Artemus drove to Amherst and the house on Main Street. He knocked on the door but received no answer. The Emily Dickinson House, now a museum, was open so he walked over.

"Do you know the Fielding family that lives next door," he inquired of the elderly lady who volunteered at the front desk.

"Oh, nobody has lived there for years," she said. "The museum has been trying to buy that property since old Mrs. Maywood died about five years ago."

"I was just here last Saturday. There was someone living in that house."

"Oh, we're closed on Saturdays. I wouldn't have seen you or anyone else in the house."

"Do you know an Allison Fielding?"

The woman thought for a bit. "No, young man, I've never heard that name before."

Nor did they have a student named Allison Fielding at Smith College. Confused and angry, Artemus returned to Deerfield, in vain trying to make sense of what had happened. He found himself slipping back into the protective shell that had opened briefly under the barrage of Allison. He vowed never again to let his guard down.

Shortly after the Thanksgiving break, Artemus was called to the dean's office. He expected another lecture about fitting in and participating in activities he regarded as infantile. Instead he received a shock.

"Artemus, I don't know how to break this news to you," the dean began.

"If it's bad, Dean Malthus, just tell me as quickly as you can. I don't need anything fancy. Am I being expelled?"

"No, that would be easy…" Dean Malthus hesitated, inhaled deeply. "Artemus, your parents have been killed. There was a robbery at your home. Both of them were shot and killed. They were found dead by a neighbor who heard the gunshots. I'm sorry."

Artemus didn't even blink.

"Why are you sorry, dean? They weren't your parents. I'm sorry I will have to leave in the morning. I truly enjoyed Deerfield Academy. It was everything I hoped it would be."

The dean stood there stunned, shocked into silence by this young man who was completely devoid of emotion, the news of his parent's death not eliciting even a blink or a shake of the head.

"I'm sorry, Artemus," he stuttered. "I didn't think you had any feeling for Deerfield Academy. It has certainly not appeared that way to us."

"There you go again, Dean Malthus," Artemus responded. "Saying you are sorry. Don't ever tell anyone you are sorry. It's condescending."

He rose and left the room.

REBECCA WALTON

"I swear, Rebecca, you came out of my womb angry. And you haven't allowed yourself or anyone in this family any peace since. Don't you ever just relax and enjoy life? Isn't there anything you are happy about?"

"Mom, how many times have we argued about this? Life isn't here to enjoy, not when things are not fair. I'll be angry until everything in my life is the same as it is for my brothers. When that day comes, I'll shut up and smile."

"That's my girl, sweetheart," Simon Walton laughed, putting down his *New Yorker*, and joining the fray, which ever since Rebecca had been suspended from Connecticut College High School, was a nightly adventure. "We didn't raise our daughter to be some sort of wilting flower, Sandra," he said to his wife, leaning across the couch and patting her arm. "The day Becky ceases to have a cause is the day we know we are dead." Simon, a professor of botany at the college, always backed his recalcitrant daughter. In his mind, Rebecca was precisely why he loved teaching.

He turned to his daughter. "I'm behind you, Becky. Just tell me what you want to do."

"I want to picket the Coast Guard Academy. I want to stop their racist faculty from ever again opening their mouths. That's what I want to do."

"What lit this fire?" Simon inquired, setting his magazine on the coffee table, gazing at his daughter with new interest.

"Didn't you see what they're trying to do to the Mohegans, Dad? They started an Eminent Domain suit to steal a piece of the tribal territory in Uncasville. They can't do that. I don't care if they are the U.S. government. You can't just take someone's land because you want to put up a brothel or saloon for their darling cadets."

"It's a different thing every night, Rebecca," her mother said, a plea in her voice. "You can't go to the wall over every issue that hits the back page of the *Times*. Give it a break. Give *us* a break."

❧

During a vicious Nor'easter in March, 1933, Rebecca Walton entered the world in the tiny coastal village of East Lyme, Connecticut. She happened to be born sixth in her family, after five brothers. Her mother wasn't far wrong in saying that she had been fighting since birth. She learned very young that if she wanted something, she better be ready to battle for it, and even though her parents tried hard to steer her toward feminine things, they had given up the struggle in that respect long ago. Rebecca grew up a tomboy of the first order. She backed down to nothing or no one. Her big brothers positively doted on her, urging her on, backing her if necessary, with their brawn. It was seldom necessary. Whether it was on the lacrosse field, or the debate team, Rebecca Walton carried her own weapons, early on developing an expertise both with words and crosse. In both skills she was a relentless attacker. Both shared in getting her a scholarship to Connecticut College if she wanted it, which fittingly claimed the distinction of being the first women's college in America.

A few of the boys in high school had tentatively suggested a date but were quickly rebuffed, which brought a considerable amount of speculation, not only from the boys but the girls as well. Perhaps the person most bothered by Rebecca's complete absence of social life was her mother.

"Rebecca, aren't you even going to the prom?" Sandra was almost afraid to broach the subject. "You haven't been on a single date your entire high school. Don't you want to have fun? Be popular? What about Ricky Gardner? He's a nice boy and from a very good family."

"You mean 'the *Gardners* of *Gardner's Island*' Mother? He's a complete boor. You'd think that he had personally arrived with old Lords Sele and Saye to found this colony, he's so pompous. I'd rather die than be seen with him."

"But you are a very attractive young woman, Rebecca. Surely there must be someone who would take you to the dance."

"That's the thing, Mother. I don't want to be 'taken' anywhere. Why do we have to wait around for a boy to ask us? Who gives them the right to make all the decisions? You should see how they walk around at the dances and size up all the girls. You'd think they were at a cattle auction."

And so, on prom night in her senior year, Rebecca and three of her girlfriends went bowling.

"Hey, for girls, you four are pretty good bowlers!"

In the lane next to Rebecca and her friends were four young men, from their dress and language, college men. The tallest of the four was standing facing the girls, arms folded, a huge smile on his face.

Rebecca was quick to react.

"What the hell do you mean, 'for girls'? I was just thinking that for guys, you bowl like babies. When was the last strike any of you got? We could beat you with our eyes closed."

"Ha! A confident one! She's been watching us. Probably trying to get some tips. What do you say, boys? Do you want to accept their challenge?"

He walked over to Rebecca and held out his hand.

"I'm Geoffrey." He paused. "Geoffrey Chaucer."

He let out a practiced laugh, almost a snort.

He does this all the time, Rebecca thought, turning to her friends with a knowing smile and quick eye roll.

"Geoffrey Macklin, actually. These are my roommates—Jared, Conner and Duncan. We all go to Yale. Sophomores.... And you are?"

Rebecca took his hand with a strong grip.

"I'm Rebecca, Isaac's wife. You probably read about me, mother of Jacob and Esau."

Geoffrey looked at her with renewed interest.

"Touché, Rebecca. Good answer."

"These are my friends, Lisa Bente, Valerie Moss and Michelle Hoover. We're seniors at Old Lyme."

Geoffrey had been joined by his roommates, all of them wearing their best pickup smiles.

"Well, are we on? For the Connecticut State Ten-Pin Championship? Two out of three. Loser buys the pizza."

Rebecca didn't hesitate, or ask her friends.

"Of course you're on. Come on, ladies. This will be the easiest pizza we ever ate."

She thought a moment. "Cumulative total of each team, Geoffrey?"

None of the girls broke 100 in the first game, while Conner came in with a 205. The other three boys weren't far behind. Rebecca maintained a forced calm as her team suffered the ignominious defeat. Geoffrey, trying not to gloat, in a poor attempt at consolation, roiled the waters even more.

"I'll tell you what, girls. We'll play left-handed."

Rebecca exploded. "Don't be such a condescending cretin, Geoffrey. We made a bet. We're not accepting anything. Lisa, go ahead, roll a strike for these jerks."

They never finished the second game. By the fifth frame, the boys had rolled a dozen gutter balls and deliberately missed any chances they had to convert a spare. Rebecca seethed at what she perceived as gross chauvinism, and while her friends were laughing and enjoying the back-and-forth banter, she worked her way into a ferocious scowl. Finally, she simply took off her bowling shoes, and tromped out of the building.

It was Geoffrey who caught her in the parking lot, having run after her, leaving the others to continue their game.

"I didn't mean to get you so mad, Rebecca. We were just having fun. Come on back in. There's nothing to get angry about."

"Maybe nothing for you, but I'm sick of being treated like some sort of helpless maid. I've had enough of male superiority."

"Hey, ease up. We were just having fun. And you must admit, it was fun in there, better than playing by yourself. Let's call a truce. I'll admit it wasn't a fair bet. We bowl at least once a week. I'll buy the pizza."

He tried to take her hand and lead her back in. Rebecca rejected the gesture, but walked quickly back into the bowling alley. Bowling had ceased among the six inside and Rebecca noticed that they had all paired off, sitting around laughing, and the girls at least, flirting.

"I called off the competition," Geoffrey announced as they walked in. "The guys buy the pizza. Come on, we'll go to Delmonico's."

"Delmonico's, where's that?" Lisa asked.

"New Haven. It's the best Italian restaurant in town. They have great pizza."

"Oh, we can't go to New Haven," Valerie protested. "We have to get home pretty soon."

"It's not that far," Jared said quietly. "Less than half an hour."

"It's after 10:00 already," Michelle said, her voice oozing worry. "My folks will kill me if I'm late."

Rebecca, who hadn't said a word since she had returned from the parking lot, settled the matter.

"We'll follow you. I'm starving. Let's go."

The girls all tumbled into Rebecca's blue Plymouth. For a moment there was silence, finally broken by Michelle, the shyest of the four.

"New Haven! Guys, these are college guys. What are we doing? We shouldn't be going to New Haven."

"What's there to be scared of, Michelle?" Lisa responded. "It's not like we're going to their apartment or anything. It's just pizza."

"I think this is cool," Valerie giggled. "I've never been out with a college guy before. This is cool."

"A guy is a guy," Rebecca murmured. "Just stick together. We'll be fine. We don't want to look like a bunch of weak chicks."

They followed Geoffrey's sleek Mercury coupe along the old Boston Post Road, turning left toward the New Haven waterfront, where they found Delmonico's at the end of a dark street in a quiet part of the city.

"Do any of you girls have a request?" Geoffrey asked when the waiter was ready to take their order. "Any vegetarians? Carnivores?"

"I only like cheese," Michelle answered timidly. "Is that okay?"

"Get a couple," Jared suggested. "Cheese and one with the works. No ground up rhino horn, though, except for Conner."

The boys all laughed. Of the girls, only Rebecca understood the joke, and her defenses went up immediately. She glared at Jared but said nothing.

When the last slice of pizza had been devoured, Rebecca stood up and started putting her coat on.

"What's the hurry, Rebecca?" Geoffrey asked innocently. "Would you girls like to see our apartment? It's not far from here, and we could put on some records and have our own prom."

Valerie, who had been flirting shamelessly with Conner, immediately agreed.

"I'm game," Lisa volunteered, her eyes darting toward Jared.

"I really have to get home," moaned Michelle. "My folks will kill me if I'm too late."

As had happened back at the bowling alley, Rebecca made the decision.

"We won't stay too long, Michelle." She locked eyes defiantly with Geoffrey, who resolutely held her gaze. "Let's see how these *college gentlemen* live."

It was only a few blocks to the apartment, a three-story block in the district behind Morey's that once was probably elegant but in old age could only be rented to students. Geoffrey quickly got out of his car and hurried back to the girls.

"Give us a minute or two to straighten up the place. It might be a bit messy. I'll give you the high sign when we are relatively sanitary. It's 2B."

"Why don't we just leave and go home," Michelle whispered. "I'm scared."

"Oh, this is fun," blurted the ever-giggling Valerie. "I think that Conner is a dream."

"I sort of like Jared too. There's nothing to be scared of, Michelle," Lisa chimed in. "What can they do to us if we all stick together? Oh, there's Geoffrey waiving. Let's go."

They tumbled out of the Plymouth, everyone but Rebecca talking excitedly.

If the boys actually cleaned anything, it was difficult to discern. There were piles of clothes against one wall, where a hide-a-bed had just been converted into a couch. Papers and books were stacked on the table near the kitchen, which had a sink full of dirty dishes. Jared swept a bunch of old *New York Times* from a well-worn coffee table, which he moved against the wall.

"Well, our dance floor is ready," he said sheepishly.

"Would you girls like a beer?" Conner yelled from the kitchen.

"Do you have a Coke or Seven Up?" Lisa shouted back, throwing her coat on the back of the couch.

"We have beer, and ... beer."

"Oh what the hell, I'll have a beer," Lisa said with a shrug, causing Michelle to gasp. Valerie emerged from the kitchen with Conner, each carrying four Rolling Rock bottles. Rebecca, who had taken a seat on the coffee table, set hers down on the floor.

"I have to use the john," she announced with a quizzical look at Geoffrey. "First door on the right down the hall," he responded, pointing. By the time she returned, the party was in full swing, the stereo softly playing Tony Bennett's "Because of You." Only Geoffrey was without a dance partner.

"I guess you're my partner, Geoffrey," Rebecca said dispassionately, taking up her beer and chugging half of it down. She turned and held out her hands.

"I'll take that as a request," Geoffrey laughed. "Not the most seductive I have seen, but at least a start."

Halfway through the Dominos' "Sixty Minute Man," Rebecca started to get dizzy. Seeing her woozy, Geoffrey led her down the hall where he guided her into one of the back bedrooms. Closing the door, he grabbed her, drawing her close, kissing her fiercely, forcing her mouth open with his tongue.

"You bastard!" Rebecca hissed as she neared unconsciousness. "You could have had me without that."

She came to with Geoffrey asleep at her side. Roughly she pushed him away and staggered to her feet, grabbing her clothes that were strewn across the floor, fumbling into her jeans and throwing on her blouse, leaving the bra where it lay. She stumbled into the hall trying to bring her eyes into focus. Lisa and Valerie were on the couch in the living room, passionately making out with their guys.

"Where's Michelle?" Rebecca yelled.

Valerie was the first to disengage. "I don't know, maybe in one of the other rooms. What the hell happened to you, Rebecca?"

"He slipped me something. We're getting the hell out of here. I'll get Michelle."

She barged through one of the closed bedroom doors. Michelle was lying on the bed, naked from the waist up. Duncan was fumbling with the zipper on her jeans.

"Get away from her you asshole," Rebecca screamed, grabbing Duncan by the shoulder and pushing him violently. Drunk, he slumped to the floor. Rebecca turned her attention to her friend.

"Michelle, can you hear me? Michelle, it's Rebecca. Can you understand me?"

Michelle opened her eyes weakly, unable to focus.

"Oh shit!" Rebecca cursed. She ran to the living room, commanding Lisa and Valerie to help her. The three girls got Michelle to her feet. With Lisa and Valerie on each side and Rebecca holding her in back, they edged toward the front door. Spotting a gym bag against the wall, Rebecca quickly emptied it, refilling it with all the beer bottles she could find in the room.

"What the hell are you doing," Jared yelled as Geoffrey slowly emerged from his bedroom.

"We're getting the hell out of here," Rebecca snarled. "Don't even think about following us, you bastards."

Carefully they guided Michelle into the back seat, Lisa getting in with her. Rebecca, shaking her head to try to control her thoughts and emotions, slammed the car into gear and roared away from the curb.

"Did you have sex?" she demanded of Valerie.

"Sex? No, we were just making out."

"Lisa, how about you?"

"Same with me. Rebecca, what happened to you? Where were you?"

"He raped me. Put something in my beer that knocked me out. I think that other asshole did that to Michelle too. He was just getting started when I broke in on him. The bastards. I'll make them pay."

It was a long ride back to Old Lyme. Rebecca stopped at a Flying A gas station to get some coffee and to straighten herself and Michelle up in the bathroom. Michelle, still groggy but getting more alert, was nearly hysterical.

"What am I going to do? It's after midnight. My folks are going to kill me."

"Relax, Michelle," Rebecca said softly, holding her close and rubbing her back. "I'll talk to your parents. We did nothing wrong except for drink a beer. I'll come home and explain it to them."

Thank God nothing happened to her, Rebecca thought, picturing the scene in the bedroom. She could only vaguely remember what had happened to her with Geoffrey. One thing she was certain of, she was no longer a virgin. For some reason, that thought didn't bother her at all. She knew that if she hadn't been drugged, she had already decided that Geoffrey would have been her first sex.

Lisa was the first to get dropped off.

"What are you going to do, Rebecca? Are you going to tell your parents? I hope you won't. We'll all be in trouble."

"I'm going to file rape charges," Rebecca responded grimly. "That son-of-a-bitch isn't going to get away with this."

"Oh, don't do that!" Lisa pleaded. It'll get us all is trouble."

"If that's the way you think, Lisa, you're already in trouble. Grow up."

Valerie, who had taken this all in, put her hand on Rebecca's shoulder. "I'm with you completely, Rebecca. We can't let them off the hook. Think what would have happened to poor Michelle here."

The hardest part of the night was getting Michelle home. She was still a bit shaky when Rebecca led her to the front door. Her parents saw them coming and met them on the porch.

"What happened? Michelle, are you all right? Did you get in an accident? You were supposed to be home two hours ago."

"If you'll let me, Mrs. Hoover, I'll tell you what happened. Nothing serious happened to Michelle. Can I come in?"

For half an hour, Rebecca went through the entire evening with Michelle's parents. She held nothing back, including the fact that both she and Michelle had been drugged. She assured Mr. and Mrs. Hoover that nothing had happened to Michelle. She did not mention that she had been raped.

"Our Michelle would never have gone with those boys on her own," Mrs. Hoover responded when Rebecca was finished. "We are holding you responsible for this, Rebecca. I don't think that you have ever been a very good influence on her. We don't want her seeing you anymore."

"I'm sorry you feel that way, Mrs. Hoover. But that's fine. Your little girl here will stay that way until you let her make decisions on her own. Good night."

Rebecca's parents were also waiting up.

"Are you okay?" Sandra Walton asked as Rebecca closed the door. "It's awfully late, sweetheart. What were you doing all this time?"

"Mom, Dad, I think you better sit down. All this time I was getting raped."

In a voice devoid of emotion, Rebecca recounted all the night's occurrences, including the rape, as much as she could remember.

"I know he put something in that beer," she said, "and I was stupid enough to chug half of it. It hit me in just a few minutes, whatever it was."

Sandra Walton was stunned to speechlessness, but her husband, more attuned to the problems of high school and college students, was more under control.

"What do you want to do, Rebecca? Should we call Doctor Strauss and get you examined?"

"I want to call the New Haven Police first. That's a major crime the jerk committed. I want him in jail."

There was silence in the room, long enough to get uncomfortable.

"You know, sweetheart, that it will be your word against his, a young high school student against a Yale man. This could be very difficult, maybe a losing effort from the start."

"Lose or not, Dad, I'm going to make that guy regret what he did. I don't even care what the result is as long as I get to be heard."

"How about the other girls? Were they raped too?"

"No, I actually stopped the guy that was on top of Melissa. The other two didn't get any drugs. They were just making out."

Sandra Walton could stand no more. "Rebecca, just listen to what you are saying! You are talking like you just took a walk in the park. You were raped! Don't you feel anything?"

"Mom, I'm pissed. No guy should be allowed to get away with that. It was intentional, not like I drank too much and deserved what I got. He put something in my beer to knock me out. It worked."

"How are you going to prove that, Rebecca?" Simon asked quietly.

"I have all the bottles."

"What do you mean?"

"I stuffed all the beer bottles in a bag. I have them. They should show what drug was used, and they are sure to have our fingerprints on them."

Simon sat there considering what he had just heard. He walked over to the phone and dialed a number. The sleepy voice of the family attorney, James Harrington, answered on the other end.

"James, I'm sorry to bother you so late, but we have somewhat of a family emergency here. I need your opinion."

He explained everything that Rebecca had said, including the retention of the bottles, then sat back in his stuffed chair and listened.

"Okay James, that would be very nice of you. Thank you."

He put down the phone, turning to his wife and daughter.

"James will be here in a few minutes. He doesn't think we should wait until morning to file a report. He will make the call after we talk it over, if that's what you want, Rebecca."

"That's exactly what I want. If he won't phone, I will."

It was after 1:00 A.M. when James Harrington arrived at the Walton's home. He was an impressive man, tall, robust with a moustache that concealed his upper lip.

"I don't think I've ever seen you without a suit and tie on, James," Simon laughed. "The girls are in here."

The lawyer assumed a thin smile as he entered the living room, giving Sandra a warm hug, and then taking Rebecca by both hands and looking deeply into her eyes.

"Rebecca, I can't tell you how sad and shocked I am by what you had to endure. I'll do everything I can to help you through this. But you must know that it will be far from easy. Do you understand that?"

"Of course I do, Mr. Harrington. I'm not a child, you know. I will be ready for anything they have to throw at me. I am very sure of my cause."

"Good girl," Harrington said, consciously trying not to sound condescending. "Let's talk about what happened. Some of my questions may make you angry, but they are nothing like those you will hear from the police, and if this goes further, from the boys' attorneys. Do you want to start now or wait until the morning?"

"Let's start," Rebecca said, not considering the condition her parents might be in. She was feeling an energy such has she had never experienced, an energy fueled by her anger.

"Tell me how you met these boys."

For nearly an hour, the lawyer grilled Rebecca on what went on at the bowling alley, what was said by all the parties, what was the extent of the flirting on both sides.

"Who decided that you girls should go to New Haven?"

"I guess I was the one who made the decision. Melissa didn't want to go. Lisa and Valerie were happy to go. They had already paired off with guys and were looking for a good time." She thought a minute, then added, "not a good time with sex, that is. None of us considered that at the time. I think it was exciting for all of us, even Melissa, to have a date with a college guy."

"What happened at the restaurant?

"We had a really good time. It was fun. The boys bought the pizza."

"And was it you that decided to go to their apartment as well?"

Rebecca considered the question. "Yes."

"Rebecca, consider this next question carefully. Did you consider the possibility that you wanted to have sex with this boy...Geoffrey?"

The silence in the room was stifling for the parents.

"Yes."

Sandra Walton let out a gasp. Simon patted her hand, with a shake of his head, telling her to stifle any outburst she might want to make.

"And if he had not used a drug, would you have had sex with him?"

Another long pause. "I think I would. I thought it was as good a time as any to lose my virginity."

This time her mother could not control herself. "Rebecca! That is awful! What an awful thing to say! Where on earth do you get such ideas?"

"Mother, I'm a normal, growing woman who has reached puberty. Sex is a perfectly normal thing. It's your generation that has the ridiculous ideas about sex, not mine."

James Harrington cleared his throat, then continued. "Rebecca, when did you realize that you had been drugged?"

"Almost immediately. I started getting dizzy and tried to get up but couldn't."

"Did you taste anything in the beer?"

"No, but I chugged about half the bottle. It just slid down."

"You wanted to get high?"

After another pause, "Yes."

"Would that have gone along with your desire to have sex with this man?"

"I think so. I think I felt that I needed some courage."

"Have you ever been drunk?"

"Yes."

Her mother simply moaned, leaning her head against Simon's shoulder.

"How often?"

"Oh, only twice. Some of the girls thought it would be fun to try. The first time, I don't think we drank more than a couple of beers each. The other time, it was vodka, but that didn't end well. We all got sick."

"Do you date often?"

"I've never had a date. I consider the boys in our school to be a bunch of infants. I have never had a desire to date any of them."

"What made it different tonight?"

"These were college guys. And they treated us with more respect than high school guys do. They actually talked to us as equals." She hesitated a moment. "At least until the beers came."

"Describe the scene at the apartment."

"Well, first off, the place was a hovel. I suppose it was a typical guys' cave, with dirty clothes, paper and unwashed dishes lying around. The guys moved the furniture out of the middle of the living room and put on some music for dancing. Valerie and Lisa were madly making out almost from the start. Michelle wanted no part of it, but finally gave in and grabbed a beer. They said they didn't have any Coke or Seven Up. I took a beer but left it on the floor and went to the john. When I came back, I chugged about half of it. The next thing I knew, I was dizzy, and the next, I woke up naked with Geoffrey next to me on a bed. I remember calling him a bastard before I blanked out."

"Are you sure you were raped?"

"I'm fairly sure. I was awfully sore between my legs."

"Was there blood?"

"Yes.

"Your father says that you collected all of the bottles. Is that true?"

"Yes, they are in that bag. I tried not to let them spill out."

"Why did you take them?"

"I wanted proof that they drugged us, at least me and Michelle."

Harrington paused for several seconds.

"You realize that even if the bottles contain drugs, and there are the right fingerprints, the defense can say that you put the drugs in after you left?"

"I hadn't thought of that. But if I had left the bottles they would certainly have been thrown out where they couldn't be found. I'll take my chances."

The lawyer turned to Simon and Sandra.

"I think you should have a physical exam done first thing in the morning, both to determine if Rebecca has actually been raped, and also to find out if there is anything in her blood."

He turned to Rebecca. "I'm going to wait until the morning to file a report to the New Haven Police. Now don't protest just yet. I want that medical examination, and I want to do a check on these boys. Do you know this Geoffrey's last name?"

"Macklin."

"Oh, no!"

"What?"

"There's a federal judge in New Haven by the name of William Macklin. Quite honestly, he's a bastard to deal with."

"That's even better," Rebecca said stolidly. "It'll make for a juicier story, politically."

"That's enough, Rebecca," her mother said, making an effort to stand up from the low couch. "It's time to get some sleep."

She turned to Harrington.

"James, I can't tell you how much Simon and I…, and Rebecca, are grateful to you. Calling you out in the middle of the night. Frankly, I am petrified at what we are going to have to endure if we carry this thing to a conclusion, but I am comforted that we have you to help us. I have to get some sleep. Thank you."

She gave him a hug, and beckoning to Rebecca to follow, left the room. "Rebecca, you come too. Let the men talk a bit."

"That's exactly what I am fighting, mother. I don't want the men to do all of the talking."

"Rebecca Walton! I said come with me. Now!"

"Mumbling in objection, Rebecca shook the lawyer's hand and slowly left the room."

"That's quite a daughter you have raised, Simon. I hope she's as strong as she says she is."

"Strength is not the problem, James. Anger might be. If Rebecca gets a cause, and she certainly has one here, there's no telling whom she might attack."

"This is not going to be easy, you know. Odds are, it will never come to court. In our society, boys are protected. You know the old saying, 'Boys will be boys, but girls should be virgins.'"

"I'll take the odds on this one," Simon said with a sigh. "Your Judge Macklin has no idea what a hornet's nest his son has stirred up with my daughter."

"The drug was chloral hydrate. We usually call it a Mickey Finn, or knockout drops."

James Harrington was on the phone to Simon Walton late the next morning.

"It's a powerful drug, very popular on college campuses because it is liquid and only takes a drop to have a significant effect. We found rather large traces in two of the bottles Rebecca took away. Both are loaded with fingerprints. We'll get them identified. What did you find out in the medical exam?"

"Rebecca was indeed raped," Simon reported. "They found traces of semen. Too soon to tell if she's pregnant though. She goes back to the doctor in ten days for that. They also did a blood test and found that drug in her system."

"Well, now it's up to you. I'll repeat that she will be in for a very tough ride. Is she still adamant on going through with the rape charge?"

"Even more than last night, James. Let's make the call. It will be toughest on Sandra. Rebecca is steeled for a knock-down fight."

"Okay. I'll pick you up at 1:00 and we'll drive into New Haven."

The sergeant was very polite at the New Haven Police department, carefully taking notes as James Harrington led Rebecca through her statement. At the end of the deposition, Harrington ushered Rebecca and her parents out of the station, suggesting that they go to lunch and talk over some important details.

"Any place but Delmonico's," Rebecca laughed.

It didn't take long for the story to take wings.

"YALE BOY ACCUSED OF RAPE!" was the headline in the *New Haven Register,* the very next morning after Rebecca's accusation. Her name was not mentioned, but the report stated that she was a Connecticut high school student. It also mentioned that the accused was the son of a prominent federal judge. And that three other Yale men were at the party. James Harrington called for a meeting that evening, telling Rebecca and her family that the politics would begin immediately.

"Believe me, they have already leaked your name, Rebecca, and you can expect the worst. I know Judge Macklin, and he will try to destroy you."

"I have been thinking about this, Mr. Harrington. I want to drop the rape charge, and file one for assault. The worst thing that jerk did to me was take away my ability to think, to act. That drug was an attack on my personal freedom. I want him to face that. The rape thing will just muddle everything up, because everyone thinks it is so awful. And they will probably try to say I consented to the sex. But they can't say that I wanted to be drugged."

James Harrington was silent for a long time. Then he smiled.

"The police, and maybe even Judge Macklin, will probably want to keep rape in the mix, but I think that's a great idea, Rebecca. Assault would be easier to prove in this case because there are witnesses. Your friends are probably going to have to testify that you and Michelle appeared to be drugged."

"I doubt that Michelle will testify to anything. She's about as timid as a baby lamb. Her parents will refuse to let her do anything."

"They might not have a choice. Their name is certain to be made public, and we will subpoena her if she isn't willing to testify voluntarily. I'm going to call all the girls and their parents to a meeting immediately. I'll advise them as to what is probably going to happen. It will be far better if you girls are a united front on this."

Before the lawyer could call that meeting, the matter was made moot by the press. All the girls' names were disclosed in the *Post*, a local newspaper based in Bridgeport. It was pointed out that they hadn't gone to their own school prom the night of the incident, implying that they represented a high school "counter-culture," loose girls out looking for a good time. The boys' names were not mentioned, but they were described as upstanding Yale students all with high grade point averages. Four sets of angry and confused parents convened in Harrison's law office the following day. They entered the conference room with grim nods to each other, and silently took their seats. Except for Rebecca, the girls all showed signs of recent tears.

"I am sure that you have all seen the newspapers," Harrington began. "I can tell you that I have already sent a very strong letter of condemnation to the *Post* for revealing the girls' names, but I don't anticipate that it will have the slightest effect. In past cases where rape was an issue, such things were common practice where it is in the interests of those involved to protect the boys.

"If you will bear with me, I will try to summarize the event and fill you in on what our plans will be. Girls, if there is anything in my report that you disagree with, please tell me immediately."

The lawyer went through the details of the night at the bowling alley and in New Haven, essentially the story that Rebecca had related to him. There wasn't a single disagreement from the other three girls, whose parents listened carefully, occasionally sighing but not speaking. When he was through, Patterson asked for questions.

"Our daughter was not involved in the drugs or rape," William Moss, Valerie's father, stated. "Will she still have to be exposed to all of this?" Lisa Bente's parents nodded, seconding the question.

"I'm afraid that Valerie and Lisa are involved at least as witnesses," Harrington replied. "If the case goes to trial, that might be a difficult time for the girls. I think that is a way off, though. We can set that aside for the moment."

Turning to Michelle Hoover's parents, he continued. "As for Michelle, she also was given a dose of the same drug. While actual rape is not an issue, from Rebecca's report, attempted rape is. I should tell you that Rebecca is of the opinion that the more serious crime is that she and Michelle were drugged. She wants to file an assault charge rather than a rape charge. Michelle would have the same assault complaint if you want to proceed."

"We want to end this now," Norman Hoover declared, his voice emotionally strained. "We are not willing to have our daughter dragged through a long court nightmare."

"You mean you don't want yourselves exposed," Rebecca blurted.

"Rebecca!" Sandra Walton exclaimed.

"It's true, mother," Rebecca responded. "If I hadn't gotten to her, Michelle would have been raped too. They just don't want their little girl to get involved. But she's not a little girl, and she is involved."

"That's enough, Rebecca," Simon Walton commanded. "The Hoover's have every right to feel as they do."

"Why don't I go over what all of you can expect in this matter," James Harrington interjected, turning the conversation. "Whether we accuse these men of rape or assault, the public will concentrate on the rape issue. Traditionally, that is very difficult on the woman's side. Frankly speaking, the courts and the public usually support the male. I personally think that Rebecca is right in wanting to drop the rape charge and pursue the assault issue. Since she is the only one that was raped, that is her decision. But both she and Michelle were drugged, and Mr. and Mrs. Hoover, that will bring Michelle into the trial whether you want it or not. You can choose not to press charges, but I will still have to call your daughter as a witness if the case goes to trial. The same applies to you other girls. You were at the scene and your testimony will be necessary. You can expect at least that there will be depositions taken."

"What's a deposition?"

"It is conducted during the discovery phase of a trial. The girls will have to go over in detail the events of that night. I will be there to advise them, but it is usually a grueling and emotionally charged ordeal."

"My husband and I hold Rebecca completely responsible for this," Gladys Hoover declared. "If she hadn't pushed her, Michelle would never have been involved."

Before Rebecca could respond, Valerie came to her defense.

"Nobody pushed anyone, Mrs. Hoover. We all agreed to everything that night, including Michelle. Why don't we get mad at those boys instead of each other?"

Rebecca, who was about to explode, nodded appreciatively and remained silent.

"I think that you can all expect your privacy to be invaded over the next months," James Harrington predicted. "I can only urge you to say nothing to anyone who calls you or asks your opinions. The best answer you can give is complete silence. The boy who has been accused by Rebecca, Geoffrey Macklin, is the son of a very powerful judge, whom I know personally. He will leave no rock unturned to protect his son, and that can include some very underhanded things. If anyone phones you, or writes you, or in any way tries to contact you, say nothing and inform me immediately. You girls may also be subjected to varying degrees of insult or intimidation, both at school and in public. Try not to respond. You four have done nothing wrong—remember that. In a perfect world, you would not have to endure this, but for women in our world, nothing is perfect."

Addressing the parents, he concluded, "I will be in touch with you as soon as I have anything concrete to say. My secretary will give each of you a packet with my card and other pertinent information. Thank you for coming today. I want to assure you that I will do everything in my power to make what you are facing as painless as possible."

The trial, scheduled for late May, a month before the end of the school year, went on for almost a week. Each of the girls was called to the stand to testify. Each, not including Rebecca, left the stand in tears. The four boys were also called. Well-coached, and well-dressed, they voiced an attitude of sheer dismay that such a thing could have happened, saying that they were simply out for a good time and were almost pushed to the final results. Geoffrey Malkin and Conner Negri both flatly denied putting any drugs into the girls' beers. As had been anticipated, the defense lawyer stated that the girls had put the drug in the bottles after the party. That argument collapsed however when the results of blood tests for both Rebecca and Michelle were entered as evidence.

Rebecca did not end her testimony in tears. Instead, she began an attack from the start of her time on the stand and continued it to the end of her testimony.

"Miss Walton, were you raped on the night in question?"

"Yes, but that's not the worst thing he did to me. Before that he attacked me both in my mind and my body."

"Can you explain what you mean?"

"By giving me that drug, he took away my humanity, my freedom to act. Because of him, I no longer was a rational human being. What he did to me after that is entirely up to him. He took away all my defenses. He couldn't have assaulted me more if he had beat me with a baseball bat."

The District Attorney turned over the questioning to the defense.

Jeremy Pontier, an expensive defense attorney, pounced quickly.

"Aren't you even concerned that he allegedly raped you?"

"Does it matter? My body can overcome what he did. And there is no 'alleged' here. I have a medical report to attest to that."

"So the rape doesn't matter?"

"Of course it does. But you represent our chauvinist society. As you would see it, it wasn't his fault. I made him do it. Isn't that right, Mr. Attorney? He assaulted me. That's more important, a bigger crime."

Pontier badgered Rebecca for more than an hour but was unable to break her down. She sat in the box, calm and under control, as James Harrington had coached her, turning nearly every question back to the assault on her mind and body. Harrington even smiled a time or two with some of Rebecca's answers.

"Rape has such a nice sound to it, if it's in a headline."

"If I had a powerful judge for a father, I could probably answer that."

The lawyer worked his way around to the question that had so shocked Rebecca's mother.

"If you had not allegedly been given a drug, would you have had sex with Mr. Macklin?"

"Probably. I thought I had been a virgin long enough. He was very attractive."

"Do you think he was aware of your desire?"

"Probably, unless he was a robot or something."

"Why then would he use a drug as you allege?'

"I never 'alleged' anything. He drugged me. And that is an unsolicited attack on my body and my mind."

"The question was, why would he use a drug, if he knew you wanted to have sex with him?"

"He's insecure. Probably because of his father."

WILLIAM DAWES

Artemus stopped for a moment when he saw the yellow police tape surrounding the Webb estate, delineating the property as a crime scene. Like most of the old houses of Hingham, the house was set well back from the sidewalk separated by a luxuriant expanse of green lawn and shaded by stately red maples and beech trees. It was the first time he had come home since his arrival back in Hingham, having spent the first two nights at the shipyard, going through his father's papers and company reports, grabbing a few hours of sleep almost by accident.

A burly man climbed out of a car that was parked on the street as Artemus pulled his Chevy up to the tape on the driveway.

"I was wondering when you would find time to come home," the man said, pulling a wallet out of his coat pocket to flash his police badge, identifying him as Inspector William Dawes.

"I've been home," Artemus said with no trace of emotion, "just not to this house. There's nothing here for me anymore."

"Aren't you the least bit curious what happened to your parents?"

"Will curiosity change anything? Bring them back?"

"No, but it is a fairly standard human emotion."

Artemus took out a pocket knife and cut the police tape, then turned back to his car.

"You can't go in there. It's a crime scene. We are still looking for clues and details."

"It's my house. I'll go in there if I want to."

He started his car, and drove in the long drive, leaving Inspector Dawes standing at the sidewalk, with a bemused look on his face, which slowly turned to a small smile. He strode after the car.

"You know this was a contract killing," he yelled at Artemus who was about to open the back door of the house. "They were pros."

Artemus stopped, slowly turning.

"It wasn't a robbery gone wrong?"

"There was no robbery. They were shot in the back of the head, kneeling, with their arms tied behind them with electrical wire."

Dawes noticed the barest trace of hesitation in the young man, and he walked up to the porch.

"You need to talk to me. You may be able to help. Right now we have nothing."

"I don't know anything," Artemus responded having regained his stoic demeanor. "I haven't been home since Christmas, and that was only for a couple of days."

"When did you last speak with your parents?"

"We don't talk much."

"Well, when was the last time."

"We don't talk at all. My father never encouraged it."

It was Dawes' turn to hesitate.

"He didn't 'encourage' it? What is that supposed to mean? Didn't they ask about your school? Your grades?"

"No."

"So you never spoke to your father about possible enemies, or problems at the shipyard?"

"I never spoke to him about anything, since…"

"Since?"

"It isn't important. If you have no reasonable questions, I have things to do here."

Artemus opened the door and walked inside, leaving the inspector standing in the cold. He ignored it when he heard the door open behind him.

"Want to know where it happened?"

"I assume you want to tell me."

"And if I don't, you're not interested?"

"No."

"What are you, some sort of zombie? These are your parents who were murdered, not some random strangers. Your parents. Don't you have any feelings at all?"

Artemus spun around, his eyes blazing.

"What kind of feelings do you want me to have, inspector? Do you want me to cry? Do you want me to yell and scream? What do you suggest?"

"I suggest the normal sort of grief that a young man would have when he finds out his parents were murdered in cold blood."

"I'm not normal. My feelings are nobody's business, especially yours. If you're so interested in my parents' murders, why don't you stop wasting time and find out who did it? If you do find out, will that bring my parents back? I don't honestly care whether you find the killers or not. It won't change a thing in my life now."

Inspector Dawes regarded the boy for some time, trying to comprehend what he was hearing.

"Did you contract your parents' murders?"

Artemus exploded.

"Get the fuck out of my house! Get out! Get out of here!"

Tears streamed down his cheeks, and his body shook violently. He balled his fists, banging them on the dining table before him. Inspector Dawes put out a hand as though to console him, then quickly withdrew it, allowing the emotion to run its course.

"They died in the cellar, Artemus," he said softly, after the boy had taken in several large gulps of air. "There was no sign of a struggle. They were simply marched down there, tied up, and shot. There is also no evidence of a break-in or forced entry. These murderers were let in by your parents. They either knew them, or for some reason trusted them. I need your help in identifying your parents' friends and associates."

Artemus had regained his composure.

"Come to the funeral. Make a list. I can't tell you who my parents knew. They never had house guests; they didn't belong to any clubs. I don't think they had any friends. If they did, they never told me about them. But they never told me about anything."

It was not a complaint; it was a statement of fact.

Old Ship Church was overflowing, the line moving down the knoll to Main Street, and almost into Hingham center. Two closed caskets, draped with white, were staged beneath the high pulpit, in a recess with box pews on both sides. Peter Milkin, the minister, had tried in vain to involve Artemus with the service, sighing with disbelief when the young man even refused to attend the ceremony and burial. It was decided to offer a generic funeral prayer and open the church up to well-wishers, followed by interment in the adjacent burial ground. Inspector Dawes made sure that there was a guest book to be signed and appointed one of his female officers to make sure that everyone who attended signed the register. Afterwards, he spoke with the minister.

"Artemus told me that his parents had no friends, belonged to no clubs. Who were all of these people?"

"Darius Webb was one of the most successful businessmen in Hingham, Inspector Dawes. He made lots of money. I'm afraid that most of these people were paying their respects to his wealth. I agree with Artemus. His father was one of the most…uh…reserved men I have ever met. There wasn't an ounce of humor or feeling in the man. He attended services every Sunday, paying a fortune for that box just to the right of the pulpit, and as far as I saw, never once spoke to a single parishioner. He was generous with his donations, strictly tithing. He walked into church with his wife trailing along and left in the same fashion. The poor woman lived without a voice."

"Did he make any enemies?"

"Not that I am aware of. Nobody knew him. Oh, I suppose there were those who envied his wealth, but I never heard anyone curse him, or even speak badly of him for that matter. He lived in a sort of bubble."

"And his son?"

"He was lonely from the day he was born. I never saw his father say a single word to him. His mother tried to dote, but that was obviously forbidden. He attended the Derby Academy. You might inquire there of his habits, but I am sure that you will find that the boy was the product of the father."

"Hingham is a small New England town. I think you know what that means, Pastor Milkin. There must have been gossip, some skeletons that folks discussed."

"Oh, there was some talk a few years ago about reprisals that young Webb took with a few of the students, but there was nothing public."

"Reprisals? For what?"

"It seems that some of the boys beat up Artemus one day. Months later, he took them on one at a time. I was told that it was done dispassionately, so to speak, without any hint of emotion. Retribution. After that nobody ever bothered him again. He went off to Deerfield Academy at the end of primary. I think his classmates were relieved."

"Retribution," Inspector Dawes repeated, looking out toward the harbor, letting his voice drop off.

"If you think that young Artemus is responsible for his parents' murders, I wouldn't agree, inspector."

"No, why not? He seems to have quite a temper. And a long memory."

"He doted on his father. He wanted to be exactly like him in every way. He told me that several times, because I was worried about him as a young boy and tried to help if I could. Besides, if he wanted them dead, he would have done it himself. I can't recall ever seeing him allow another person to do anything for him. He was very independent."

Inspector Dawes heard the same story both at Derby Academy and at Deerfield. Artemus Webb was a loner, who worked hard, and didn't care at all about the things most young people considered important. That he was impressive, everyone agreed. A few teachers described him as "high principled." "Antisocial" was the common refrain, but "highly intelligent" was not far behind as an observation.

"He is brilliant," Sydney Phelps stated simply. "But he was out of place in a normal school environment. He is a mature man in a teenager's body. The other kids were brutal toward him, but they were also in awe. If their attitude bothered him, he never betrayed it."

"You seem to have gotten as close to him as anyone, Mr. Phelps. How did you do that?"

"I gave him goals to achieve and room to move. I got out of his way and let him teach himself. As I say, he's brilliant."

"What do you expect he will do now?"

"After watching Artemus for two years, I have no expectations, about anything. The man is completely different from anyone I have ever known."

"Seems that is the consensus, Mr. Phelps. So was Jack the Ripper."

In the week following the funeral, Artemus met with Winston Haverill, the family attorney, who handled both the personal and business affairs of Darius Webb. For several days, they reviewed the financials of the family as well as Webb Shipyards. Artemus was named as the sole heir, with authorization to step in immediately as the sole owner of the company.

"Your father changed his will last summer, Artemus," Haverill said. "He told me that you were already the most qualified person to run his company. Were you aware of that?"

"No, he never spoke to me about anything. In fact, he got very angry when I told him that Webb Shipyards either had to change or die."

"Precisely, that impressed him very much. He was a picture of pure pride when he related the story to me."

"He threw me out of his office."

Haverill cleared his throat and shuffled through the stack of papers in front of him. More than thirty years of dealing with Darius Webb had trained him well to work with the son. Nothing has changed, he said to himself, betraying the thought with a small sigh.

"I should tell you, Artemus…"

"I prefer 'Mr. Webb'."

"I should tell you, Mr. Webb, that you are a very wealthy young man, not only personally, but your company is possessed of tremendous equity and cash surpluses. Your father was probably at the financial high point of his career when he was… when he died. And he made sure that you would not be hit by large estate taxes. Essentially, you are free and clear financially."

"Precisely, what does that mean?"

"Personally, you inherit an estate, which after minimal taxes, is valued at approximately $15 million. Webb Shipyards shows cash reserves of more than $10 million, and assets of nearly $80 million. By any standards, in just about any industry, those are very impressive numbers."

"And what is your fee, Mr. Haverill?"

"My contract is very reasonable. About one percent."

"One percent of what?"

"One percent of your company and personal net receipts."

"Always one percent? Or does that increase in certain instances?"

"Well, when there are sales, and, uh… commissionable transactions…"

"Mr. Haverill, please have all of my personal and business files delivered to my office by the end of the day. I will inform you whether or not your services are still required after I have looked at our books."

Artemus abruptly stood and left the office, without further comment, leaving the lawyer in stunned silence.

❧

"I want every foreman in the conference room in an hour," Artemus commanded as he walked into his father's office at Webb Shipyards. "And tomorrow I want every contract and subcontract we have on my desk. I don't want to be disturbed the rest of the afternoon."

Mrs. Sheffield, the long-time personal secretary of Darius Webb, was startled by Artemus' sudden appearance and brusque demeanor.

"Oh, Artemus, I'm so sorry…"

"Don't even go there, Mrs. Sheffield. I don't have time. There are more important things to worry about right now."

"More important, Artemus?" she blurted out. "More important than the murder of your parents? How can you even conceive such a thought?"

Artemus stopped, halfway across the room. He turned and faced the woman.

"Mrs. Sheffield, it seems to me that you have been too long in my father's employ. That is evident from the weak emotions you are trying to express, at a time when this company is in great peril. I think that you should seek employment elsewhere immediately. I will give you two week's severance."

With that he spun and entered his father's office, calmly closing the door behind him. Without sitting, he dialed a number on the phone.

"Sydney, I need to see you. Immediately. How soon can you get here?... Where?...I'm at Webb Shipyards in Quincy. I have a proposal to make to you."

Finally, he sat behind the large mahogany desk. He leaned back in the stuffed chair, entwined his fingers behind his head, and let out an audible sigh.

"I am eighteen years old, and I have my own company," he intoned aloud without a trace of emotion. "And I am more than ready."

WEBB SHIPYARDS

Webb Shipyards was a sprawling complex of open drydocks and large closed workshops along the southern shore of Rock Island Cove near Quincy, Massachusetts. The Cove, just off of the Weymouth Fore River that dumped into Quincy Bay, provided some protection from the furious Nor'easters that hit the coast every winter. What had begun as a small ship painting yard had been expanded during World War II by Darius Webb into a center for the rehabilitation of old war ships and supply tankers. In the yards, those rusting relics were sanded, painted, welded and refitted back into functional ships to be sold to small countries looking for a defense fleet or to merchant corporations in search of sturdy tankers. Most of the ships came via the Panama Canal from mothball fleets in the Asia, Hawaii and the West Coast, having completed their tour of duty in the War in the Pacific. Darius Webb had ridden the wave of euphoria at the end of the war, which resulted in tremendous economic gain and almost tripled the size of his yards. Despite his previous objections to his son's declaration that the industry was dying, deep down he had believed that himself for some time. The ships he was refitting were old and slow and soon would be overtaken by sleeker, larger and more efficient vessels. But a lifetime of non-conversation with his son, could not bring him to reveal those doubts to the one person capable of continuing his legacy.

A freezing December wind swept through the yards at the Webb Shipyards as Artemus made his way from the dry docks to the office. He cursed New England weather which could at a whim whip up a raging nor'easter and choke the land of all moving life. The day had commenced in cold sunshine, but he was not dressed for the afternoon.

"I was born here," he muttered out loud to himself, "and I still don't know how to dress for the winter."

With a grim, determined look on his face, he entered his office where he gathered a sheaf of papers before going to meet the foremen in the conference room.

His arrival yesterday had left the company in chaos. Within minutes of his encounter with Mrs. Sheffield, the news had spread to every employee in the shipyard, from the welders to the janitors. The reaction was a mixture of shock, fear, and anger. Mostly fear. Webb Shipyards had settled into the complacency inspired by success, satisfaction from the booming post-war business. Workers received adequate wages, even augmented by a bit of overtime. Contracts flowed in, creating an optimism that was impossible to ignore. The entire firm was in a state of disbelief over the grisly murders of Darius and Melinda Webb. Since Webb Shipyards was a family company, no one wanted to even guess as to the future. While most of the workers knew Artemus from his summer work in the factory, they couldn't imagine that he was capable of actually assuming control of the business.

Ten men sat around the conference table when Artemus entered, the foremen who represented the entire production team of Webb Shipyard as well as the accountants and sales people. Each had been summoned with a cursory message, to present himself with a description of his division and duties. None of the foremen had the least idea what was expected in such a description. Work at the yard had come to a complete halt as the leaders scrambled to put some sort of report on paper.

"Why has there been no work done this morning?" Artemus demanded to nobody in particular before he took his place at the head of the table. "Who told the workers to stop?"

The question was met with nervous silence. A burly man wearing a leather apron slowly rose to his feet.

"I told them to hold up work, Mr. Webb. Nobody is certain what is expected of us, given the shock of your parents' murders, and your arrival yesterday."

Artemus ignored the second half of the man's declaration.

"The murder of my parents has nothing to do with the building of ships, Mr. Murphy. It will be dealt with by the police."

Frank Murphy didn't falter. "Yesterday you fired one of the most loyal employees in our company, for no apparent reason. Is that what we are all to expect?"

A murmur of surprise passed around the table. Several heads nodded as each man focused on Artemus, awaiting his response.

"Yes."

As though a cork had exploded from a champagne bottle, protests burst from every mouth, the room filling with exclamations. Artemus regarded the agitated men without a hint of concern. Only he and Frank Murphy remained silent, their eyes locking. Slowly Murphy folded his arms.

When the furor diminished after several minutes, Artemus raised his voice.

"You will all kindly sit down and be silent."

Only Murphy remained standing, not having moved since his original statement.

"Sit down, Mr. Murphy," Artemus said quietly. "I accept your decision. Do you have a report for me?"

One by one, the veteran ship workers rose and gave their reports, some hesitantly, some tersely, some with defiance. It was clear that none of the men, save perhaps Murphy, knew quite what to make of this youngster who was apparently suddenly their boss. Including Murphy, none knew what to expect. The reports concluded, each deposited a file in front of Artemus, and silently left the room.

Once clear of the office, they separated into two groups, suits and boots, the men who worked the assembly lines heading for the workshop; the coat-and-tie administrators walking to their cars in the parking lot. Without speaking, the latter group knew that they had to discuss events away from the shipyard. For the line foremen, the open air was a sufficient meeting room. The men burst verbally with released tension.

"What the hell was all that about?" Samuel Outlander, a twenty-year veteran muttered. "Does that little asshole think he can actually run this company?"

"He can go fuck himself," another man declared. "I've never had to write a report in my life. What the hell does he expect from us?"

Among the six men, only Frank Murphy remained calm.

"Take it easy, you guys. Let's just wait and see what happens. He's no fool, that boy. Did you notice he addressed each of us by name? And he knew exactly what we all did. Let's wait and see."

"Wait for what, Frank? To get fired on the spot like Mrs. Sheffield?"

❧

Sydney Phelps looked around the office of Webb Shipyards, noting the empty desks with interest. The glass door behind that desk read simply "Darius Webb," printed in block letters. The door was closed. Finding no one in the large room, he knocked tentatively on the glass, receiving a loud "Come in!" He found Artemus behind a large mahogany desk that was cluttered with papers.

"Oh, Sydney, I'm glad you're here. Sit down. I'm just reading these reports."

Phelps pulled up one of the old oak armchairs that were strewn around the office, and sat down, studying his erstwhile student closely. For a quarter hour the two sat without so much as a word exchanged. Finally, Artemus put down a file and looked up.

"We have some decisions to make," he said simply.

"I assumed you would say that. Those are departmental reports?"

Artemus didn't betray his surprise at his former teacher's astute assumption.

"They are, and I don't like what I'm reading. They are all positive evaluations, almost glowing."

"And you find that disturbing? Why?"

"Because in this world, nothing is glowing."

"I know where you are going with this, Artemus, but tell me anyway. Why do positive reports bother you?"

"Because, if you are going to grow and develop, you have to know what's not good instead of what is good. You have to know what to change."

"Did you ask the foremen for that?"

"No, they should know that. That's why they are foremen."

"Not necessarily. Maybe they just advanced by attrition.

"Precisely. I think they all got to where they are just because they lasted the longest. I think I am going to clean out all of them."

"And who do you expect to run the company?"

"I'm going to sell it."

"If you fire all the managers who is going to buy your company?"

"Webb Shipyards shows fine profits. That will sell the company."

"Would you buy it?"

"I'm selling it."

"You didn't answer the question. If you saw a profitable company that just lost its long-time owner and the administration was newly fired, would you buy it?"

Artemus sat back in his chair, glaring at his former teacher. He took a deep breath and let it out.

"No."

Phelps calmly regarded the young man behind the desk, not showing the triumph he felt at winning the argument. Seconds passed before Artemus dropped his gaze.

"I'll pay you $100,000 a year."

"And what would I do for that huge amount?"

"Exactly what you just did. Every time. I want someone who will be loyal, and above all, honest."

"And if you don't like what I am telling you?"

"I don't intend that I'll ever like what you're telling me. That's why I want you next to me."

"When do I start?"

"You have. I will put a full year's salary in escrow, just in case you get fired unexpectedly. I never asked, do you have a family?"

"I have a wife. We'll have to find a place to live. I would like a week to make the arrangements."

"Three days. And I want you to do two other things."

Phelps stood waiting.

"Find out who killed my parents. And find a woman named Allison Fielding."

"I'll need a budget."

"You have whatever you need. These last two tasks—be quick."

Artemus turned back to his reports. Without looking up, he said in a low, threatening voice, "And Sydney, don't ever call me Artemus again."

Frank Murphy pulled off his heavy coat and hung it on a clothes rack near the door. He shivered, but still unbuttoned his shirt sleeves and rolled them up a couple of turns while looking around the office building. No one occupied the receptionist desk, which didn't surprise him. It was 7:00 in the morning and snowing outside. Too early and too cold. He shook his head a couple of times, waved his hand across his graying hair and knocked.

"Enter!"

"Good morning, Mr. Webb," he said politely. "I got your phone call this morning." He didn't mention his wife's reaction to a 5:00 A.M. phone call that woke the entire family and sent a shock wave through the house.

"Sit down, Mr. Murphy. We have to talk."

Artemus looked as though he had spent the night at his desk. His eyes were heavy, his hair unkempt. He needed a shave.

"I'll be blunt, Mr. Murphy. We need to overhaul Webb Shipyards."

"I don't understand. We aren't lacking in work. We have contracts stacked up, waiting to be filled. We…"

Artemus cut him off. "I have spent the night reading through all of these reports. None of them are honest. We are losing money on bad bids; we are producing last year's product; our equipment is outmoded or broken; we are standing still, and our shadow is consuming us. These reports are those of complacent men. I want hungry men."

Murphy moved uneasily in his chair, unsure how to answer, or even if he was expected to answer. Silence filled the room like a suffocating cloud. Finally, Artemus broke the tension.

"I am making you the plant superintendent, effective immediately. I expect your full and complete effort, and your loyalty. If you accept, you can expect a good bit of unpleasantness in the days and weeks ahead. I want to root out anyone who isn't willing to give his soul to Webb. We are going to fashion the finest shipyard in the world, and we are going to start tomorrow. I will expect your answer by 9:00 this morning. There will be nothing easy if you accept, but you will be compensated liberally."

"Why me, if I might ask," Mr. Webb?"

"Because you came closest to an honest report, and yesterday you were the only one of your colleagues who showed any sign of having balls. I will await your answer at 9:00."

"You can have it now. I accept."

"Good, you just passed the first test. If you had waited 'til 9:00, I would have withdrawn the offer. Sit down. We have work to do.

❧

Sydney Phelps had nothing to report when he arrived at Artemus' office the day after the funeral.

"There is no record anywhere of an Allison Fielding. At least not in New England. And there are no leads on your parents' murders. I have hired a private investigator for both cases. He will report back weekly."

"Have you spoken with Inspector Dawes from the Hingham police?"

"Yes, or rather, he spoke to me. It seems that you are one of the prime suspects, Mr. Webb."

"I know. If I were in charge of the investigation, I would focus on me too. I still want you to pursue both subjects. Allison Fielding is a young woman, in case that comes up."

"I assumed that," Phelps responded stoically.

Artemus abruptly changed the subject.

"Now, about selling Webb Shipyards. We need to expand our sales."

"Why?"

"To show prospective buyers that the new administration is growing the business."

"That will take time, at least two quarters to register the growth."

"I'll accept two quarters for sales growth, but I also want a new product, one that hasn't yet been developed. Find out if there are any shipyards on the market right now, anywhere in North America. I want to buy one. Secretly."

❧

Artemus closed the shipyard for four days in memory of Darius and Melinda Webb. On December 20, the workers returned to work, the cloud of uncertainty even thicker and more ominous. Every detail of the funeral had been spread and amplified among the ship workers and their community. Artemus' cold demeanor and apparent indifference to the murders of his parents was the scandal of the entire Boston area.

Speculation about his complicity in the crime was rampant, even hinted at in the *Herald American*. Thus far the *Boston Globe* was silent on the subject, but talk shows were having a field day. The financial pages were filled with the history and profitability of Webb Shipyards, broadcasting a picture of profit that was the envy of the industry. There were dire predictions about the company, now in the clutches of an eighteen-year-old boy.

A stage with a public address system had been set up in the main warehouse at the shipyard. The workers were directed to take seats for important announcements, which only heightened the dread they were feeling. Artemus, dressed neatly in suit and tie, stood on the stage with Frank Murphy, who was in his usual work clothes. There was no need for a call to order; silence filled the room in advance of the people.

"Good morning to all of you," Artemus began. "It has been a very difficult week, but one which I intend to put behind us quickly and permanently. I am here to announce to you that Webb Shipyards is about to enter a new era, one in which we will become the envy of the ship building world. We will begin this morning, by introducing Mr. Frank Murphy as the new plant superintendant. It will be his duty to oversee our production and to make sure that every employee is producing to the maximum of his abilities. During the next week, each one of our employees will be interviewed and will have a detailed job description assigned, carefully listing not only his duties but our expectations of production. Some of you are content with the output of Webb Shipyards to date. I am not. I intend to double that output in the coming year. To that end, our sales staff will be increased. We are looking into plant expansion along the Hingham shore already. That is all. Each of you is to report to your normal work station, where you will resume the work you were on prior to our recent problem. Thank you."

With that, Artemus walked off the platform, disappearing in the direction of his office. Frank Murphy took the mike and called for a meeting with the various plant foremen. The rest of the workers, at first confused by the abrupt end of the meeting, slowly began to work their way silently toward their job sites.

"What the hell was all of that, Frank?" one of the foremen shouted.

"Take it easy, Billy," Frank responded. "Take it easy. All of you, sit down and shut up. There is a new rule at Webb now, and you all better listen up."

Murphy passed out a thick packet of forms to each man. Every foreman was asked to produce a list of all his workers, a description of their duties, and to rank them in order of their value to Webb Shipyards.

"What kind of shit is this, Frank?" one of the older men yelled after looking at the first form. "If you think I'm going to write up a hit list of my men, you're fucking crazy. I'll quit before I do that."

"That's your decision, Mikey," Murphy responded. "It may also be your job. That goes for all of you. I had a long talk with Mr. Webb, and I agree with his ideas about building this shipyard. We are going to get trim and mean. If you want to be part of it, part of running this place, then you are going to have to prove you can be a leader. If you can't, you're going to be history.

"What'd he pay you Frank? I hope you got your blood money."

Murphy ignored the grumbling. He looked hard at the men, most of whom were life-long friends.

"Give this a chance, men. I don't want to lose any of you. Give it time. I know you'll be surprised."

He didn't mention that as plant superintendent he also had a list to complete, a quality ranking of these very foremen who were standing there grumbling. He also didn't tell them that the bottom third of every list was about to be fired.

REBECCA

The conviction of Geoffrey Malkin and Conner Negri not only sent a shock wave through Yale University, but throughout New England. The story made news in the campus newspapers of universities across the country, sending a warning shot all along Fraternity Row. Both Malkin and Negri were sentenced to three years in prison, shortened by half because of their previous clean record. The defense legal team immediately filed an appeal, but it was withdrawn just a week following the trial with no explanation.

Rebecca returned to high school life and a wide range of responses. The details of the trial were disseminated among the student body that was bent and folded by the whispers of gossip. Generally, she was a hero among the girls, who had always regarded her as something of a crusader for women's causes. But to that was added the impossible achievement of standing up to the entire legal system, indeed even standing up to the men of Yale. As for the boys, there was no end to the levels of their responses. If there was one statement from the trial that was reported accurately it was Rebecca's declaration, "I thought I had been a virgin long enough." That drew responses from the high school boys that ranged from astonishment to near reverence. None of them even considered asking her out on a date.

While Lisa Bente and Valerie Moss remained close friends, Michelle Hoover, ordered by her parents to banish Rebecca from her life, walked away whenever their paths threatened to cross. Rebecca was perfectly content not to care, although she pitied her erstwhile friend for being such a "wimp."

She graduated number one in her class, which automatically made her the valedictorian to the considerable consternation of most of the school community. When her honor was announced, more than a few parents filed protests with the administration, all of which were disregarded. Her speech was the most anticipated in Connecticut College High School history.

"If this school, or any school does their job properly, they will teach their students to be radicals," she opened, to the shock of her mother and pride of her father. "We should be educated to look at the institutions around us and try to tear them down, to build something better. We should accept nothing at face value, until we have analyzed it and found it logical and good."

It was a speech that was designed to be shocking but was in fact uplifting, greeted when Rebecca concluded with a communal exhalation of relief and a warm ovation.

"Oh Simon," Sandra Walton whispered, clutching his arm, "thank God it's over!"

"It really was a very good speech," he responded, kissing her on the cheek.

To the complete shock of her parents, teachers and classmates, Rebecca didn't accept the scholarship to Connecticut College. Instead she applied for pre-law at Yale, with twin majors in English literature and creative writing. Causing even greater shock, her application received early acceptance with a scholarship offer that took care of more than half of the room, board and tuition.

"Rebecca," her friend Valerie protested, "are you crazy? They will murder you at Yale. That judge is a big alum. He'll make life miserable for you in law school."

"I hope he does," Rebecca responded with a smile. "That will make me work harder."

"Dad, I don't want to get a job this summer," Rebecca announced the day after her graduation. "I want to start preparing for law school and I need the time."

"That's okay with me, sweetheart," Simon Walton said. "What do you mean by 'preparing?'"

"I am going to take a look at seminar papers on file at the college, and I am going to start keeping a journal."

"I can understand the seminar papers," her father told her, "but why the journal?"

Rebecca was silent for a moment, considering.

"It won't be a normal journal. I want to start observing people and describing them."

She let out a small laugh.

"Dad, if I'm going to be a great trial lawyer, I need to know what makes people tick. I need to know what they are thinking even before they know it themselves."

"Where are you going to find these people?"

"I'm going to hit the streets, start bumping into people, make them talk to me."

Sandra Walton had been listening silently. More and more she had found herself outside the conversations of her husband and daughter and had developed a dread where Rebecca's future was concerned. Listening to her now, drew her into the dialogue.

"Becky, you can't just walk down the street and start up random conversations. People are going to react."

"Of course they will Mom. That's exactly what I want them to do and their reactions are going into my journal. I had a teacher who told us that we should never leave a person without having made them say something. That's what I'm going to do, make them say something."

"Rebecca," her Dad asked quietly, "what is it you want to be able to do with all of this? You must have a plan."

"Dad, I want to be able to ask anything I want, to say anything I want, without being embarrassed or afraid. We have a first amendment that gives me free speech. But everyone is afraid to ask or say what they really feel."

She paused, taking a deep breath.

"I want to learn not to be afraid. I want to be able to ask the question I am pondering, to state the argument I am feeling. I want to look an asshole in the eye and tell him he's an asshole, without fear or inhibition. I want a blank slate in front of me that I can write on."

Her mom was silent, dumbfounded by Rebecca's outburst. Her father silently arose from his chair, walked over and embraced her.

"Rebecca," he whispered, "go for it."

It was a summer of pure adventure. Rebecca engaged everyone she encountered, the toll collector on the Connecticut Turnpike, the cop in Old Saybrook giving parking tickets, the cadets at the Coast Guard Academy, the old folks visiting Mystic Seaport. She confronted authority; consoled crying children; enraged librarians; befriended tramps and railroad hobos. She forced everyone to talk to her, or scream at her, or cry with her. And everyone she encountered found their way into her journal. She recorded their eyes, their tears, their anger, their passion. She learned what made them tick. But she also learned what made her tick, what was difficult for her to say, to do, or to ask. In the course of confronting people and their hang-ups and problems she learned about herself, and her strengths and weaknesses. It all went into the journal.

Rebecca hit the Yale campus like a tornado. Her reputation preceded her because of the sensational trial in the spring. The older students, aligned by gender for or against her, were frankly astonished that after the trial she had still applied to Yale.

"She's got more balls than all the guys that tried to rape her," one of the more outspoken frat boys had laughed. But for the men on campus, Rebecca was a bitch of the first order; for the women, she was a hero. She walked around campus leaving a large trail of whispers in her wake.

The college system at Yale was only in its infant stages, purportedly designed after those at Oxford and Cambridge in England. Freshmen were not allowed to enter one of the colleges. Consequently, Rebecca was assigned to one of the freshmen dormitories for women, a situation she immediately refused to accept. With three women of like mind, she moved off campus into a nearby apartment house. A week into the school year she found herself summoned into the office of Virginia Saugus, the Dean of Students.

"Miss Walton," the Dean stated flatly, "I understand that you and three of your classmates have taken an apartment in town. That is unacceptable. We do not allow freshmen to live off campus."

"Why is that?" Rebecca snapped back.

"We feel that leaving your homes and coming off to college is a major adjustment for any student. There are dangers and pitfalls that we would like to protect our students from."

"Dean Saugus, I am perfectly capable of defending myself against pitfalls and dangers, and even if I weren't it would not be your responsibility. I am eighteen years old and considered no longer a minor by law. I do not want to live in a dorm."

"I'm afraid that is the rule, Miss Walton," the Dean responded with a tired voice. "If you do not wish to abide by it, I'm afraid you will have to find another university."

"Dean Saugus, have you been inside of one of the female dorms lately?" Rebecca asked pointedly.

"Not for some time. Why do you ask?"

"I ask because if you had visited those dorms you would refuse to allow your own daughter to live in them. They are filthy, unpainted, over-crowded, stifling hot in summer and freezing in winter. Convicts have better facilities than freshmen students at Yale. I refuse to live in such squalor."

"I'm sure that you are exaggerating the condition of the dorms, Miss Walton. I haven't heard a single complaint about them."

"Then, Dean Saugus, you are either blind and deaf or dead. Would you allow me to give you a tour of the dorm to which I was assigned?"

"There is no need…" the dean began, and then she changed her entire tone. "I accept your offer, Miss Walton. Shall we go now?"

They walked briskly over to Old Campus, the site of a quadrangle of Victorian Gothic dormitories that had all been built during the 1920s. Rebecca had been assigned to one of the dormer rooms on the fourth floor at McClellan Hall. Three girls were lodged in each room. Since she and two of her roommates had never actually occupied the room, it was still empty, so she marched the dean up four flights of stairs to a hallway that in September was positively stifling.

"Cockroaches," she declared dryly, pointing at a corner of the landing, as a couple of the dreaded bugs scurried for cover.

There was debris—empty cans, papers, food wrappers—strewn around the stairwell and especially evident on the top floor when they arrived. Rebecca pointed out three mice feeding toward the end of the hall.

"Let's start with the shower room, Dean Saugus," she said, waving toward the middle of the floor.

"Would you care to shower here?" she asked, as they entered a steamy room with peeling paint, lipstick messages on the mirrors, overflowing cannisters filled with towels, paper, tampons, and other female sanitary items. The dean was speechless.

"Let me show you the room that was assigned to three students. It measures twelve feet by fifteen feet.

There were three small narrow single beds lined up against the outside dormer wall. A door-less closet set into the right wall was divided into three vertical compartments, the only storage except for under the beds. Three small desks were scattered around the remaining walls. There was a decided odor of sewage in the room.

"Well, Dean Saugus, would you stay here?"

She looked at her watch.

"I'm sorry but I have a class to attend."

Rebecca left without another word, leaving the dean behind in the awful room.

The following morning she was again called into the dean's office.

"Miss Walton, I want to thank you for your tour yesterday. I fully agree that the conditions of that dorm, and others I inspected, are not acceptable. We will begin a program of upgrading immediately, and for that we are indebted to you and the other young women who are living with you. As a result, we have decided to accept your present living conditions with the proviso that you will take your meals with the other freshmen students.

"Dean Saugus, would you like another tour of the freshmen cafeteria?"

The dean let out a laugh.

"That too?" she asked.

"I would suggest that you visit the cafeteria when it is in full use, and then go to the dining rooms of any of the colleges. Yale has relegated its new students to a grossly substandard quality of living. I am thrilled to be able to learn at this great university, but I absolutely refuse to accept that quality of living that you are demanding. I will pay for tuition, but I refuse to accept your room and board."

The smile disappeared from Dean Saugus' face.

"You are making it very difficult, Miss Walton."

"I will commute the fifty miles from my home in New London before I will stay in those dorms or eat in that dreadful cafeteria.

"We will make a decision by tomorrow," the dean said dryly. "Good day, Miss Walton."

❧

For a third straight morning, Rebecca found herself sitting in the dean's office. This time she was forced to wait more than half an hour before she was called in.

"Miss Walton, we have been called to attend a meeting at the president's office. Please come with me."

They walked briskly to Woodbridge Hall, in the center of campus on Wall Street. Inside they were ushered into the impressive chambers of President Franklin Wilmington. He rose and greeted them warmly.

"Dean Saugus, welcome," he said graciously. "And you must be the irrepressible Rebecca Walton. I must say you have firmly established your place at this university, perhaps quicker than anyone in history. Please sit down."

"President Wilmington, believe me, I don't want a place except as a hard-working student."

The president smiled.

"There is undoubtedly a 'but…' that follows that statement.

For the first time in several days, Rebecca smiled.

Nodding to the president, she concluded her statement.

"…but I don't want to live in sordid conditions while attending one of the world's great institutions."

The president nodded, ceding the point.

"I am not sure what to do with you, Miss Walton. I agree that the conditions you so correctly pointed out are not acceptable, but we also have a firm tradition that all freshmen will live on campus. I find it impossible to make an exception for one student."

"Four students, Mr. President," Rebecca corrected. "But it could easily be four hundred."

"I'm not sure I understand," he responded.

"Sir, I am not alone in being appalled by the condition of the freshmen dorms and cafeterias. If you were to make an announcement that while those conditions are being upgraded, freshmen students would have the option of finding lodging off campus on a month-by-month basis, I think you would find a great many who would jump at the chance. As for the food services, those could be improved immediately, and freshmen could still be required to eat on campus. Once the dorms have been cleaned and free of vermin, and the overcrowding has been resolved, students could be required to return to campus lodging."

President Wilmington was silent for a while, pondering Rebecca's suggestion. Finally, he smiled and stood.

"Dean Saugus, I think that is all for now. Thank you for bringing all of this to my attention. If you don't mind, I have a few more things to discuss with Miss Walton."

The dean left, and President Wilmington resumed his chair and looked directly at the young woman in front of him.

"Miss Walton, it seems that Judge Macklin's appraisal of you was spot on."

Rebecca was startled.

"Judge Macklin? I have nothing to do with that man."

"I believe you do, Rebecca. It was Judge Macklin who got you early admission, and it is Judge Macklin who is keeping you in school right now."

"I don't understand," Rebecca began to protest, then went silent.

"Nearly everyone at this university is sadly familiar with your story, and its connection with Geoffrey Macklin. I'm sure you know that. But what you apparently don't know is that Judge Macklin was so impressed by your behavior and ideas at Geoffrey's trial, he insisted on your being admitted to pre-law at Yale. He feels you have a tremendous future in the law. He has asked me to have you drop by his office this afternoon."

He handed Rebecca the judge's card.

"2:00. Be prompt."

For once in her life, Rebecca was speechless.

WILLIAM MACKLIN

She arrived at the judge's office fifteen minutes early, having no idea what she was doing there. Almost immediately, the inner door opened, and a smiling Judge Macklin emerged, holding out his hand to Rebecca.

"It's nice to see you again, Miss Walton. And not in an unfortunate courtroom. Please come in."

He ushered her into the very prototype of a law office—huge walnut desk, relatively uncluttered, three walls of book shelves filled with the august leather tomes of the law. A Remington bronze was about the only ornamentation, a cowboy trying mightily to remain in the saddle of a wildly bucking bronco. She was directed to a pair of chairs on the side of the room. She took one and the judge sat in the other, removed from the power of the massive desk.

"It seems you have hit the campus running," the judge said with a laugh. I'm told you have the whole place in an uproar, trying to figure out how to skirt tradition without destroying the institution. Well done!"

Rebecca ignored the statement.

"Judge Macklin, do you mind telling me what is going on? The last time I saw you, I insulted both you and your son, and I got your son thrown in prison. Why am I here today?"

"Let's get something clear, Rebecca Walton. You did not get my son thrown in prison. My son got himself thrown in prison. And it may have saved his life. Quite honestly, I was prepared to take you and those other girls down, to have you destroyed for daring to accuse my son of rape. But then I watched your performance in the court room, and I reminded myself what it means to honor the law. You made me reevaluate everything I had been doing and thinking in the years prior to that trial. I accused myself and found myself guilty of arrogance. I decided it was not you and your friends that deserved to be taken down, but the whole patrician atmosphere that I and my son and his friends represented."

Rebecca sat there, shocked at the judge's frankness, not knowing how to respond.

"I acted completely out of anger," she said. "I was tired of being treated like an insignificant female."

"The point is," the judge observed, "that you channeled your anger into a plan, and you pulled that plan off beautifully. You never even blinked. It took me a couple of weeks to realize that and that is why I helped you get into Yale. I want to watch you grow."

He rose and walked over to his desk, then turned and faced her.

"Miss Walton, I would like to serve as your mentor."

❧

"Miss Walton, anger is only useful in the courtroom if it's concealed. The minute you expose it, you provide an opening that will most certainly be used. Sarcasm, which is a not so subtle form of anger, works only when a male uses it. In a woman it is a negative. Irony is basically useless because few people, especially in the jury box, understand it."

Rebecca had accepted a position as a clerk in Judge Macklin's office. It gave her the opportunity to scour the library of law decisions that filled his shelves. Gifted with a near photographic memory, she absorbed the decisions and the would-be precedents as if she were drinking a glass of water. Her reading was punctuated by a continuous flow of questions from the judge who had mentally placed his entire professional fortune on this precocious woman who combined mental acuity with driving work ethic, complete lack of inhibition where questions needed to be asked, and an imaginative mind that could construe solutions where none seemed to be available. For three years, while she was maintaining a complete course in the classics and writing, she virtually put together a law curriculum as well.

She had won her initial battle over freshmen housing. The reaction of the students when they were told they could temporarily move off campus while the dorms were being revitalized was exactly as she had predicted to President Wilmington—so many students moved out of the dreadful dorms that the school was able to empty Durfee and McClellan dormitories and could expedite their remodeling. By the second semester, they were finished, and students were moved from other dorms to repeat the process. By year's end, all the freshmen dorms were upgraded.

Rebecca had been designated for Saybrook College, one of fourteen residential colleges on the Yale campus. Her complaints about dorm living were eliminated when she was assigned lodging at Vanderbilt Hall, perhaps the best on campus. Compared to that first dorm room at McClellan Hall, she was living in a palace.

"Dad, I'm going to get out of school in three years," she told her father, "less if I can swing it."

At eighteen or twenty units a semester she easily completed the course work a year ahead of time. That academic schedule, combined with her clerkship with Judge Macklin gave her no leisure time, something that worried her parents considerably.

"Becky, you have to relax sometimes," her mother scolded. "You can't just work all the time."

"It's what I want to do, Mom," she always replied. "I'll relax when I am finished with school."

Her father laughed and broke in, "Becky, I can guarantee you that will never happen. If you think you are driven now, just wait until you start your profession."

In 1954, at twenty-one years old, Rebecca graduated, Summa Cum Laude from Yale and was immediately accepted into their prestigious law school. Judge Macklin hosted a graduation party at his old Queen Anne Victorian near Wooster Square. He positively doted on his new graduate who in his mind had become the daughter he had never had. Rebecca was the center of attention, this outrageous, outspoken prodigy who had conquered the Yale humanities curriculum in an unheard-of three years.

She was the center of attention until, halfway through the evening, the judge introduced a new guest—his son Geoffrey, who had been released from prison and had spent the last two years working with the National Park Service in Yellowstone and the Southwest. He walked in, trim, tanned and smiling to general applause, a surprise to all in the room.

Judge Macklin had spirited him off to the National Park Service the day he was freed from the ancient Cheshire Correctional Institute just north of New Haven. He had spent his time healing his mind and body and had only recently returned to the East to resume his schooling at Yale.

"Hello, Rebecca," Geoffrey said quietly, after he had made the circuit of his old friends and family. "I hear from my father that we are virtually brother and sister by now."

Rebecca looked up at him, unsuccessfully trying to match the new Geoffrey with the boy who was etched in her memory.

"I hope for both of us that that is not true," she said coquettishly. "I am happy that you are back home."

"I understand that you are bound for law school."

"Yes, largely thanks to your father. For a reason I can't begin to understand, he has taken me under his wing and pushed me through."

"Well, I understand if you don't," he responded. "You will remember that I saw you in action three years ago. It is something I don't ever want to forget."

"Well, welcome home, Geoffrey. Maybe someday we can go back to Delmonico's and begin this whole thing over, the proper way."

She walked away and joined a group of fellow graduates around the food table.

Judge Macklin had watched the conversation with interest.

INSPECTOR DAWES

William Dawes was frustrated. He had been in law enforcement for more than twenty-five years with the Boston Police Department and he had never encountered a case like this. In more than a month of combing the Webb estate, forensics hadn't turned up a single bit of evidence. Except for the pair of bodies, this wasn't a crime scene at all—no fingerprints, no footprints, no signs of a fight or even an argument, no evidence of forced entry—nothing. Two people had apparently admitted their killers, been walked to the cellar and executed. Except for the peculiar reaction of Artemus Webb, a reaction that was completely within the general description the boy had broadcast to his world, there was not a suspect of any sort. Dawes had spoken to all of Artemus' teachers and many of his classmates in two schools. He had even spoken to the boys whom Artemus had beaten up. Everyone had the same report—Artemus Webb was anti-social and didn't care if anyone liked him. That was hardly grounds for murdering his parents.

As he arrived at the office of Webb Shipyards, he bumped into Sydney Phelps.

"You're a long way from school, Mr. Phelps," the inspector said by way of greeting. "Here to visit your lost student, who I understand is now a filthy rich young man?"

"No, actually, I have been hired by Mr. Webb as an advisor."

"Really, does that surprise you?"

"Nothing surprises me about Mr. Webb. He most certainly doesn't follow any normal path as far as his predictability is concerned. No, he hired me, in his words, 'to be honest with him.' Thus far I have been."

"Does that mean you are advising him on business as well as personal matters?"

"I suppose so. He hasn't really spelled out my duties yet."

"Can I ask you, did he ever mention his parents in your talks with him at Deerfield?"

"He never mentioned anything at all. Most of our conversations were a sentence or two at most. I would give him a project; he would accept it and walk away. I would ask him a question and receive a curt, but prompt answer, one that was almost always spot on. He may be antisocial, but he is a very analytical thinker, and at the same time, capable of synthesizing some rather complex subjects."

"You seem very captivated by Artemus Webb."

"Frankly, I have never met anyone like him, at any age."

"Is he capable of killing his parents?"

Phelps stared at Inspector Dawes.

"Are you serious? You suspect that Artemus murdered his parents?"

"I have to ask every question I can come up with."

"That is an absurd question. Good day, Inspector."

Phelps walked away from the office, heading for the shipyard, leaving Inspector Dawes standing on the steps. The policeman watched him leave, then entered the office, asking for Artemus Webb.

"Good morning, Artemus," Inspector Dawes said with a smiling greeting as he entered his office, knowing full well that Artemus insisted that everyone call him 'Mr. Webb.' I have a few quick questions and I'll be out of your hair."

He didn't wait for Artemus to respond.

"Did you make any phone calls to your parents the day they were murdered?"

"No, I never phoned them the whole time I was at Deerfield. My father forbade it in no uncertain terms. He said I was supposed to grow up and hanging on his shirttails was no way to do it."

"Did you resent that?"

"Of course I didn't. He was right."

Artemus couldn't hide his interest though.

"Why do you ask anyway? Were there calls made from Deerfield that day?"

"We think your parents died around 9:00 P.M. There were seven phone calls made from Western Massachusetts, between 1:00 and 5:00 that afternoon. He handed Artemus a list. One was DE 4-2682.

"That's the payphone at the Deerfield Inn. This one, NA 8-1011 is from Millers Falls. There are calls from Manchester, New Hampshire, Hartford, Southwick, Amherst and West Springfield. The numbers are all payphones. Does that list mean anything to you?"

Artemus stared at the list for several seconds. He put it down and looked at the detective.

"Except for Amherst and Deerfield, they were all places where I visited plants and mills for my research project."

"And your father was aware of that project?"

"It's what we argued about. Those plants were all dying or dead. I told him that Webb Shipyards would be the next to go. He didn't like hearing that and threw me out of his office."

"Do you think he was checking up on your research work for some reason?"

"I have no idea," Artemus replied with a wave of his hand, then paused a moment, seeming to consider something. "If he hired someone to follow me around, you ought to look at his expenditure records. He would have to pay them."

He paused again.

"But if he didn't want anyone to know, he would have paid in cash."

"I checked. There were no apparent payments made. Why would you think he would want to keep that secret?"

"I didn't say I thought that. I have no idea what my father thought."

"Your lawyer says that your father was proud of your project, that he changed his will to turn the company completely over to you on his death. That doesn't sound like a man who wasn't interested in his son."

"It sounds like a man who talked to everyone but his son," Artemus replied bitterly. "Is there anything else you need, Inspector? Oh, by the way, were there any calls from Boston that day?"

"I don't remember any. I'll check though. Why do you ask?"

"Curiosity."

Shortly after Inspector Dawes left, Sydney Phelps returned to the office. Artemus handed him the sheet of phone numbers.

"See what you can do with these, Sydney," he said. "Those were phone calls made to my parents' house the day of their murders. Whoever made them would have had enough time to drive to Hingham and commit the crime. That seems to be the avenue the police are taking."

"Do you find it odd that Inspector Dawes gave you this list?"

"Yes."

"Did you make any of these calls, Mr. Webb?"

Artemus glared at his former teacher.

"I want you to make a list of the five-best legal-accounting firms in the country. I am going to need a new lawyer. And Sydney, get me a housekeeper and a cook."

Phelps left without another word. He was not gone long before Artemus had another visitor, Attorney Winston Haverill.

"I got your imperious message that you wanted a meeting," the lawyer announced dryly without any other greeting, not even removing his hat on entering. "I was told it was important. I have several more appointments this afternoon."

"It is only important if you want to hear that you are fired," Artemus retorted without looking up.

"You don't have the right, young man. We have a long contract which I have no intentions of abrogating."

Artemus looked up, glaring at the man. "Then your next conversation will be with the police. You have been stealing money from this company for ten years, milking my father as though he were a senile cow. For a high standing lawyer, you aren't very good at cooking the books. I will give you a very clear choice, Mr. Haverill—you will deposit $1.75 million in the Webb Shipyard general account and tear up our contract or I will take what I have found to the police. You have until tomorrow morning at 11:00. Now get out of my office."

Haverill started to blurt out an objection, swallowed hard, then spun and bolted out of the door. His exit produced the first smile of the day.

JOE AND NEMO'S

Christmas in New England is a special time, "White Christmas" coming alive most years. Every one of the traditional houses in Hingham proudly displays its tree, festooned with lights, some actually with candles. The streets glow with yew bushes decked with lights. Doors are bewreathed, many with branches of hemlock or fir, filled with cones and glass ornaments. A few shout out the season—bright red, with circles of local cranberries frozen in the winter air. In the stately houses, candle lights shine from every window, the traditional form of welcome in colonial inns, announcing hospitality and warmth. There are no plastic figures or commercial displays ruining the perfect lawns, which on a good year are white with new fallen snow. Given a recent storm, the inevitable snowman pops up here and there.

It was Christmas Eve. Artemus drove his Chevy down Seal Cove Road to a dark, forbidding house, a house that displayed none of the Christmas spirit enjoyed by his neighbors. Not wanting to shovel the driveway, he parked at the end of it near the street and trudged through the snow, which was crusted by the cold night air, crunching under his footsteps. He had the idle thought that his parents' killers couldn't have perpetrated their crime if there had been a snow storm. Inside, the house was also dark. His mother had always been responsible for Christmas decorations, but this year the boxes of ornaments, garlands and a few crèches lay stacked and unopened in the basement.

Weary from a long, contentious week, and unending reports, he plopped down with a heavy sigh in an overstuffed chair in the living room, not even bothering to turn on the lights. In seconds he was sound asleep. He awoke several hours later, still weary, but famished, knowing full well that there was nothing he could do about it because his house was empty of food. Still hopeful, he walked into the kitchen, opened the bare refrigerator. There were a few chips left in an old Lay's bag and a single banana, black-skinned with age. His shoulders slumped, and he stood there for a moment, angry—angry at himself for not having anything to eat, angry at the world for his isolation. For the first time in his memory, he felt sorry for himself. He realized he missed his parents. Shaking himself from his depression, he grabbed his heavy Lodencoat and walked out into the winter night. It was already 10:00. Most of the restaurants would be closed by now. He headed for a Friendly's café on Hanover Street in Quincy, arriving to find it closed and dark. Absentmindedly, perhaps attracted by the distant lights, he turned north onto Highway 3 toward Boston.

"There must be some restaurant that stays open on Christmas Eve," he murmured to himself, turning onto Cambridge Street, heading for city center and Scollay Square. There, as it has been for more than thirty years, was a bright neon sign advertising Joe and Nemo's. He had seen the place as a young boy, but it was far beneath his father's tastes to consider stopping there. Breathing a sigh of relief, Artemus pulled up on Stoddard Street and walked into the place. It was filled with people, standing in lines waiting at the counter or conversing loudly at tables strewn haphazardly around the large main room.

The man in front of him, well dressed, with bowler hat and scarf, turned in triumph when he finally arrived at the front of the line.

"I made it!" he yelled, donning his hat and bowing to the room, receiving a loud applause in return. He turned to one of the waiters, "I'll have two all around, my man, and regular coffee."

"What the hell does all that mean?" Artemus asked him.

"Where have you been, young man?" he retorted with a laugh. "This is Joe and Nemo's. They served dogs that way to my grandfather—mustard, onions, relish and horse radish—that's 'one all around.'"

"I'll have the same thing," Artemus ordered when his time arrived.

"Go find a seat, Mac. We'll bring it to you."

Artemus turned to find the man with the bowler waving him over. "Here's a seat. Better grab it while you can."

"Jeffrey Belcher," the man introduced himself, holding out his hand. "Merry Christmas!"

Artemus, taken back a bit by this unrestrained bonhomie, responded in kind, taking his seat at the long table that already held ten other diners.

"There's not a better dog in all the world," Belcher boasted, as their orders appeared. "New York brags about Nathan's, but they break the skins on their dogs, and they grill the buns. No class. I was out in California last year and they have a little shack in Oakland called Casper's. That's as close as I've ever come to Joe and Nemo's. They steam the buns, but they also steam the dogs, don't boil them the way Joe Merlino does. And they don't have horseradish."

Artemus realized that he was genuinely famished and waded into the hot dogs without replying. He devoured the two dogs, nodding when the waiter asked if he wanted more coffee.

"I ordered regular coffee," Artemus told the waiter. The coffee you brought me was filled with sugar and cream."

This brought a laugh from both the waiter and Belcher.

"Regular coffee in Boston has about three sugars and a couple of pulls of cream," Belcher said. "You really are new here."

This actually brought a laugh from Artemus.

"Native born," he told the man. "But my parents never let me have coffee. Is there irregular coffee?"

"Just black. Nobody around here would drink it that way."

"You seem to be a connoisseur of the world's hot dogs, Mr. Belcher" Artemus changed the subject. "What's the story about this place? Are they always open, even on Christmas?"

"They only close for an hour and a half every day, from 3:30 in the morning to 5:00. Otherwise they churn out the dogs, all day and all night. And yes, I have been eating hot dogs my whole life. I am ashamed that Boston also must tolerate those Fenway Franks out at the Sox games. But then you don't go to a baseball game to eat hot dogs, do you?"

Artemus assumed the last question was rhetorical.

"Is there that much business to keep this place open all night?"

"You *are* new here, that's for sure. See that building over across the street? That's the Old Howard. And down the street is the Crawford House and the Casino Theater. Strip shows, my boy. There is never a shortage of customers. That's the slogan of the Old Howard— 'Always Something Doing.' And there's always a dog to eat at Joe and Nemo's whatever you're doing and whenever you are doing it. You should go see the show at the Howard. You're just in time. They have a Christmas special tonight."

Acting on Belcher's suggestion, Artemus walked across the street to join a crowd, mostly men, who were queued up at the ticket office at Howard Theater. He found his seat in the left rear of the orchestra just before a trumpet announced the beginning of the show and the lights dimmed. A pretty young woman appeared on stage, clad entirely in red balloons. She led a monkey on a long leash. She began dancing, the balloons fluttering provocatively in all the right places. Suddenly she stopped, smiled lasciviously at the audience and handed the monkey an object, a sharp nail. Cleverly she danced around the animal, every so often stopping to expose a particular balloon to his nail. "Bang!" and the audience roared as slowly the woman's delightful attributes came graphically into view. The final balloon brought down the house.

It was part of the warm-up acts for the main show—the star of Boston burlesque, Lilyann Rose. Artemus was completely absorbed, finding himself yelling more than once, then quickly stifling his enthusiasm as soon as he realized he was enjoying the scene. It was 1:00 A.M. when the crowd pushed back onto the street. Heading to his car, he was stopped by a very well-dressed young woman.

"Buy a girl a drink, sailor?"

"I'm not a sailor," Artemus responded, feeling himself smile.

"The question still stands whoever you are."

"Sure, got a bar in mind?"

She led him down Cambridge Street to the Crawford House theater bar, still packed at this time of the morning.

When they were settled in a corner at a small table, the young woman, introduced herself as Beatrice Woolsey.

"And you are?" she inquired of Artemus, who was busy surveying the patrons, all of whom were theater-dressed.

"Just a visitor, no one important."

"Well, Mr. Visitor, welcome to Boston."

She turned to the waitress and ordered a Tassel Tosser.

"I'll have a beer," Artemus ordered, turning back to the woman. "What the hell is a Tassel Tosser?"

"It's a brandy drink, named after Sally Keith. She performs here."

"Tossing tassels?"

"Exactly, she can rotate them in opposite directions from each of her breasts."

"That I would like to see!"

"Too late. She's already finished tonight. But you're in luck. I can show you how she did it."

Artemus stared at her, at first not comprehending, then a light seemed to go on and he took a closer look the young woman.

"You're a hooker!"

"You don't have to be such a boor, Mr. Visitor. I call myself a professional if you please."

"Well, Miss Professional, I would like to see you do that."

"It's cost you. A sawbuck will get you a quicky, but that's hardly worth your time, or mine. But for a twenty, Sweetie, I'll take you right around the world."

Artemus pulled a wad out of his pocket, thumbed through it and pulled out a hundred-dollar bill.

"And where will this take me?"

Beatrice took the bill from the table, quickly stashed it in her bodice, stood, and grabbed Artemus' hand.

"Honey, I'm going to show you the galaxy!"

She led him to the elevator of the Crawford House.

❧

It was mid-afternoon on Christmas day when Artemus got home. Inspector Dawes was waiting for him in his driveway.

"Merry Christmas, Artemus," he said with an expansive smile.

"Do you get overtime for working on Christmas?"

"Only when I have a corpse to explain. You were out late, last night. Enjoy Scollay Square?"

"You followed me? Are you crazy?"

"Well, you are my only suspect, you know. Who else am I supposed to follow?"

"Get out of my way. I'm tired and I'm going to bed.

"Why didn't you tell me about Haverill? If you had, I might have saved his life."

"What are you talking about? What about Mr. Haverill?"

"He's dead. Hanged himself last night. Horrible Christmas present for his family. He blamed you in a note. Said you fired him, and he was ruined."

"Shame," Artemus said without expression or emotion, walking away to the back door of his house. Dawes followed him.

"Did you fire him?"

"Yes. He had been stealing from my father for ten years. I told him I wanted the money returned to the company bank account and our contract with him cancelled."

"You can prove that?"

"Didn't I just tell you he was cheating? Of course I can."

Artemus was about to slam the door on the inspector when he turned to face him.

"Are you sure it was suicide? I also checked Haverill's books and he was rolling in dough. A couple of million would barely have hurt him. Merry Christmas, Inspector."

Dawes stood there looking at the closed door. Suddenly the cold made him shiver.

ALLISON

By spring, Webb Shipyards was back in full production. To the surprise of Frank Murphy, the assembly line was noticeably more efficient once the number of workers had been reduced, a fact not lost on the workers themselves. When the first quarter results were made public, all the foremen received substantial bonuses, and the shipworkers' salaries were increased, for the first time in more than five years. Darius Webb had fought the unions all his life, successfully keeping them out of his company, but at a cost of occasional strife, as well as several threats to himself and his family. Artemus' salary raises put Webb Shipyard at the forefront of workers' compensation in the east coast shipbuilding industry, a fact not lost on the unions.

"Mr. Webb, you are increasing your labor costs," Sydney Phelps pointed out when they were reviewing the first quarter reports. "You said that was one of the reasons that American plants were closing. Have you changed your mind?"

"You wanted two good quarters, Sydney, before we could sell Webb Shipyard. You have your first one. If I'm selling the company, I don't care what kind of time bomb I place in it, so long as it detonates after the sale."

"I've found you a shipyard to buy."

Phelps pushed a thick file across the desk, its tab identifying "Wilkins-Owen Shipyard, Houston, Texas."

Artemus opened the file and glanced briefly at the content page.

"Thank you, Sydney. I bought it yesterday."

Phelps didn't betray his surprise.

"Do you mind if I ask what you are going to do with it?"

"I am going to create a demand for supertankers."

"Supertankers? Larger than we have now? What will you do with them, once they're built?"

"Now Sydney, you disappoint me. I don't actually intend to build them, just plant the idea. We are going into the land business. Get me a plat map of downtown Manchester, New Hampshire. And I'll want them for Plymouth, Lowell and Fall River too. And I want you to find me a detailed map of the greater Boston area. I think we are going to need a ring road."

"How did you know it was murder?" Inspector Dawes asked as he barged into Artemus' office, again without being announced,

It had become a type of game by now between the two, for the Inspector, a continuing source of frustration, increasing now that William Haverill's apparent suicide had been changed to a murder, leaving him with three unsolved homicides revolving around the enigmatic Mr. Webb. And with no solution in sight.

From Artemus' view, the inspector provided a welcome source of entertainment, a bit macabre to be sure, but in his own unstated way, he was also vitally interested in both cases. Because there wasn't a hint of a clue in either murder, Artemus was the suspect by default.

"I told you before, Inspector, William Haverill was a very wealthy man. Webb Shipyards wasn't his only victim. He was a multi-millionaire and my little bill wouldn't have put him over the edge."

He paused in his reading of reports and looked up at the lawman.

"How did you discover it was a murder, Inspector? It's hard to hang someone who doesn't want it to happen."

"We discovered knockout pills in his system. He probably wasn't even awake when he died."

"Who do you suppose will be the next victim?"

"If I were in your chair, Artemus," Dawes said dryly, "I would be commencing to worry. You are either the main suspect in both murders, or the potential victim in a third."

That drew an actual smile from Artemus.

"Only three, inspector? I was hoping at least to get into double digits."

"I'm serious, Artemus. People with money seem to be falling over dead in these parts. If you're not the murderer, then you can easily become a target."

Artemus did get serious.

"I'm surprised at you inspector. Think about it. Who is there who would benefit from the deaths of my parents and my attorney? I lost when Haverill died because I'll probably have an impossible task getting money out of his estate. It would have been idiotic of me to kill him or have him killed. I don't think that anybody but Haverill and I knew he was fired. Oh, and Sydney. Clearly, I was nowhere near my house when my parents were murdered. If you rule me out, and I can tell you that I must be ruled out, there can't be too many people who connect to the victims. Now that I think of it, have you considered Sydney?"

Inspector Dawes, who had been scanning the titles of books on a side wall of the office, spun around.

"Why would you suspect Sydney Phelps?"

"I didn't say I suspect him of anything. I simply asked if you had considered him. He certainly knows me, was probably in contact with my parents about my school project and knows just about everything I am doing here. I think I told him I fired Haverill."

Dawes was frankly taken aback, almost at a loss for words.

"Are you actually offering up your trusted assistant as a murder suspect, Artemus? That is incredible, even for you."

Artemus put down his report and glared at the policeman.

"If I thought for one second that Sydney had murdered my parents, he would not be here today, inspector. Now, why don't you do your job and stop bothering me?"

Dawes turned, almost in disgust, but was halted by another of Artemus' suggestions.

"Before you go, inspector Dawes, you said at the beginning that this was a professional murder. Have you checked with any of the Boston mob sources to see if my father had any money dealings with them? Or Haverill for that matter?"

The envelope arrived on a Monday morning with the day's mail, in a hand-written envelope addressed simply to Mr. Webb, c/o Quincy Shipyards. Inside was a scrap of paper, with a very simple message: "You can find her at Maddie's."

Artemus sat there looking at the note, ignoring the stack of other mail lying on his desk.

Her? he thought. And what or where is Maddie's?

He punched the intercom for Sydney. When his assistant entered, he handed over the paper without a word.

"It must mean your Allison," Sydney stated in a matter-of-fact voice. I'll find out what Maddie's is, probably a restaurant."

Sydney walked back to his office, leaving a much bemused Artemus to fumble through the rest of the mail. His mind was years away in the past.

"Maddie's is a bar and restaurant on State Street in Marblehead," Sydney came back with the report. "Maddie's Sail Loft to be precise. It's been an institution there since the '40s. It's always crowded. I'm told they serve huge drinks."

He handed Artemus a sheet of paper with the address and phone number, noting, almost with amusement, that the information seemed to provoke an odd response in his boss—a certifiable emotional response. First love, Sydney thought, his observations completely hidden.

For the first time in his adult life, Artemus Webb was confused, battling the note and its contents the entire week. It was a week bereft of precision, immediately noticed by his assistant. By week's end, it was time for intervention.

"Mr. Webb, why don't you drive over to Maddie's tonight and have dinner. I've been told they have wonderful chowder and decent bay scallops. I've also been warned never to have a second drink. They serve them in milkshake glasses."

Artemus didn't even look up.

❧

The restaurant downstairs was packed. Artemus was directed to the bar upstairs where he found mostly young people, jammed into every possible nook. A bearded bartender, Billy Barrigan, presided over the melee, with a gin bottle in one hand and a tonic quart in the other. Both entered the glass at the same rate.

"What'll you have, Mac?" Billy bellowed.

"That looks good," Artemus responded, not really knowing what to order.

"Good. It's all I make here."

He took his drink, which was indeed in a huge glass as Sydney had warned and jammed himself into the far corner of the bar where he could scan the entire room. At 6'4" he could easily see over the crowd. An hour went by and he was about to give up when he saw her.

And she saw him. Their eyes locked for only a moment. She smiled, ducked behind a large man, and was gone. Artemus fought his way through the packed room literally bursting through the last group of patrons out to the second-floor landing. Allison was nowhere to be seen. The sidewalk was filled with weekend revelers, some waiting for a table at Maddie's, others giving up and wandering down to The Landing on Front Street, which survived on Maddie's overflow. Artemus didn't even bother to try to find her. He was content with the realization that he could.

"Sydney, who is she?" he demanded of his assistant the first thing Monday morning. "I know that you arranged that whole thing back at Amherst. Who is she?"

Sydney Phelps looked up at his boss, his eyes filled with confusion.

"Who is who?" Mr. Webb. "And what was the matter in Amherst?"

"Allison Fielding, Sydney. You know who I'm talking about. I want to know who she is and where I find her."

Sydney was completely taken aback.

"Mr. Webb, I know absolutely nothing about that woman. The first time I ever heard that name was the day you hired me and told me to find her. I remember her name vividly because I have failed miserably with the first two tasks you assigned to me—finding her and your parents' killers. I know nothing about her, and I certainly know nothing of whatever might have happened in Amherst."

He paused, considering something. Then he slowly stood up to face Artemus.

"If you don't believe me, I am forced to tender my resignation."

"Did you send that note telling me I could find her at Maddie's?"

"I did not."

"Sit down, Sydney," Artemus commanded, deep in thought.

Then he pulled up a chair and sat down himself.

"I believe you, Sydney," he said, "but that reveals another, far more serious problem. Someone, probably my parents' killer, has been manipulating me since I was at Deerfield. Not only did they find this girl who could actually run at my pace, but she was also beautiful and spectacular with sex. They furnished an empty house without the neighbors noticing it and emptied it the next day. That took money, and a lot of planning. They just showed up again with that note about Maddie's."

For one of the few times in his life, Sydney was confused.

"Mr. Webb, what possible reason would someone have to want to get you laid by a girl who then disappears?"

"Control, Sydney. Control."

Artemus got up and walked out of the room.

SYDNEY PHELPS

Artemus had just returned from a long run north along Route 3A. He had gone almost to Scituate, through several of the beautiful New England villages. In this part of the world, where spring is a fleeting weather emotion highlighted by azaleas and rhododendrons that thrive in the cool coastal climate, the joggers were all out celebrating even though the temperature had barely reached 40º. Even Artemus changed his routine to enjoy the season.

"Mr. Webb, I have a dozen letters asking you to address various organizations on your business plan," Sydney announced when he arrived at his office.

"Screw them! I'm not talking to anyone."

Sydney was expecting this response and was ready.

"If you really want to sell Webb Industries, you might rethink that. Right now, you are the talk of the business world, a very young man who has taken an established business and in its first quarter brought it to an unheard-of level of efficiency and production. It wouldn't hurt to get your name out to a wider public."

Artemus was silent for some time, considering the matter.

"Sydney, I don't know how to give a speech. I would be a total mess in front of an audience for which I have very little respect."

"Mr. Webb, I can't get into the matter of your view of the business world, but I think you can double the price of your company by explaining how you made it so profitable."

"Where are these invitations from, Sydney?"

"It's a very wide range of organizations," he responded, flipping through a sheaf of letters. I have them from the Harvard Club, part of a series they are doing on local industry; from the Kiwanis in Boston; the Quincy Chamber of Commerce; the South Shore Businessmen's Association. A very interesting one is the Commonwealth Club in San Francisco. There are three from local universities: Northeastern, Boston State and Simmons College. I might suggest you start with one of the local groups, to stay within your comfort level. If you make a mistake in Quincy or Plymouth, it won't go very far."

"I don't give a damn about mistakes. And I don't give a damn about helping fools correct their mistakes."

"Mr. Webb, I recall at Deerfield that someone asked you what you were doing there, and you answered, 'I'm here to learn how to get rich.' Spreading your name across the country will help you do that."

Sydney reached up to a shelf behind him, grabbed a cardboard-bound report and placed it in front of his boss.

"You can read the paper you wrote at Deerfield. It is now more relevant than ever."

Artemus snorted.

"No one wants to listen to a high school term paper, Sydney. They would laugh me out of the hall."

"That's no ordinary high school term paper, Mr. Webb. It should be considered the business manifesto of our time. You are proving yourself correct with your own company."

Artemus was again silent for an extended period, wandering around the room and finally facing his assistant.

"Will you help me write the speech, Sydney?"

It was a startling question. For the first time in their relationship Artemus Webb was actually asking for help with something.

"Of course."

They decided on the Quincy Chamber of Commerce, since they were members themselves. Sydney counseled against the "old money" clubs such as the Algonquin or the Harvard Club. Secretly he wanted to schedule the Commonwealth Club, but that was no place for a novice speaker. In his response to them he held out the possibility of a future date.

"I'm willing to give you an hour of my time, Sydney, to teach me how to give a speech. If it takes longer, I will refuse to do it."

That declaration sent Sydney into a frantic effort to outline the contents of the talk and to prepare his boss on its delivery. He decided that simplicity was essential.

The next morning he was ready. He handed Artemus an outline based on the research paper he had written:

I. Industry as we have known it in America is dead.
II. Cost is the major issue.
  A. Labor
  B. Taxes
  C. Regulations

III. We have moved from makers to users.
IV. Education is stifling imagination.

"We can fill that out or add to it if you want. But let's talk about your delivery. Keep it simple. Be yourself. And talk slower than you think you should. If you can, look around the audience and make eye-contact wherever you can. You will draw energy from the responses you see."

They ended up working the entire morning, with Artemus the student in a class he had neglected to take while in school. It was totally in keeping with his personality—public speaking was a skill he needed to increase his wealth and he intended to learn how to do it.

When they were finished, Sydney received yet another shock, actually two shocks.

"Thank you, Sidney," Artemus said with firm eye contact. "I am taking you to lunch."

They drove the eleven miles from Quincy to Boston, Artemus pulling up at the Fish Pier near Southy. Without a word he led his assistant down the grimy elevated sidewalk, entering a restaurant that didn't even boast a sign.

"It's called the "No Name Restaurant," Artemus said. "I found it on one of my wanderings from Scollay Square. The best seafood in Boston."

Sydney was amazed. The place was tiny, only a single long counter with round swivel stools covered with red vinyl material, and half a dozen mismatched tables on the other side.

"Two bowls of fish chowder," Artemus ordered when the unshaven waiter walked over. "And we'll share a plate of scallops. Two beers."

"You got it, buddy," the man answered with a heavy accent.

"He's the owner," Artemus said softly. "They're Greek."

He was back almost immediately with two huge bowls overflowing with seafood, and a plate of scallops that was big enough to cast a shadow. The two men dived in.

"This is positively delicious, Mr. Webb," Sydney gushed, savoring the chowder.

"The first time I was here, some guy was on his seventh bowl and he ordered another one. They refused to give it to him and threw him out."

When the meal was finished, Artemus placed $15 on the table that was enough to include a good tip. Nick, the owner, huge smile on his face, handed them their coats.

"How on earth do you serve so much great food for so little?" Sydney asked him.

"It's easy. We steal it."

❧

To his utter shock, Artemus discovered that he really enjoyed putting his business thoughts into some sort of order. He worked on his speech every night that week, even speaking it out loud to his mirror. When he thought he was ready he announced to Sydney that he was to be his audience, demanding that he be as critical as he wanted to be.

"You're useless to me if you overlook any criticisms to save my feelings. That's not what I am paying you for."

Sydney was stunned by both the content and the power of the speech. It was the essence of logic, blunt and in several places almost insulting to American industry and education. But the kicker was a cogent vision of the future that challenged business leaders to change their goals and create a new purpose.

"Mr. Webb," Sydney said quietly, when the half-hour oration was finished, "I was going to suggest that you open the talk with a disclaimer that you were not totally comfortable with public speaking, but I drop the suggestion. I am very impressed with your delivery. It was totally in keeping with your history and your personality."

"How about the content, Sydney. I don't give a shit whether the audience likes my delivery, but I want them to understand what I have to say."

"It is generally good, but you need to enforce your ideas with some relevant statistics. You do a pretty good hatchet job on the colleges. There are forty of them in the Boston area, so you are going to attract a lot of attention. I think you should analyze curriculums in view of where you say America is going. You say they aren't teaching for the future. Hit them with data. Tell them what the future is going to require of a student.

"Your picture of heavy industry in New England is extraordinary. And true. Everyone in the audience probably lives in the shadow of a crumbling factory. But few people will make the jump from your depressing picture to your vision of the future. You are moving a whole society from the cities to the shores and the suburbs.

"I very much like your ideas about Americans becoming users instead of makers. You could probably find lots of numbers on exports and imports to back you up, but I don't think a long procession of numbers is useful in a speech like this. Maybe just the gross import and export figures."

Artemus had been taking notes. When he finished, he picked up all the papers and left the room, without a single word being spoken.

Good, Sydney thought with a wry smile. I thought I was going to have to endure another "Thank you."

❧

Artemus' lecture for the Quincy Chamber was only a week away. He had gone over it so many times it was committed to memory, something that surprised him in the extreme. He had a hard time comprehending why it was so important to him, because he didn't have the slightest interest in the audience he would be addressing. In fact, if he truly analyzed himself, he would have realized that at heart he was contemptuous of the entire modern business world.

Sydney considered asking if he was ready for the talk but deferred to his own common sense that such an inquiry would be met with stark derision. He decided to just wait for the event and hope that it went off well. Deep down, he prayed that there would not be a total meltdown by his boss, who had never once spoken in public and was the apotheosis of the anti-social man.

The talk was scheduled at the Tirrell Room on Quarry Street in Quincy, a venue that could hold up to 300 people. Within two days of the announcement that Artemus Webb was the featured speaker the event was sold out. Everyone in Quincy, indeed, most people in the greater Boston area, had heard about this nineteen-year-old who had taken over a major shipyard and thrived, who was a major suspect in his parents' murders, and who had fired a third of his employees within weeks of taking over Webb Shipyards. There were more stories and rumors adrift in the population about Artemus Webb than anyone in recent memory. The Chamber of Commerce was giddy; Sydney Phelps was fearful; Artemus Webb was unfazed.

"He can't be nineteen," a lady in the audience whispered to her friend when Artemus walked out on stage. "He's at least thirty-five. And very handsome!"

Stone-faced and calm, Artemus took his seat at the head table, not moving a muscle during the various pre-speeches and introductions. Finally, it was his turn and he slowly rose and strode to the podium. Without a greeting of any sort he began his talk, speaking of his journeys to dead and dying factories a few years earlier. Without a note, he carefully catalogued the ills of New England manufacturing, not forgetting the ship building and tanker companies in Quincy and Watertown.

"If the economy of our region has died, what are the schools doing about it? Nothing. We have more than forty colleges and universities in the Boston area, and they are doing nothing. They are still teaching the same broken curricula they taught when the industrial revolution began. We are going to have to dismantle our industrial sites because they are a blight on our land, a blight on our people, but it is really the Harvards and the Yales that should be torn down and started again. We need new ideas, new teachers, new students and new goals.

"Our industry has failed for several reasons and there is no change in sight. First, labor is too expensive; second, modern industries are not going to, of necessity, be on water; third, the unions have destroyed the factories, both in morale and in expertise."

He didn't even stop for a reaction. In a couple of paragraphs, Artemus had condemned the industrialists, the academic world and the unions.

"We will have to switch from a blue-collar to a white-collar world. We have to transform the human landscape that was imposed by heavy industry, start living on our lake fronts and sea shores instead of working there. We are going to have to face the fact that we have become a nation of users, not a nation of makers. We have let the world become our supplier while we sat around coddled by the educational system of the past. If we don't change, we will become a second-rate nation. I personally believe we already are."

He walked to his chair and sat down.

There was a smattering of applause as the stunned audience tried to take in what they had just heard. Then a man near the back of the hall stood, whistled and began clapping wildly.

"That was incredible!" he shouted. "Finally, someone capable of telling the truth. That was incredible!"

The audience remained silent.

The director of the Chamber slowly rose and walked tentatively to the podium.

"I would like to thank Mr. Webb for that extraordinary speech. I am certain it is going to provoke more thought among us than anything we have heard in the past few years. Almost as an afterthought, he asked if there were any questions. Hands shot up around the hall.

"You say the unions have ruined factory workers. How?

Without standing, Artemus responded.

"They have become the security blanket, the pacifier of workers who are either lazy or incompetent. The good workers need no union. It is only those who can't that they represent."

That brought out more than a few boos.

"You say you are against unions, yet apparently your factory pays workers higher than union wage. At the same time, you say that labor is too expensive. Can you explain?"

"You are a good example of why this country is failing," Artemus said, his eyes skewering the questioner. "Webb Shipyards has reduced our labor force by 50% and raised our salaries by 25% because now we don't have to pay for union waste. Our workers are better trained, more capable and far more efficient. And, in my view, happier."

"You are condemning the universities," a well-groomed man began, acid dripping from his voice, "but I don't believe you finished high school. How are you qualified to talk about higher education?"

"They are training students today the same as they did my grandparents. In nonsensical subjects like rhetoric and metaphysics. They require two years of foreign language but teach it in such a way that it is impossible to learn it in that time. How can I comment on higher education? First of all, I refuse to call it "higher," and secondly, I can comment on it because I have a brain and am capable of making a logical statement. Most college students have neither."

He continued.

"From the patches on your sport coat, I assume you are a professor. If so, answer me this: Why does Harvard have a football team? And why do they give scholarships for pole-vaulting and cheerleading and not for marine biology? What is the academic value of 'The Game' that has wasted our time and money for over a hundred years? And please, please, tell me the metaphysical value of Hasty Pudding?"

That outburst produced an appreciative smile from the erstwhile professor.

There were dozens of hands in the air when a halt was called after forty-five minutes of piercing sometimes caustic questioning. Artemus never rose from his chair and handled every attack with calm confidence. When the final question was fielded, applause began and then slowly spread throughout the hall. A few persons stood and in seconds, everyone was on their feet. Without a word or gesture, Artemus left the stage. Sydney was waiting at the car.

"Mr. Webb, that was a *tour de force*!

I don't want a *tour de force*, Sydney. I want a steak. Let's go to the Golden Rooster.

LINDA ALLENBY

He remained an isolated man. Devoid of social niceties and completely without any human relationships, Artemus moved from home to office to gym. Once or twice a month he ventured north to Boston, where he enjoyed a pair of Joe and Nemo hot dogs with Jeffrey Belcher, the hot dog aficionado he had met his first Christmas. That was followed by a show at the Old Howard and a romp with Beatrice Woolsey at the Crawford House. He was always her most generous client.

"Why don't we make this a permanent thing?" she asked him one Saturday night. "We could start by you telling me your name."

"I don't want anything permanent," he said dryly, "and my name doesn't pay your fee."

"Well I know your name anyway, Mr. Webb. You would have plenty of room in that big house of yours and nobody would even know I was there."

Artemus was as silent as a rock, slowly pulling on his clothes.

"Leave town tomorrow morning, Miss Woolsey. If you are still here at noon, I will have you arrested as a whore. And I will see to it that you don't get out of jail quickly."

He threw five twenties down on the bed and stormed out.

His timing was perfect. A few months later the Crawford House closed, the last remnant of the Boston's wild burlesque district. The Old Howard had already been boarded up when Vice Squad officers filmed the lewd dance of Mary Goodneighbor a couple of years before and the halcyon days of Scollay Square were numbered.

When he heard the news, Artemus was shocked and he realized he was going to have to look elsewhere to find another Miss Woolsey.

"Sydney," he said laconically to his assistant the next morning, "I need a wife. Find someone for me."

Sydney Phelps didn't register the slightest evidence of shock. He was quite used to inscrutable orders from his boss. Any surprise that he might have had over the last five years was offset by the incredible power and insight of the man. Artemus was always completely informed, no matter what the subject was. Always. Ultimately Phelps began to look forward to watching powerful business men and civic leaders stagger out of Artemus' office following a meeting. Some were red with fury; others looked like they had been emotionally trampled. All knew that they had lost something or failed to achieve what they had wanted. On the other side of that back desk sat a man who had just finished a pleasant walk in the park.

"How on earth do you work for that man, Sydney?" Lucille Bradford from the Quincy Board of Selectmen asked one day following a meeting with Artemus. "I have never met a more obnoxious, mean, intimidating man. He doesn't have a drop of humanity in his body."

"What was it you wanted of him, Lucille?" Sydney inquired blandly, ignoring the question.

"We would like to expand the waterfront park. I told him the city was going to assess each resident business for the project."

"How much are you seeking to raise?"

"We estimate the project will cost $650,000," the woman stated.

"And the assessment is based on what? Gross revenues?"

"What other way would be fair?" she spat, still angry at her encounter with Artemus.

"And what did he say?"

"He said he had no intentions of using that park, that it was a sop to the townspeople that would only promote idleness and crime. He told me to assess the people who were using the park."

She stopped to take a deep breath.

"I told him that they couldn't afford it, but that, if he felt charitable, he could easily finance the entire project without batting an eye."

"I can imagine what he said to that!"

"No you can't, Sydney. He said that there are 19,503 households in Quincy. If we assess each household $22.03, we would have our park. And then he told me that we in government would have to stop robbing the people, because the park improvement should be costing less than $300,000."

"My experience is that he is usually right on something like that," Sydney said quietly.

"He had the blueprints for the project sitting on his desk," Mrs. Bradford said. "How did he get them? We just got them yesterday. And he told me he had already contacted the *Quincy Gazette* to tell them how we were robbing the people. Imagine!"

She got up to storm out of the office but turned and threw an envelope down on Sydney's desk.

"He told me he was giving me his $22.03 personally!"

❧

Good employee that he was, Sydney put an ad in the *Harvard Crimson* the following month:

"Well positioned twenty-two-year-old man seeking a wife. Send qualifications with photograph to P.O. Box 1433, Rockland, Massachusetts."

He waited a week and then drove south to Rockland to pick up any responses that had come in.

"You're going to need a bigger box, Mac," the postman bellowed as he pushed out a cart with three large tubs filled with letters. "Whatever it is you're selling, I want in on it."

Sydney let out one of his infrequent laughs and asked if he could borrow the cart to take the load to his car.

"Oh, I'll wheel them out, sir," the man said. "That's the most mail I've ever seen in a week. I think I want to get to know you."

Back at the office, Sydney carted the tubs to Artemus' office, a smile on his face the entire time. He left a note. "Applicants for the new position of Mrs. Webb."

The following morning, he arrived to a bellow from the inner office.

"Sydney, get the hell in here! What the hell is all of this?"

"Those are the responses to a ten-word ad I put in the Harvard newspaper. You should be able to find a wife somewhere in there. I told them to include a picture."

"Cancel the damned ad, Sydney. Tell them the position is filled. And throw away all this rubbish."

"You really should at least look at the pictures, Mr. Webb. You said you wanted a wife. How are you going to find one without talking to anyone? Open them up; take a look; and discard any one you don't like. Just from a photo you might find one that is at least interesting."

He walked out without waiting for a reply, his smile reappearing the second he closed the door.

⁂

Artemus walked past the tubs the rest of the week, unable to look at the letters but also unable to throw them out. Early Saturday morning he opened the first envelope.

"Dear Sir:

As you can tell by my picture, I am not very good looking, but if you will just look beneath the surface you will find a wonderful woman, who wants with all her heart and soul to become a loving wife and a happy mother.

Sincerely,
Rachel Eaton"

The simplicity of the woman's message came close to winning the day, but Artemus put her letter on his desk and opened another envelope.

"Dear Future Husband:

My picture speaks for itself. But what you can't see is a mind and a body that yearns for you. Look no further.

Maggie Tembrink"

That one was immediately discarded in the waste basket. Artemus continued to open letters the entire morning, amazed by the variety and complexity of emotions that his ad had inspired. They were pleading, boastful, condescending, passionate, and most commonly, downright salacious. By the afternoon, he had only three letters sitting on his desk. All were written by quiet, apparently timid women. He was on the third bin and almost dozing off when he opened a letter written in a very attractive calligraphic hand.

"Hello Deerfield:

It's about time you started looking for a wife. You just have to find me.

Allison"

He leaned back in his chair staring at the letter. After several minutes where his mind went blank, he threw it on his desk and stormed out of the room. He drove to the South Shore Fitness Center where he worked out until his body could take no more. After a long steam bath, his mind was functioning again, and he drove home. He ignored the impulse to dwell on the woman who had so invaded his emotions and sent him into a confusion that he could not begin to understand.

"Sydney, I want to discuss this ad you placed at Harvard," Artemus said that following Monday as soon as his assistant arrived.

"As you can probably see, I went through the whole batch, most of which was garbage. I want you to look at the four letters I kept. The first three I find interesting and I want your observations of them."

Sydney read the three letters carefully, then looked up.

"You selected these three as wife prospects?"

"Yes."

He put the letters down on the desk.

"I think they are all the same woman."

For an instant, Artemus betrayed a look of surprise.

"Why do you say that?"

"They are all in the same handwriting."

Artemus picked up the letters, scanning them carefully.

"I guess she is my type of woman," he said, nearly laughing. "But this fourth letter is more serious."

He handed Sydney Allison's letter.

"I don't understand," his assistant said. "How would she know it was you?"

"Precisely. Did you tell anyone you were placing that ad?"

"No."

"Did you pay for it with a company check?"

"No. I paid for it in cash."

"Did you phone it to the newspaper?"

"Yes. I phoned the text and then sent it with the payment from Hanover."

"Get our phones and our offices checked for bugs. And your house and mine. Do it today."

Sydney nodded and got up to leave.

"What should I do about the other three letters?" he asked Artemus.

"Have that woman come in to interview for a job."

❧

Sydney, a curious look on his face, escorted the young woman into Artemus' office. A tall woman, almost 5'10", she was dressed in a light blue skirt and top with a navy blouse. Her hair, shoulder-length, was clasped above both ears, revealing a broad face, that while not by any standards beautiful, had an air of elegance. It was clear that she was by no means intimidated by the imposing figure of Artemus Webb.

"Which of these three women is actually you?" Artemus asked, holding up the letters he had selected from the barrels that had arrived in his office.

"My name is Linda Allenby. I made up the other two names."

She hesitated.

"Well not actually. Rachel Eaton and Humility Cooper were both young girls who came over on the *Mayflower*. I live in Plymouth and have worked at Plimoth Plantation for several years. I just like the sound of their names."

"Why write three letters?" Artemus asked gruffly.

"I really wrote more than a dozen. I figured it would increase my chances."

"I am going to give you a job," Artemus announced, not bothering to look at the woman.

"I'm not looking for a job," Miss Allenby said firmly. "I'm looking for a husband."

Artemus put down the report he had been reading and glared at Miss Allenby who stood there almost defiantly before him.

"Will you always do as I command?" he asked.

"As long as it isn't immoral."

"Will you willingly share my bed?"

"Yes."

"Can you cook?"

"Very well."

"Are you a virgin?"

"Yes."

"If you have a business card, give it to my assistant. He will contact you if this matter is to proceed any further."

With a curt wave, he dismissed her.

"I see you are still in one piece," Sydney smiled as she came out of the inner office.

"I think he likes me," Miss Allenby said happily, handing him her card. "I am sure I will hear from you shortly."

Sydney watched her leave with a bemused look on his face.

Artemus never mentioned the matter when he left for the day, but the following morning he told Sydney to call the woman and bring her back.

"I have a proposal to make," he said as Miss Allenby entered his office. "We will live together for one month. If after that period, either of us is dissatisfied with the other, we will go our separate ways. If we agree at that time, we will be married immediately."

"That is more a proposition than a proposal, Mr. Webb," she responded immediately, never taking her eyes from his. "I would be the only loser in such an arrangement, and I refuse."

"How would you be the loser?" he asked.

"If we were to separate, you could simply call in another woman for a month. You could have a dozen live-in paramours a year. And I would no longer be able to tell my future husband that I am a virgin. I am disappointed in you, Mr. Webb."

She turned to leave.

"Then it is next Friday, a week from today," Artemus said as she was grabbing the door knob.

"Next Friday?" she asked, turning back to him.

"Our wedding day."

"Are you sure you want this, Mr. Webb?" Sydney asked when Artemus had informed him of his decision. "You don't know anything about her. Who is she?"

Even he was shocked by the marriage announcement.

"She was born in Carver, one of seven kids. Her parents own several cranberry bogs and are quite well off. There has never been a divorce in the last three generations of her family. She attended Silver Lake High School and graduated from Emmanuel College in Boston, Summa Cum Laude. She is presently on the research staff at Plimoth Plantation. Her specialty is 17th century English accents. Her birthday is August 2 and she is twenty years old."

Sydney looked down at his feet, astonished at the information that had just spewed out of his boss's brain. I should know better by now, he thought.

"I want you to prepare a marriage contract. If it fails, she will receive a modest sum, but in no way even a tiny part of my business."

"I will arrange for a Justice of the Peace in Boston, Mr. Webb. You will need two witnesses."

"You will serve in that role for me, and Miss Allenby's sister will do the same for her. I don't want anyone else there."

❧

The two were married the following week in a quick civil ceremony at the Old City Hall on School Street in Boston. The bride and groom and two witnesses walked across the street to the Parker House where they enjoyed a lavish dinner at Parker's Restaurant before the bridal couple took the elevator up to the Presidential Suite.

The wedding night was a disaster. Linda Allenby-Webb was a virgin, and while he had some sexual experience, Artemus had always been with experienced women who knew how to please a man. He had no idea how to deal with this young woman. Frustrated, he stormed out of the bed and fell asleep in the suite's second bedroom, leaving his bride trembling with shame, tears flowing freely.

Without a word spoken the next morning, they checked out of the hotel and drove to Hingham and his house. It was two weeks before the marriage was consummated, that achievement due solely to the counselling Linda sought from her mother, and the extraordinary cuisine she had ready every night when her husband came home. As for Artemus, absolutely nothing changed in his life, except he was enjoying fine meals and all the sex he required. If Sydney had expected any change in his boss, something he really didn't hope for, he was pleasantly surprised. The only change was that ironically, he acquired a new conversational friend in Mrs. Webb. The two of them gradually formed a formidable alliance in the support of the enigmatic Artemus.

Unbeknownst to Sydney, Artemus was in fact considerably changed. This woman who was now his wife had somehow created the tiniest crack in his psychological armor. Only once in his life had he opened a corner of his mind to another person—Allison Fielding. She had hit him with a broadside for which he was unprepared, and when she disappeared, he had vowed that never again would he give in to another person.

And now he had a wife, Linda…

BILLY FRANCOBALDI

Billy Francobaldi was born premature, brought into the world by an Italian midwife in the North End of Boston in January, 1918. There was rejoicing throughout the city. Folks paraded on Hannover Street, walking through the quarter with a full bottle of Chianti that would be finished before they had walked three blocks. The more pious were praying their thanks at the Old North Church on Salem Street, where once a very un-Italian Paul Revere had made his imprint on history. But none of that was because Billy was born. The Great War had just ended, and hundreds of Italian men would be coming home from the agony that had taken place in the muddy trenches of Europe. For Billy, only his mother celebrated at his birth. Her time of agony was over, and he had arrived safely into his world. Or so she thought. Along with the troops from Europe came the Spanish flu, the greatest pandemic to ever hit the planet, and much of the North End was decimated during the months following the war. Billy's mother died along with hundreds of other vibrant and healthy men and women. The city, in a near panic, established the Home for Italian Children, a place that could care for the many orphans born by the deadly plague. Billy was one of them, although at first an elderly aunt tried her best to keep him alive. But the effort was too much for her.

Billy was in the second grade when Zia Mara died. There was no one to take him in so he was transferred to the Boston Farm School for Indigent Boys on Thompson Island in the harbor. There he would spend the next seven years, enduring a regimen of hard work, hours of study and a good amount of bullying by boys who were bigger and stronger than him. He grew inward, afraid to voice an opinion, happy to be of service to whomever demanded it. Many times, he was abused and came to take it as a matter of life.

Billy was in his sophomore year when a stranger appeared at the school.

"You have a young boy named Francobaldi?" the man inquired. "I want him. He is family."

And so, in 1930, at the beginning of the Great Depression, Billy returned to the North End. He found himself in the home of Rocco and Maria Fitopaldi who lived at 12 Moon Street, not far from North Square. They were not family, and while they gave him room and board, they paid him almost no attention. He seldom attended school at Michelangelo High, and generally roamed the streets doing odd jobs and menial tasks for the merchants. Billy Francobaldi became known as a young man who would never have a thought of his own but was a trusty errand boy.

"Who are my relatives, who took me off of Thompson Island?" he asked his foster mother one day.

"Oh, you have some cousins living in New Bedford," she said with a sneer, "but they didn't want any part of you, boy. They paid your way out of the school and brought you here. We agreed to house you, but it was obviously a mistake. You cost us more than you bring in."

Before he was 20, he was running numbers for the local mob leader, and doing errands for many of the prominent underworld figures. He lived around the quarter and seldom left the North End, which had changed from Yankee to Irish to almost totally Italian by the time he reached the age of 30. By then Billy was the consummate "go-fur," living in a small room off Garden Court.

He was sitting one afternoon in Giro's Restaurant on Hannover Street when a man in a nice suit approached him.

"Billy, I'm told you do jobs for people. I have one for you."

"What is it?" he asked in his simple way.

"I need you to visit one of the shipyards in Quincy. I want you to learn about the old war ships they are bringing in from around the world."

"How do I get to Quincy?" was his unexpected reply. "I don't drive, and I don't even have a friend with a car."

"You can take the T to Neponset Circle and hitchhike from there. I'll give you the train fare. I just want you to get to know the ships and workers at the dry docks down there. That's all."

"Why?"

"I'll tell you later. I'll pay you $20 every time you go. You walk around the yards and talk to the men. We'll pick you up in the afternoon and bring you home. Deal?"

"Sure, but how do I get into a big shipyard? They don't just let you walk around the place."

"Just walk in. Take a camera. They won't bother you if you aren't fooling around with the machinery. Don't get into anyone's way."

He was such an unassuming, non-threatening man, it was almost as if Billy was part of the shipyard. After a couple of visits, he found he could almost wander around at will, talking easily with the workers on break, asking about the ships they were working on and the process of rehabilitation that was carried on at Webb Shipyards. After half a dozen visits, he received another visit from the man in the suit.

"Billy, there is a ship coming into Webb from the Far East," the man told him. It's a freighter, the *Orient Jewel.* Ask around if there are any men interested in making a few extra bucks when it arrives."

It was the real beginning of Billy's work at the shipyard.

Frank Murphy was admitted to Artemus' office late in the afternoon, on a crisp fall day in 1956.

"Mr. Webb, we may have a problem," he announced.

Artemus had been engrossed in some steel bids he had just received from Pittsburg and had already commenced an angry mood. His head snapped up.

"What kind of problem, and what do you mean by "we?"

Murphy had grown used to the gruff demeanor of his boss and he realized that it was the center of the man's personality and would probably never change. He had learned to think past that demeanor.

"The problem is a legal one, and when I say 'we' I mean that both I and the company are most likely going to be hauled into court."

"Explain."

"There has been a guy hanging around the plant, trying to talk to the workers. I have seen him for years. Your father had him thrown off the property half a dozen times, sometimes literally thrown out into the street.

He was at it again last month and I told him to get out and not come back. He was back again last week and started a row out on the line. I grabbed him and tossed him out on the sidewalk. He has filed a lawsuit naming me and the company. For physical assault."

"So, we'll countersue him for trespassing. Did you post those signs about visitors coming through this office?"

"I did. The day you told me," Murphy said, a tinge of defensiveness in his voice.

"Have you been served?"

"No."

"Then we'll worry about it when and if that happens. Go back to work, Frank."

"Sir, I think there's something more to this. I think someone is behind this, someone who wants to harm Webb Industries."

Artemus looked up again.

"Who?"

"This guy, Billy Francobaldi, is a squeaky little runt, not someone who deliberately looks for a fight. He was sent here, but I don't think he's union. I asked some friends at the union office. They've never heard of a Billy Francobaldi. There's something fishy here, Mr. Webb."

"Why would someone non-union be wanting to talk to our workers?"

"That's my question exactly. It doesn't make sense. He was asking for three or four of the men we laid off when you took over."

"Okay, let's wait and see what happens. If he shows up again, call the police and have him arrested. If they file a lawsuit, I may just let it happen to find out what's going on. And send in the men he talked to. I want to know what he was asking."

Artemus punched his intercom.

"Sydney, have your private eye get everything he can on Billy Francobaldi. I think he's local. I want everything he has done back ten years at least."

❧

Several weeks passed with no more news of the threatened lawsuit.

"Most of these threats are just that," Sydney observed during his Monday morning planning session with Artemus. "Lawsuit threats are common when someone has just been hurt or embarrassed. But actually beginning the hassle and expense that a lawsuit implies is another matter."

Artemus had interviewed seven of the workers who had talked with Francobaldi, with some curious results.

"He never even mentioned the union," Walt Malpensa said. "He just likes to hang around and look at the ships we're working on. He's always asking a bunch of questions about the ship classes and ages. I think he's just a nut that way."

"Did he talk about any one ship or class of ship?"

"Yeah, a couple of times. He wanted to know if we were going to get a light cruiser in anytime. He said he had never seen one, but he had heard of one that was being scrapped out in San Francisco."

Freddie Mayers reported along the same lines.

"He was constantly asking the names of decommissioned ships we were going to be getting in for rehab. He even suggested a couple of names that he had read about as being available. He's more of a pest than a threat."

All the men Artemus interviewed described the man as interested in the ships and types of ships that were coming through the Webb drydocks. But the last man he spoke with, Vincent Henry, corroborated what Frank Murphy had said earlier.

"He asked about three or four of the men you fired when you took over. He said he really liked them and wondered where they were working now. I knew about a couple of them."

"Do you remember their names?" Artemus asked.

"I know there was Joey Giambo and Ralph Menicotti. I think he also asked about William Brodsky. Oh, and Martin Witt. I think that's it."

When he was finished with his questions, Artemus wrote out his notes, which he handed to Sydney.

"See if you can find any of these four men, Sydney. I have a strange feeling about this Billy Francobaldi."

It didn't take Sydney long to make a startling discovery.

"Joey Giambo was killed about a month ago in a mysterious car crash," Sydney reported. "The brake fluid had been drained and the accelerator pedal was frozen. He ran into a stone wall at the bottom of Bunker Hill."

Artemus' head snapped up.

"He was murdered?"

"It appears that way, but that's not all. William Brodsky was found hanged. Very similar to Attorney Haverill's murder. We can't find any trace of the other two men on your list."

Sydney looked at his notes.

"...Witt and Menicotti. They disappeared almost the day they were fired."

"Are their families gone too?"

"No, just the men. Their families both filed missing person reports. They are frantic."

"They are probably in a land fill somewhere, or at the bottom of the harbor," Artemus said without emotion. "Someone powerful and dangerous has reappeared at Webb Shipyards, Sydney."

He picked up his telephone and dialed a number quickly.

"Inspector, you will want to see me right away."

He slammed down the phone, angry.

A half-hour later Inspector Dawes was sitting in his office.

"Your list of murder victims is increasing rapidly, inspector," Artemus opened the conversation, "more than doubled."

"I don't understand, Artemus. I keep pretty well informed about such things, and I am still working on your parents and Haverill."

"You can add four of my former employees to your list," Artemus replied, handing Dawes the list of the fired men.

"These men were sacked the week after I took over the company. If you recall, I reduced the workforce by a third at the time."

"And what made you think of them now?" Dawes asked, leaning forward intently in his chair.

"Billy Francobaldi."

Artemus filled the inspector in on the story of Billy Francobaldi, from the past few weeks stretching back to the time when his father was still alive and running the plant.

"Francobaldi was asking about these four, maybe four months ago, and was a bit upset when he found they had been fired. I did a check on them and found them either dead or missing."

Artemus paused to let his revelation sink in.

"Curious, wouldn't you say, inspector?"

Inspector Dawes was silent for some time mulling over the information he had just received. It didn't matter to Artemus because he had already gone back to the report he had been reading. Finally, Dawes looked up.

"I assume you think that this has something to do with the murder of your parents, Artemus."

"And Haverill," Artemus responded. "If you dig up Brodsky and do an autopsy, I'd bet that you will find the same drugs in his system as Haverill's. There was and still is something sinister going on at Webb Shipyards, Inspector. And I intend to find out what it is because it probably killed my parents."

"Inspector," Artemus continued, "someone, a person or an organization, has been manipulating me since at least my junior year in high school. I am certain of it, but I haven't the slightest idea why. Sydney and I have been discussing it for months now and we are no closer to an answer than you are. I only know it is happening."

"You have a reason for suspecting this?" the policeman asked.

"I don't suspect it; I know it."

"Artemus, you are going to have to enlighten me."

Artemus related the story of Allison Fielding, not omitting the smallest detail, including his brief sighting of her in Maddie's Sail Lounge.

"At first, I thought that Sydney had orchestrated all of it, wanting to get me laid as a normal part of growing up, when he saw it would never happen if it were up to me. I figured that he had also written that note about finding her at Maddie's. But when I confronted him, his reaction of denial was completely convincing."

Artemus got up and walked to the window that looked out on the shipyard.

"Not long after that, my parents were killed, leaving me, a teenager, in charge of the company. And then came the Haverill murder. Somebody is very interested in my life, but I can't explain why."

"Has anyone tried to strong-arm you, or change the way you do business?"

"Nobody. You know how social I am. I don't even have friends suggesting anything because I don't have any friends. If somebody is trying to benefit from me or my business, they aren't very good at making themselves heard."

Inspector Dawes fidgeted in his chair.

"So Artemus, you don't have any better Idea than I do."

"Somehow, I think that Haverill is involved, and now these new murders drag in Billy Francobaldi."

Dawes looked past Artemus out the window and was silent, considering the suggestion.

"Do you think Haverill was silenced?"

"I don't know. He was certainly not a professional killer, but he might have known who to call. If you were a betting man, inspector, where would you find such a killer around this area?"

The answer was swift in coming.

"The mob or the unions."

"I agree. I'll tell you what—you check out Haverill and any contacts, meetings, financial arrangements he might have had with the unions, and especially any meetings that seem odd in the last two or three months before his death. Lawyers always keep logs, so my guess is that Haverill's is complete. I'll do the same with my father's schedule. Maybe we can find something they have in common. Let's draw up an alphabetical list of names and see if there is anyone on both lists."

Looking down at the floor, Dawes nodded but didn't say anything. Then he looked up at Artemus.

"Do you mind my asking why for almost five years you could care less about this thing, and now you are completely involved?"

"Now it's personal. I want to find out who wanted to get me laid back when I was in high school. And why."

Another thought occurred to him.

"Inspector, Haverill was stealing from my father, more than a million dollars over the years. Maybe he was doing the same to other clients. Maybe he was a funnel for money to someone else."

Inspector Dawes got up from his chair, almost exuding energy. For some time he had nearly given up on the case of the Webb murders, there being not a single clue he could follow. Now suddenly, there were clues everywhere and his spirits were unexpectedly on the rise. He also noted that for the first time since he had met him, Artemus was also interested.

Darius Webb had been a very meticulous man. Artemus had noticed in his office an entire shelf of identical old meeting planners, leather-bound with the year incised in gold on the spine and "Darius Webb" and the year on the front cover. But after a cursory look he had dismissed them as an antiquarian collection of an odd man. Now he looked at them in earnest because they detailed just about the entire life of his father, going back more than thirty years. He carried a stack of them out to the front office.

"Sydney, make an alphabetical list of every person my father had a meeting with and the dates of those meetings."

REBECCA

Rebecca had continued her summer practice of confronting people wherever she was and analyzing their reaction. By the summer of her sophomore year at Yale she had begun experimenting with causing that reaction, and even manipulating a person into the reaction she wanted. She was developing a formidable weapon.

"It's really interesting," she told her father one day at dinner. Every person has a tell-tale thing that gives them away. You can tell they are lying because they blink… or scratch their chin or pull their ear. They say the good poker players watch for those hints and that's what makes them good."

"Becky," her mother responded almost with a laugh, "you have been causing mayhem on the sidewalks for three years now. When will you let up and give New England a rest?"

"I think I am going to have to stop pretty soon, because Judge Macklin wants me to work for him this summer. I am doing his precedent research which is really interesting."

The law school seminar was a venue made for Rebecca. There she could put her phenomenal memory, her insight into people, her skill at debate, and her natural attack mentality to complete use. Within a few weeks, the word spread that she was not a person to be taken lightly if one were looking for a verbal fight. Her long hours spent in Judge Macklin's law library provided her with a data base that no other student could match.

Where her undergraduate curriculum had been filled with formal lecture and seminar classes in writing and literature, law school offered her the chance to put her knowledge to practical use. Her writing of briefs was clear and precise; and her arguments were enhanced considerably by her wide literary background. But it was her mentor, Judge Macklin, who made the greatest contribution to her arsenal of tools. He taught her to analyze herself.

"Rebecca, you can't always be on the attack. You have to figure out the best approach at any given time. You have to be able to read the people and the circumstances and adjust your behavior and your arguments accordingly."

"I thought I was doing that with my summer program," she responded.

"But you are only using the aggressive aspect of your own personality. There are times when confrontation is the worst thing you can do. In a courtroom every jury is different. Some will respond to an aggressive lawyer; others will be repelled. Try out different personality approaches in your summer wanderings. Make an attempt at being nice and watch how people respond. Force yourself to act counter to your own instincts and see what that gets you."

Each Monday when she came to work at the judge's office, he would quiz her about her weekend encounters, and brainstorm what she had learned or failed to learn.

"It is incredible," he told one of his colleagues, "what an ingenious program that girl has devised. She goes out on the street, in parks and public buildings and initiates conversations and arguments with everyone she meets. She has developed a skill at reading people that I have never seen before. Add to that her inherent verbal and linguistic skills and she is going to be one of the finest trial lawyers Yale has ever produced."

In law school, she was no longer subject to the housing regulations of the undergraduates, although she had thoroughly enjoyed her stay on campus at Saybrook College and Vanderbilt Hall. Now she lived in a small studio apartment near the harbor.

Geoffrey Macklin phoned one Friday evening in early December.

"Rebecca, how about that revisit to Delmonico's tonight?"

She didn't hesitate.

"When will you pick me up?"

"I'll be there in half an hour."

It was her first actual date.

Geoffrey was right on time, double-parking in the narrow street and running up to her second-floor apartment.

"I almost honked," he laughed, "but then I figured that wouldn't be a very good way to restart our friendship."

"And you were right," Rebecca answered. "If you had honked, I would have sneaked out the back stairs and gone to the library."

Delmonico's was almost an institution in New Haven, an old- fashioned Italian restaurant only a few blocks from Rebecca's apartment. Here if you wished you could get a meal that included minestrone, a salad, pasta and whatever entrée you desired—for a very reasonable price.

"I love the linguine and clams," Geoffrey enthused, not even looking at the menu. "I think I have had it a dozen times here. No need to look for anything else."

"Then that's for me too," Rebecca declared, putting down the extensive menu.

They laughed their way through dinner, Rebecca relating the highlights of her street encounters with people, Geoffrey telling of his wildlife encounters out west.

Dinner finished they drove into the city to a popular pub, Cave A' Vin, for an after-dinner libation, continuing the conversation they had halted at Delmonico's. Rebecca found that for the first time in her memory she was completely at ease, not looking for any tell-tales, or prospective arguments.

"I don't think I have been this relaxed in my life," she confided to Geoffrey. "Thank you for getting me out of my rut."

"I'm willing to 'get you out of your rut' anytime, Rebecca. I am so happy we came out tonight."

It was midnight when they pulled up at Rebecca's apartment. Geoffrey double-parked once again and came around to open her door. She was barely out of the car when she grabbed him and kissed him passionately.

"To be continued," she promised. "Thank you for a wonderful evening, Geoffrey."

She literally ran to the apartment door.

Rebecca finished Yale Law School in January, 1956. She had completed her undergraduate degree and law school in only five years. Her parents, Simon and Sandra, and her five brothers and their wives, were joined at the ceremony by Judge Macklin and Geoffrey. Since Rebecca's family were all from out of town, the judge had offered to host a reception at his home. He invited many of the law faculty as well as a number of other students who had just received their degree.

"*Juris Doctor*!" Rebecca's brother Max exclaimed. Who could ever have guessed that our little sis would become a Doctor of Law?"

"It was either that or a prize fighter," another brother, Stephen, laughed. "She was always in a fight, or at least a loud argument. Well done, Rebecca."

Rebecca worked her way in hugs around her "boys" as she called her big brothers.

"You guys were the ones that made me fight," she disclaimed. "I would have been a retiring little sissy if it weren't for you."

Judge Macklin was in his glory. The young woman he had watched in court five years before had fulfilled the prophecy he had made following that trial. He walked over and gave Rebecca a hearty, ersatz-father bear hug.

"Rebecca, it is just beginning. I know you are signed up for the bar exam in February. Do you need anything from me?"

"I think I need six recommendations, Judge. Can you write them all?"

"I'll take care of that right now. You know you don't have to take the MPRE," he said, referring to the Multistate Professional Responsibility Examination, "because of your grade in the ethics class."

"Yes," Rebecca answered, "Thank God we live in Connecticut."

The judge walked away to join a group of professors who had gathered near the food table. He returned a few minutes later.

"I have your six recommendations, my dear. Now, go enjoy the party. We'll plan for the bar exams next week."

She breezed through the two-day Uniform Bar Exam (UBE) which are held annually in Connecticut in February and July, finishing the first day written exams in less than half the time allotted. She followed that with the second-day multiple-choice question sessions with a spectacular 96% score. The announcement of her acceptance to the Connecticut Bar Association came on May 1. In the meantime, she had applied for the bar examinations in both Massachusetts in July, and New York, scheduled for February of the following year since all the eastern states held their exams on the same days.

Following the Connecticut exams, Rebecca retained her apartment in

New Haven. More than a dozen offers came in from law firms throughout the state. She consulted with Judge Macklin as each offer arrived, narrowing down her choice to two firms in the capital.

"I'm afraid we are going to lose you, Rebecca," the judge said sadly, "but Hartford is calling, and it makes the most sense, until you decide you want a bigger stage like Boston or New York."

That night, lying with Geoffrey at her apartment, she related the judge's emotional goodbye.

"I'm not sure who is going to miss you more, Rebecca. Are you sure you won't accept my offer? You know you are already my father's daughter, so why not add daughter-in-law to that?"

"You know I can't, Geoffrey," she whispered earnestly. "But I want to see how far I can travel before I decide to settle down. It's not that I don't love you. I do. You know that."

She sat up with a smile.

"Besides, Hartford and New Haven are not very far apart."

"39.35 miles," he laughed, kissing her and drawing her back to him.

MALCOLM SALTONSTALL

The name carried cachet all by itself. It was just about all he received at birth. From his earliest years he felt himself patrician and privileged, far above those he bumped up against in his school and on the playgrounds of Sherborn in summer, even though most of them also came from families of Boston Brahman status. The child of parents who were far too old and busy to care for him, he was raised by nannies and staff, pampered in the extreme, urged always to let others do the "dirty work" of living. The one important thing that was hammered into his brain was his pedigree. After all, his ancestor Richard had been lord mayor of London and that man's nephew had arrived with Winthrop for the founding of Massachusetts Bay Colony. Nathaniel Saltonstall was a judge in the Salem Witch Trials, and even more importantly he began a generational string of family members that was unbroken to this day—graduates of Harvard University. It would become Malcolm's only obsession, to be his generation's representative who carried on that tradition. Later, while he was at Harvard he glowed with importance when his uncle Leverett was elected Governor of the Commonwealth.

His path to that great university was one filled with broken glass and boulders. He struggled in school from kindergarten on and his view of his peers got him in constant scuffles. He was a poor reader and mediocre at math, on the verge of failing in many of his elementary and high school classes. But he had one ability, if it could be classified as such—he could get others to do his work.

"Want to go to the Sox game?" he asked his high school friend, Jacob Lodge, one weekday during their junior year.

"I can't," Lodge replied. "We have those term papers to turn in on Friday. Did you finish yours already?"

Saltonstall laughed.

"My staff is finishing it!" he exclaimed. "I have better things to do than write some stupid paper on the Civil War."

"Like going to the Sox game?" Lodge asked sarcastically. "Do you ever do your own work, Malcolm?"

"Not if I can help it. What good is having money if you don't use it?"

His money bought him a 2.5 Grade Point Average at Andover, and his name got him into Harvard. There he struggled mightily, unable to hand off as many assignments as he did in high school, where both the teachers and the administration were intimidated by his family name. At Harvard, however, Malcolm found that just about everyone he ran into seemed to have an equally impressive lineage. He was constantly bumping into students with names such as Endicott and Winthrop, Adams, Cabot and Peabody, many preening just as adroitly as he. He didn't even smile when he heard the old ditty, "This is Boston, the land of the bean and the cod, where the Cabots talk to the Lowells and the Lowells talk to God."

He barely scraped together enough passing grades to emerge after four years with a bare 2.0. But in his mind, it was enough. There would be no tests after graduation.

❧

For Artemus, the years should have been exhilarating, with a new marriage and a shipyard that was fabulously successful. But his stoicism never wavered, and if he was ever inclined to be happy, outside forces continued to repress such emotions. The string of murders that surrounded him didn't outwardly affect his behavior, but the inner pressures were rising.

The years had wrought a remarkable change in the young man. He had always been intimidating, even as a teenager, but now, at 23 years of age, he was beyond that. Most people who encountered him considered him to be frightening. He was a huge man, 6'4" and about 250 pounds of muscle, clean-shaven with a bushy moustache and eyebrows that almost connected above the nose. His jaw, massive cheek bones and shaved head were Borglum-sculpted. He had the coldest eyes, knife-throwers that could skewer a man before he had opened his mouth. You would guess him to be about 40 and you would be off by nearly two decades.

His management of Webb Shipyards created six straight quarters of skyrocketing profits; triple what Sydney Phelps had suggested. Not only had he streamlined the rehab process of older ships; he had instituted a new generation of supertankers both at the Quincy shipyards and at the Wilson-Owens shipyard in Texas. Artemus turned down several offers For Webb Shipyards until the price reached an impossible $150 million. Without any sign of emotion, he accepted the offer. It would take more than a year to iron out all the conditions of the sale and close the escrow. Meanwhile Artemus was already mentally into another endeavor.

"What now, Artemus?" Sydney asked him the day the deal was accepted.

"Now we begin to demolish and redesign industrial waterfronts, and make living circles around big cities, Sydney. Since we are going to become a nation of users rather than makers, the waterfronts are going to become very valuable for housing and our cities are going to expand in area."

"Are you so sure that American manufacturing is dead?"

"It died two decades ago, but nobody was willing to admit it. The shoe industry is gone; textiles are made in the Far East; the steel industry will move to China; cars to Japan. Drive along any river in the east, along any Great Lake shore, along the ocean. You will see dead, empty, rusting factory buildings and no life. We must remove the corpse and bring in that new life. And that will take houses and apartments, with water views. We don't need water anymore for transportation or power. We will use it for landscaping."

It was the biggest flow of words he had ever heard his boss utter. Sydney was silent, trying to conjure up an objection to the vision he had just heard.

"What will the people do to be able to buy these waterfront houses?" he asked.

Artemus was quick with his answer.

"Banking, insurance, research and development and computers. We are going to replace factories with labs and offices, blue collars with white ones. We will let the rest of the world do the manual labor. The industrial revolution is finished. We are now entering the technological revolution."

"Mr. Webb," the man on the phone began, "my name is Malcolm Saltonstall and I would very much like to schedule a meeting to discuss some matters that could be of great importance to both of us."

Without waiting for Artemus to answer, he continued in a distinctly Boston Brahman accent.

"I am a long-standing member of the Harvard Club," he said, pausing for a moment to let Artemus be impressed. "And I and some colleagues are very much interested in the talk you gave to the Chamber in Quincy. You made quite an impression, young man."

Artemus broke into the monologue stream.

"What do you want, Mr. Saltonstall? That talk was a long time ago. I have things to do."

"We would like to host you at the Club next Wednesday."

"Who is 'we'?"

"I, Jacob Lodge and Michael Winslow. You would be a fourth at our table. Do you play dominos?"

"I don't play games," Artemus declared flatly, "but I will accept your offer for lunch. What time should I be there?"

"We meet at 11:00 in the morning to discuss matters of importance to us, and we dine at 12:00."

"I'll be there at 11:00," Artemus said.

Just before he hung up, Saltonstall coughed and added, "Mr. Webb, a coat and tie are mandatory to dine at the Veritas Restaurant at the Club."

Artemus hung up without a comment. He wrote the three names on a piece of paper and called Sydney in.

"Get me a financial background on these three men," he said without further comment. "Oh, and Sydney, they have invited me to lunch at the Harvard Club. Tell me about that."

"The Harvard Club?" Sydney said slowly. "It's got to be at least fifty years old, a private club open to graduates of Harvard and I think several other schools like MIT and Yale. It's very upper crust. Why do they want to talk with you?"

Artemus almost growled.

"Saltonstall said he had a proposition of mutual interest. That means he wants me to do the work for him and his buddies."

"Work?"

"He mentioned my talk at the Chamber. He probably wants me to start buying property for them, or he wants me to give him the blueprint of what we are going to do."

He stopped for a moment, considering the matter.

"I would say the latter is more likely. He wants my plans."

Artemus picked up the map of greater Boston he had been studying.

"He may be making an offer I can't refuse," he said cryptically.

For several weeks prior to Saltonstall's phone call, Artemus had been poring over the maps of Greater Boston area with Sydney, connecting old factory towns about twenty miles around the city.

"We are going to make Boston the hub of a greater technological area," Artemus declared. "Bostonians always called their city 'The Hub' so we'll make them live up to their nickname."

There was a makeshift half-loop highway already in place, called the Yankee Division Highway, an artery that harkened back to the early days of motorways before numbers had begun to be applied to roads.

"Let's begin our loop here at Quincy," Artemus suggested.

"You might want to consider Braintree, Mr. Webb," Sydney suggested. "Then you could tie up to Route 3 that is coming up from the Cape."

"Okay," Artemus agreed, pulling out a protractor. "If we begin with Braintree, fifteen miles south of Boston, let's see what our line crosses."

After an hour of juggling, they had connected Braintree to Dedham, Needham, Newton, Waltham and Lexington. The northern arc took in Woburn, Stoneham, Wakefield, Lynnfield, Peabody and ended in Salem, the old witch city. It was a string of former factory towns that perfectly supported Artemus' theory. Dedham was famous for its peculiar blue and white pottery. Needham had grown wealthy on the Carter Knitting Mills that recently had moved to the Carolinas. Newton, with the Stanley Motor Works, had created the famous steam car and once had lesser mills churning out glue, paper, chocolate and snuff. Waltham had just closed their famous watch factory, a victim to cheaper, more reliable models like Timex. And the once massive Boston Manufacturing Company had ceased to produce household textiles. Woburn once had many tanneries, sending leathers south to the boot makers in Brockton; Stoneham manufactured machine tools; Wakefield boasted of their South and Anthony Stove Company, the Boston Ice Company and the Wakefield Rattan Company.

Peabody tanned the leathers that were used in Salem's and Marblehead's shoe factories. All of that industry had disappeared by the time Artemus was studying his maps.

"Sydney, I want you to set up at least half a dozen land development corporations, based in several states and unrelated in any way. Start looking for properties within a mile of our line, preferably including the line itself. Look in particular for the old, empty factories. They will provide us with land that is unrestricted, where we don't have to buy out homes and local businesses."

Artemus stood for a moment on the sidewalk along Commonwealth Avenue gazing up at the stately entrance of the Back-Bay Harvard Club. While he had no previous associations to the place, the name carried a caché that even he couldn't entirely resist. He had not taken two steps inside the lobby when a tall, rather frail man approached with a smile and a hand extended.

"Mr. Webb, I am Malcolm Saltonstall. Welcome to the Harvard Club."

Artemus accepted the handshake reluctantly, especially when Saltonstall's grip could only be described as that of a dead fish. His mind registered dislike immediately.

"Winslow and Lodge are waiting at the bar," his host said, walking toward the back of the building. They found the pair deep in conversation, their backs to the lounge.

"Jacob, Michael, I'd like you to meet the famous Artemus Webb. Artemus, this is Jacob Lodge and Michael Winslow."

"I prefer to be called by my family name," Artemus said dryly, extending his hand to the two men.

"Well, Mr. Webb it is then," Lodge answered, a bit unsettled, glancing over at Winslow, who returned a slight smile.

"What can I get you to drink, Mr. Webb?" Winslow asked. "We have over a hundred different single malts in the club."

"Soda water and ice will be fine," Artemus responded. "I never drink during the working day."

"Well, you are certainly not working today," Saltonstall laughed. "Are you sure you won't take something stronger?"

"I am always working, Mr. Saltonstall. Now, suppose we get down to the reasons you invited me here. I can give you an hour, less if the topic is of no interest to me."

"Well, fair enough," Saltonstall responded stiffly. "Gentlemen, shall we adjourn to the card room? It appears our lunch will have to wait."

They settled in at a round poker table, Saltonstall removing a couple of decks of cards and a rack of poker chips to a nearby side table. Then he coughed uneasily and made an attempt at beginning a conversation.

"Mr. Webb, we were all very impressed by the reports we received about your talk at the Quincy Chamber of Commerce. To say that your views of industry, labor and government are unique would be a gross understatement."

There was a moment of embarrassed silence when Artemus didn't respond, fixing Saltonstall with a stony gaze.

Winslow broke the silence.

"Your declaration that American industry is dead or nearly so was quite a shock to most of us in the business world, Mr. Webb. We are very interested in…"

Artemus interrupted him.

"Are you three in the business world at the moment?"

Winslow ignored the question.

"Let's get right to the point. We agree with most of the points you made in Quincy, Mr. Webb, and are particularly interested in your ideas for the rehab of old factory assets. We have considerable resources, all liquid, to invest if you are interested in working with us."

"What do you mean when you say, 'working with us?'"

Jacob Lodge spoke up for the first time.

"You indicated in your speech that you were recommending the rehab of waterfronts that formerly housed factories. You also mentioned a future of expanding cities. You obviously have ideas of where best to place your time and money. We would like to propose that you accept us as financial partners on these ventures."

"Why would you want that?" Artemus asked.

"We think you are on to something, and that it could be very big. We want to be part of that dream."

"And why would I want to let you into that dream as you put it?"

"Because," Saltonstall interjected, "with our backing you will have tremendous leverage."

Artemus was silent for an uncomfortable time. Even as a youth he had been aware of the tremendous power of silence as a conversational or debating tool. When he finally spoke, his eyes scanned the faces of the three men.

"You say that you have considerable liquid wealth. Might I ask the source of that wealth?"

"Each of us inherited family money," Saltonstall said. "That got us into a club like this. But we have also been very successful with investments over the years."

Artemus' gaze turned to a glare.

"Gentlemen, your investments have been major disasters. You don't have a cent from most of them. And you used up your inheritances with those idiotic investments."

All three men erupted as one.

"You are out of your mind, man," Michael Winslow hissed.

"Am I? Mr. Winslow, three of your major investments have gone bankrupt—Millers Falls, Union Plastics and the Boston Company. Mr. Lodge, you lost almost every cent you own in textiles in Lawrence, Lowell and the Fall River Knitting Mills. And Mr. Saltonstall, you were heavily invested in Brockton Work Boots, half a dozen paper mills in Maine, not to mention major holdings in Waltham watches and Plymouth Cordage, both of which are about to go under. Now I will ask you again, gentlemen, what is the source of your reputed 'liquid wealth?'"

The three men sat in stunned silence glaring at this impudent young man who undoubtedly had access to information they had thought to be well hidden.

Without another word, Artemus rose and left them sitting there.

ARTEMUS

The papers were served shortly after the New Year. Artemus was named in the civil lawsuit as well as his company, Frank Murphy and several other workers. They were charged with assault in throwing Billy Francobaldi off the premises. Francobaldi was asking for millions.

"Good," Artemus growled to Sydney, "the little weasel has finally gotten around to what I wanted him to do months ago."

"Why are you anxious for a trial that is sure to be a nuisance?" Sydney asked quietly.

"I don't want the trial. I want the depositions."

"I'm afraid I don't understand, Mr. Webb."

"Sydney, I want to turn Mr. Francobaldi into a pot of mush in the depositions. I want to find out why he was really poking around the shipyards, especially in my father's time."

"How much time do we have?" Sydney asked.

"The court date is set for March. That gives us three months. We can always get a delay if we need it."

Sydney got up to leave. Then he turned back.

"By the way, Mr. Webb, they found Ralph Menicotti. He washed up on the shore near the Boston Light on Little Brewster Island in the harbor. He had been garroted."

"That leaves only Martin Witt," Artemus mused, naming the last of the four workers Francobaldi had inquired about. "He'll wash up somewhere too."

Inspector Dawes was admitted to Artemus' office. He carried a briefcase from which he took several papers and put them on the desk.

"It took a while, going through Haverill's log books, but here is a list of every person he dealt with over the last ten years.

"Are they alphabetized?" Artemus asked, pulling out a file drawer in his desk.

"Yes," Dawes said with a smile. "As you had asked."

Artemus extracted a similar stack of papers, the names from his father's business diaries.

"Start reading, Inspector."

They worked their way through the alphabet, without finding a match, until they got to Billy Francobaldi, who was on both lists.

"Now that is interesting, Inspector," Artemus said. "I assumed that he would be on my father's logs because he was always getting thrown out. But let's come back to him after we finish our lists."

The next name that matched was Jacob Lodge, which drew an immediate response from Artemus.

"He's one of the Harvard Club trio I met a while back. Is there a Saltonstall or a Winslow on your list?"

"Saltonstall is entered three times. But Lodge comes up more than a dozen times," Dawes said. He had written after each name the number of times that person came up in the lawyer's log books.

"There is a man named George Knowland who appears the most," the inspector continued. "He had twenty-one meetings with Haverill."

"He's not on my father's list," Artemus said. "Do you know who he is?"

"I can't find him anywhere," Dawes answered. "That's why I'm most interested in him. I'll keep digging."

They found another five names that matched on the two lists. Three were lawyers who practiced corporate law, something that Haverill was not involved with. They agreed that these were probably referrals from Haverill to Darius Webb. The other two names were business men in Boston, whom Dawes agreed to contact. When they were finished with the list, Artemus went back to the man he was most interested in.

"What about Francobaldi?" he asked. "He appears often in my father's log, a couple of times where he got paid for something. I think it had to do with his recommendations for mothballed ships that we brought in for rehab."

"His entries in Haverill's logs indicate he came in for advice, but it doesn't stipulate what type of advice. There are no financial transactions."

"How about that man named Knowland? What type of meetings did he have?"

The inspector shuffled his papers and went back to the "Ks."

"There were two checks that Haverill wrote to Knowland. Sizeable ones—$20,000 and $10,000. There is no note as to what they were for."

"When were they written, Inspector?"

Dawes looked at his notes and almost snorted in dismay, slapping his forehead.

"Two weeks before your parents were murdered."

"Artemus," his wife murmured late one night after they had made love, "we have been married for over a year and you have never once taken me to dinner. Haven't I fed you well?"

"Your kitchen is better than any restaurant, Linda. Yes, you have fed me very well."

She was silent, using one of the tools she had watched him use against verbal combatants.

"Okay," he said, realizing he was trapped. "Do you have a place in mind?"

"Locke-Ober in Boston. I have never had French cuisine before."

Artemus sat up in bed, regarding his wife closely.

"You've been planning this, haven't you?"

"I have," she admitted, "but for a special reason."

"What reason?"

"I'll tell you over cocktails."

They drove into Boston the next Saturday. Locke-Ober Restaurant had a long reputation in the city, the third oldest in Boston, after the Union Oyster Shop and Durgin Park. But it was not at all like those two, which served up what everyone in New England considered to be "local food"—lobsters, seafood, chowder, prime rib, scrod, and of course, Indian

Pudding. Locke-Ober on the other hand was purely continental and somehow had managed to survive in this provincial part of the country.

Since his childhood, Artemus had never been to dinner with a woman before, and even though his confidence could hardly be measured, he had a feeling of insecurity as they sat down at the small corner table.

"Bring us your best champagne," he told the waiter as he was still approaching the table.

"I have two that are about equal," the waiter said without changing expression, Dom Perignon and Perrier Jouet 'Flower Bottle.'"

"Bring them both," Artemus replied with a glare. "We'll let you know which is better."

"Artemus," Linda whispered, "We can't drink two bottles of champagne."

"I don't care. He should have suggested just one of them."

When the waiter returned, accompanied by one of his colleagues carrying the Perrier Jouet, Artemus glanced at both.

"Bring two more glasses and we'll compare them for you," he said icily to the waiter.

"Of course, Sir," came the reply, accompanied by a slight bow.

They were left in peace to try their comparison.

"Which do you like?" Linda asked.

"I don't like either one," Artemus responded. "I hate champagne."

"Oh, Artemus, then why did you order them?"

"Because Sydney told me that was the way to start a fancy French dinner."

Linda laughed out loud and patted his hand, noticing that he didn't withdraw it immediately.

"Well, I like the one with the flowers."

"Maybe you just like the bottle," he said.

"Is that teasing, Artemus? You've never teased me before."

"What is your surprise, my dear? That's why we're here, isn't it?"

She picked up her glass and held it out for him to clink. He hesitated, but then realized the custom, took his glass and touched hers.

"Artemus, I'm pregnant," she murmured, looking at him carefully, hoping desperately for any sign that he was pleased.

He sat there like a rock, motionless, without expression. After what seemed to her like an eternity, he smiled.

"When?" he asked.

"Late June. I waited to be absolutely certain. I'm four months along."

He sat there looking intently at her.

"Are you okay?" she asked, almost shivering with emotion.

"I won't know how to act," he said, ignoring her question. "My parents barely talked to me. I don't know how to be a father."

"You'll know," she said, again putting her hand on his. "At least you have a guidebook on what not to do."

The elaborate dinner flashed by, Linda completely happy for the first time since the day she married this strange, powerful man. Also for the first time, they actually discussed things—her family, where she learned to cook so well, what she did at Plimoth Plantation. There might have been no one else in the restaurant, so intense was their conversation. Three hours later, when coffee was served, Linda let out a gasp.

"Artemus, we drank both bottles!"

"We'll take a taxi home," he smiled and then broke out in a full laugh. "I'll come and get the car tomorrow." Then he added, "You have made me very happy, Linda."

FRANCOBALDI

"I think I found you a lawyer," Sydney announced when Artemus arrived the Monday after his dinner at Locke Ober and Linda's unexpected announcement.

"She has just passed the bar in both Connecticut and Massachusetts."

"She?" asked Artemus, with an edge to his voice.

"I spoke to my friend at the law school at Amherst. He is very close to one Judge Macklin, a Superior Court judge in New Haven. According to my friend, Macklin says this young woman is going to be one of the great trial attorneys in the country. He says she is very bright, works hard, accepts nothing at face value and has an incredible killer instinct."

"So I will be her first case?"

Sydney didn't back down at all.

"To be honest, Mr. Webb, the Francobaldi case is nothing a big lawyer would even consider. It's a case of simple assault, if that. If you are interested in making Francobaldi uneasy in the depositions, this young woman might be perfect."

"What's her name?" Artemus asked.

"Rebecca Walton."

"Get her in here. I want to talk to her."

Rebecca Walton entered Artemus' office with no trepidation. She had done a quick check of Webb Shipyards and its young owner and concluded that there would be no subterfuge in his dealing with her. Reports on his anti-social personality intrigued her and she was fully prepared to engage with him.

"You are very young to be a lawyer," Artemus said as she was introduced. "And you are a woman…which gives you two marks in your favor."

"How many do I need?" she asked, preparing for a fight.

"Two is enough," he said, beckoning to a chair in front of the desk.

"I want to fill you in on what you are getting involved with," he said. "Several of Boston's best legal minds turned down this case as being too insignificant for their august persons. This is going to be one of the biggest cases in the city's history by the time you are finished."

"As I understand it, Mr. Webb," Rebecca responded, "this is a case of minor assault. Isn't that true?"

"The first chapter. We didn't assault Francobaldi. He was trespassing on our posted property after being asked several times in the recent past not to enter our yards. He was picked up by the armpits and placed outside of our gates. I called the police to report his trespass."

"Why hasn't a court thrown it out as frivolous?"

Artemus actually smiled.

"Because I don't want them to."

"Why not?"

"Because I want Francobaldi torn apart in the depositions. I want to know everything about him by the time you are finished with him."

"Is this a vendetta, Mr. Webb? Just because he trespassed on your shipyard?"

"Miss Walton, almost five years ago my parents were murdered in what appeared to be a contract job. My father's lawyer was murdered a few days later. In the past couple of months three of my former employees were murdered. And a fourth has disappeared. There has not been the smallest clue as to the murderers, until Francobaldi showed up. I believe that he is the key to solving those cases, and perhaps preventing more killings."

Rebecca inhaled visibly, sat back in her chair and held Artemus' stony glare.

"I accept your case, Mr. Webb. But if you want this Francobaldi broken down, it will take a bit of investigation and lots of work."

"What is your fee?" Miss Walton.

It was something Rebecca hadn't even considered. She had never been involved with a potential criminal case, and the few jobs she had clerked for since passing the bar hardly demanded high fees.

"My fees are $40 an hour and transportation costs from Hartford or lodging in Boston if it is necessary."

"Miss Fleming, those fancy Boston lawyers would have cost me five times that amount. Let's agree on $50 and I'll double that rate if you do your job well."

"I have just one more question at this time, Mr. Webb," Rebecca said. "Why on earth is Francobaldi bringing this lawsuit? He doesn't have a chance of winning it and it could get him in a hell of a lot of more trouble."

"Miss Walton, my assistant Sydney and I have been asking that question since the whole thing started. There's something very strange in all of this and we can't figure it out. Let's find out, shall we?"

He turned away from her and grabbed a report from the table behind him.

"Sydney will fill you in on everything that has transpired to this point. Good day, Miss Fleming."

Sydney was waiting for her when she exited Artemus' office.

"Well, Miss Fleming, are you going to work with us?"

"As I understand it, Mr. Phelps, I just got a raise on my first case. Yes, I'm told you can fill me in on some details."

"I can," he responded. "And please call me Sydney." Then he added with a small laugh, "Only the back-office personnel demand family names."

"Well then, you can call me Rebecca. But please not Becky. That's reserved for my parents."

They spent nearly four hours discussing the history of Webb Shipyards, the multitude of murders, and Francobaldi's activities with the workers both when Darius Webb was still alive and more recently. They agreed to subpoena all Francobaldi's financial data—Federal and state tax returns, bank statements, house and car payment history.

"We have a private investigator in our employ," Sydney volunteered. "Would you like to speak with him? I would be happy to put him at your disposal."

"Yes, that would be very helpful. I'd like to speak with him as soon as possible."

Sydney picked up the phone.

"Melvin, this is Sydney. Can you come by our office? I want you to meet our new lawyer....an hour? That would be fine."

He turned back to Rebecca.

"You heard that?"

"Yes," she answered looking at her watch. "I'll get a quick lunch and be back in forty-five minutes. I saw a Friendly's Restaurant down the street."

Melvin Judd was waiting in Sydney's office when she returned. He was a middle-aged man, graying at his sideburns, and a bit overweight. Formerly a military intelligence officer, he had been in the investigation business for just over ten years. A Boston native, he was very familiar with the local scene as well as the politics.

"Concentrate on Francobaldi," Rebecca requested. "I want to know everything there is about his life—what restaurants he goes to; who he hangs out with; what kind of car he drives; how much he spends on the side; does he have a girlfriend—everything."

She handed him a business card.

"Call me if you get anything. Anything. I don't care how small it is.'

She turned to Sydney.

"You mentioned an Inspector Dawes. Can you give me his number? I'd like to talk to him this afternoon if possible."

She was about to leave when she turned back to Sydney.

"May I take the logs of Darius Webb?" she asked.

"Let me ask Mr. Webb," he responded and picked up the intercom phone.

"I assumed she would want to look at them," Artemus responded. "I had them delivered to her car."

Rebecca shook her head, smiled and breezed out of the office.

❧

A month went by without a word from Rebecca Walton. Melvin Judd kept Sydney informed about his progress in filling out the life portrait of Billy Francobaldi and reported that Rebecca was in contact with him at least twice a day. For his part, Artemus never once asked about the progress of the case, having entered March 15 in his calendar as the date of the first deposition, and then put the matter out of his thoughts.

Inspector Dawes appeared unannounced one afternoon. Artemus was away at a meeting in the South Shore, so Dawes pulled up a chair to speak with Sydney.

"That is an impressive young woman you hired for the Francobaldi trial," he said. "She doesn't miss even the slightest detail. Where did you find her?"

"She was recommended by a friend. She just passed the bar in Hartford and Boston with the most glowing recommendations. She seems to have won Artemus' confidence because he hasn't even asked about her progress since he hired her."

Sydney changed the subject.

"Is there any new information on the murders of the three workers?"

"Nothing. I now have six murders and there isn't a single clue on any of them."

"And no word on Martin Witt?"

"Nothing. We are assuming that he is dead. His family has given up hope."

He paused for a moment.

"I agree with Artemus that Francobaldi is our best lead in unraveling this whole mess. But I can't tell you why I feel that way. It's more a gut feeling than anything I can measure."

"If he is somehow involved," Sydney wondered, "why would he want to instigate this lawsuit? I would think he would want to stay as far away from Artemus and Webb Shipyards as he could."

Dawes nodded.

"I was thinking the same thing. There is something larger behind this that is escaping us. Logic is absent all along the way."

"I don't think so, inspector," Sydney replied. "It's just that we are only looking at the conclusion; we haven't yet uncovered the premises."

On the first of March, Rebecca appeared once more. She carried a heavy briefcase into the office.

"I need to coach you on your upcoming deposition," she told Artemus. "There are some definite rules I want you to follow."

"Why do I need coaching?" he replied with his usual hard stare. "I know what a deposition is."

"Do you?" she responded with an edge to her voice. "Let's try it out. I did a little research on you in the past couple of weeks."

"Mr. Webb, are you aware that on seven different occasions in the last six months, your workers have been arrested in assault cases?"

"That's not true," Artemus almost exploded.

Rebecca reached into her brief case and withdrew a batch of papers that she threw on the desk.

"Here are the arrest warrants, Mr. Webb. You are named as an accessory in three of them."

"Those are phony papers," Artemus hissed.

"I understand that you have been in a Southy bar called 'The Q.' Were you involved in any fights there?"

"That's none of your goddamned business. I was only there once as a young boy."

"You were underage, Mr. Webb?"

"My age was irrelevant," Artemus snapped.

"Alright, stop," Rebecca commanded. "Mr. Webb, Those things were mostly true, but you have already made several mistakes, if this were your deposition. First, if you aren't aware of something, say so and no more. A simple 'I don't know' is all you need. Second, keep your cool. If you allow anger to show in the deposition, I can guarantee that the lawyer will goad you into repeating that in the trial. Third, volunteer nothing. In a deposition everything is the opposing lawyer's business. And you volunteered that you were drinking as a minor, which could have all sorts of implications down the road."

She stopped and fixed Artemus with her own stony glare.

"Now are you going to listen or not? You hired me as your attorney. If you think you have all the answers, I'll walk out that door right now."

Artemus held her gaze, then relaxed his arms and shoulders which had tightened up without him realizing it.

"You win, Miss Walton. Tell me what to do."

"As I said before, there are some rules to follow. If you don't like the question, or you don't know the answer, say either 'I don't remember,' or 'I don't know.' Answer with as few words as you can. And please, don't volunteer anything. Make them drag every word out of you. If I think you shouldn't answer something, I'll tell you not to answer it."

Artemus nodded.

"I understand, Miss Walton. One thing I am good at is not saying more than I should."

"But you just did, Mr. Webb. You should have limited that statement to 'I understand.'"

"And one more thing, you have a very intimidating demeanor, Mr. Webb. I would say that you scare the shit out of most people. You can glare all you want during the depositions, but that won't work in front of a jury. Glare at them and you will turn them all against you. You are going to have to try to act nice, or at least, neutral."

They spent more than an hour going over what Artemus regarded as minute details, but what Rebecca considered fundamental issues.

"I served Notice of Deposition the day you hired me, Mr. Webb, so we will get to depose Mr. Francobaldi first. That's an advantage because we can refer to his answers during your deposition. I also gave him about ten pages of discovery materials we expect at least a week prior to his deposition. If he doesn't respond in a timely fashion, it will probably extend the trial date."

❧

The deposition was only two days late. Francobaldi didn't send all the information Rebecca had demanded, but she wasn't concerned.

"I found almost everything I asked for on my own," she confided to Artemus. "We have enough to make it pretty hot on him for a few days."

❧

"Mr. Francobaldi, please tell us why you were always hanging around the Webb Shipyards."

"I like old ships."

"Is it a hobby of yours, old ships?"

"Yes, I've always been interested in the World War II ships."

"Always? Do you collect models of them?"

"No."

"Do you have a library of books about old ships?"

"No."

"Here are some pictures of World War II ships. Will you identify them by class, please?"

He scanned the half dozen pictures.

"Which one is a light cruiser?" Rebecca asked innocently.

"I don't know."

She took one of the pictures back and showed it to him.

"What type is this?"

"I don't know."

"Can you identify any of these ships?"

"I can't.

Rebecca removed a stack of reports from her briefcase.

"Mr. Francobaldi, what is the source of your income?"

"I work as a consultant for various companies."

"What companies?"

"I can't think of them right now. I'm too nervous."

Rebecca leaned forward over the table, establishing eye contact, which was quickly broken by Francobaldi.

"Did these companies issue you 1099 forms for the work you did?"

"I don't know what that is."

"Did you ever receive any money from Webb Shipyards?"

"No."

"Are you sure of that, Mr. Francobaldi?" Rebecca asked, taking two cancelled checks from her pile of papers.

"Oh, I remember. I got paid for alerting them to ships they could restore. It was what they did after the war."

"Do you remember what ships those were?"

"No."

"What is your average income each year, Mr. Francobaldi?"

"I would say it is about $8,000."

"Are you sure?"

"No. You have the tax returns right there. I never look at those things. They are all done for me."

"Who does them?"

"I have a friend who is a tax person."

"What's this friend's name?"

"I can't remember."

Rebecca smiled, looked at a couple of the tax returns, and leaned back in her chair.

"So, Mr. Francobaldi, you are a lover of old ships, but you can't identify any of them. You don't know how much you make a year and you can't remember who you work for or who does your tax returns. Is there anything you actually know?"

He sat there, his eyes down, without moving.

Rebecca again changed course.

"Mr. Francobaldi, do you have a bank account?"

"No."

"How do you pay your bills?"

"I use cash. Or I have a friend pay them for me."

"What is that friend's name?"

He hesitated, looking at his lawyer, who shook his head.

"I can't remember."

"Where do you live, Mr. Francobaldi?"

"In the North End."

"Where in the North End?"

"On Garden Court, near North Square."

"Do you own your house?"

"It's an apartment."

"How much is the rent?"

"I don't pay any rent. A friend lets me stay there."

"The same friend that you don't remember?"

Francobaldi smiled.

"No, a different friend that I don't remember."

"Do you own a car, Mr. Francobaldi?" Rebecca asked

"Yes."

"What kind?"

"A Lincoln Continental."

Rebecca let out a small whistle.

"A Continental. That's an expensive car. How much did it cost?"

"It was a gift."

"From a friend?" she asked sarcastically.

Rebecca shuffled through her notes and withdrew a single sheet.

"Mr. Francobaldi, do you know a man named Joey Giambo?"

"Yes, he was one of my friends who worked at Webb."

"Have you seen him recently?"

"No, he was fired, and I haven't seen him since then."

"Then you don't know that he was murdered?"

Rebecca watched his eyes dilate.

"He was murdered? No, no, I didn't know that."

"Do you know a William Brodsky?"

"Yes, he was also a friend from the shipyard."

"Do you know that he was murdered?"

This time the shock was visible, and Rebecca watched his entire body slump.

"How about Ralph Menicotti?"

"He also worked at Webb."

"Do you know that he was murdered?"

"Oh, no! That can't all be true," he stammered. "They can't all be dead. How about Martin Witt?"

"You tell me, Mr. Francobaldi. How about Martin Witt? He's been missing since he was fired at Webb Shipyards."

"Oh, my God!" the man moaned, and cast a pleading glance at his lawyer.

"I believe that this is quite enough for one day, Miss Fleming," his lawyer said. "As you can see, my client is very distraught."

"We will continue this tomorrow at 9:00," she said firmly.

❧

Neither Francobaldi nor his lawyer appeared the next morning. Artemus and Rebecca remained in the conference room going over details of the case when they finally decided there was no point in waiting any longer.

"That's a very expensive law firm he has representing him," Rebecca said. "They wouldn't normally just ignore a deposition. I'll file for a Court Order to get them to appear."

They were about to leave when a legal clerk handed them a large manila envelope, addressed "Artemus Webb."

Artemus glanced at Rebecca and ripped open the envelope.

In rough hand printing, on a half-sheet of paper was a message:

"Francobaldi's suit is dropped. A warning to you and your lawyer—be careful."

Artemus picked up the phone that served the conference room and dialed his office.

"Sydney, call Dawes and have him meet us at the office in half an hour. We are leaving Boston now."

INSPECTOR DAWES

Without a word, Artemus handed Inspector Dawes the note he had received in the deposition room.

Dawes read it, turned it over to see if there was anything on the back side, and read it again.

"I would take this very seriously, Artemus, and you too, Rebecca. There are too many dead people piling up around here and we don't need any more."

"What about Francobaldi, Inspector?" Rebecca asked. "He is obviously a tool for someone powerful. He lied in every one of his answers except one, so he is definitely hiding something."

"How do you know that?" Artemus demanded.

"I have been studying faces for years," Rebecca told him. "Francobaldi's eyes dilated every time he lied, and he usually rubbed his chin at the same time."

Artemus registered that without changing expression.

"I'm going to call him in for questioning," the inspector said. "You still have a trespassing complaint against him, Artemus. Let me see if I can get something out of him without his lawyer around."

"If he's still alive, Inspector."

Rebecca took up her briefcase and pulled out some papers.

"Inspector, Mr. Francobaldi denied that he had a bank account, but that was one of his lies. He had a checking account at Rockland Trust, in Hanover. There are some curious items I think you should look at."

She handed him two monthly statements.

"These show the payments from Webb Shipyard. They are from March and August, 1959."

She pulled out more papers.

"These are bank statements from each of the four men who were fired by Mr. Webb. All four show identical cash deposits of $500 in April and September of the same year."

Inspector Dawes was silent while he scanned the bank statement.

"That's too much to be a coincidence," he said. "They were certainly working together on something."

"There's more," Rebecca went on. "Mr. Francobaldi's April and September statements show deposits of $1,000 each."

Once again, Dawes considered this new information. He turned to Artemus.

"Can you find out what ships came into the shipyard around those dates?" he asked.

"I'm sure they are noted in my father's log, and if not, they will be in the annual corporate tax statements. I'll have Sydney look them up."

"You don't need to," Rebecca interjected as Artemus was about to leave the room. "The ship names are on the checks paid to Mr. Francobaldi—the *U.S.S. Altamont*, a destroyer and the liberty ship *Willard Tipton.* Those ships were logged in about a week before each of the checks were drawn."

Dawes and Artemus exchanged glances.

"Would you like a job, Miss Walton?"

"I already have one," she snapped back, not at all pleased with the surprised reaction of the two men. "What do you think I have been paid for the last month?"

Artemus smiled.

"The timing is too exact to ignore, Inspector," he said. "There has to be a connection between Francobaldi, those four workers and the ships. Those two vessels have to have been carrying something, probably drugs."

"Can you provide a list of what present workers were on the payroll in 1959?" Dawes asked.

"Just about all of them," Artemus said. "You can begin with Frank Murphy. He's the best informed of them all."

"I'll start to interview them. Someone at the yard must have heard something or thought something was strange."

He changed the subject.

"On that other matter," he said, looking at Artemus and Rebecca, "that note is a definite threat, especially in view of what has occurred around Webb. I am concerned for your safety."

"What can you do, Inspector?" Rebecca asked curtly. "If someone wants to hurt us, there is not much we can do to prevent it."

"There are precautions you can at least take..." the lawman started, but Artemus interrupted him.

"Actually Miss Walton, now that the Francobaldi case is closed, you don't have to remain in Boston any more. I think it would be safest for you at home, away from all of this."

Rebecca was taken back a bit. It hadn't occurred to her that her contract was in fact concluded. She was about to object, but then started packing all the papers on the table into her briefcase.

"You are right, Mr. Webb. I guess I had gotten so involved in the mystery surrounding you that I had forgotten what I was actually hired to do."

"Wait here, both of you," Artemus said and quickly left the room. He returned after several minutes with an envelope, handing it to Rebecca.

"Miss Walton, you have done remarkably well. I thank you. Here is your fee with a sizeable bonus. I am most impressed, and believe me, I very seldom say such things."

He glanced at Dawes, who nodded, fully in agreement.

"Miss Walton," Artemus continued, "I would like to have you on a sort of permanent retainer if that's what it is called. I am certain that this little event with Francobaldi is not going to be the end of my legal problems. Can I count on you if something else comes up?"

"Mr. Webb," she responded with a slight smile, "I'm afraid I don't have the slightest idea of what a 'permanent retainer' is or costs. But you are my very first legal client. I would be happy to work with you on whatever comes up."

She hesitated, then held out her hand.

"Good-bye for now."

She shook hands with Artemus and Dawes and walked to the door.

"I'll be back in a couple of weeks, Mr. Webb," she said.

As Artemus had feared, Billy Francobaldi was nowhere to be found. The day after his meeting with Artemus and Rebecca, Inspector Dawes was told he had moved out of his apartment in the North End and left no forwarding address.

"Who moved him?" he asked the landlady, a plump woman who had a heavy Italian accent.

"A large van came up yesterday morning and he was gone by noon."

"Was there a name on the van?" Dawes asked.

"One of the normal ones, Mayflower, I think?"

"You think?"

"It was Mayflower. How could you forget that?"

"Were there people other than the movers?"

"There was another man who was giving all the orders. I thought that was strange, to be honest."

"What did he look like?"

"Big, burly guy," she said. "With really thick curly black hair. I noticed the hair because it looked like it had been done in a beauty shop it was so perfect. He looked pretty tough though."

"Did you notice anything else?"

"Mr. Francobaldi wasn't very happy to be moving. I could tell that because he kind of sulked around the whole time, like he was lost."

Dawes spoke to several of the neighbors who knew Francobaldi. They described him as a quiet but friendly man who never bothered anyone. They couldn't recall anyone ever visiting him, a fact that most of them thought was very odd.

"We're a very small neighborhood," one man said. "and very nosy. If Mr. Francobaldi did anything, we would all know it, and talk about it. We never talked about him."

He paused, then laughed.

"We did kid him about his cannolis."

"Cannolis?" Dawes asked confused.

"Oh, he went to Bova's bakery over on Salem Street every day and came home with a bag of cannolis. He always ate at Giro's down on Hanover Street and he would take a couple of those cannolis with him for dessert."

Dawes talked to the managers at Bova's and Giro's and received pretty much the same report as the neighbors gave—Billy Francobaldi was a quiet, gentle man who was almost invisible if you weren't looking for him. He was always alone and seldom had anything to say.

"He didn't know a thing about the Celts, the Sox or the Bruins," the manager at Giro's laughed. "How can you live in Boston and not know about them?"

Dawes contacted Mayflower Movers in Charlestown. He found that the truck with Francobaldi's furniture was delivered to a big warehouse in Salem, next to the Parker Brothers factory. The driver said that neither Francobaldi nor the big man with the curly hair accompanied him but left the apartment in a '58 two-toned blue Chevy Malibu.

Dawes drove to Salem to look at the goods that had been stored there. He found them in a messy pile. Apparently, someone had ransacked Francobaldi's things looking for something. It took Dawes more than an hour to rummage through what was a sad collection of nondescript furniture and decorative items. He found a small roll-top desk that had been tipped over and was littered with papers that revealed nothing about the person who had sat there. He was about to move to other items when he opened the top drawer and, on some impulse, reached his hand inside and discovered a small shelf suspended from the desk writing surface. Wedged on the shelf was a simple spiral notebook, a rough diary that listed four pages of items and dates: the names of ships and when they had arrived at the Webb Shipyards. For the first time in almost five years, Inspector Dawes felt his heart beating faster. Scanning the list, he found the *U.S.S. Altamont*, and the *Willard Tipton.* He counted a total of sixteen ships over a period of ten years, each with a check mark behind their name. There were two more with no check marks. They had not yet arrived at Webb Shipyards.

❧

Billy Francobaldi was nowhere to be found. Inspector Dawes had put out a general warrant for his arrest to no avail. He was either in hiding, or, more probably, dead. Despite that, Dawes walked into Artemus' office with a smile on his face, something the younger man noticed immediately.

"What makes you so happy, Inspector?" Artemus asked.

"Progress. I have news that is going to involve you."

He explained the list of ships he had discovered in Billy's old desk.

"Are you expecting these two ships for refitting—the *Dartmouth* and the *Albuquerque*?"

Artemus reached to a shelf behind him and brought out a thick, leather-bound volume. He flipped the pages until he found what he was looking for.

"Yes, both are due within the next couple of months. They are both Omaha Class cruisers."

Dawes showed him a copy of the list he had gotten in Francobaldi's desk.

"Both were on Francobaldi's list, but they weren't checked off."

Artemus scanned the list carefully, then picked up the phone.

"Sydney, get Murphy in here."

Ten minutes later, Frank Murphy walked into the office.

"Murphy," Artemus asked. "The four men who were fired and later killed, what shift were they on?"

"Graveyard, I think. We were really busy back then, what with all of the rehab government business. We ran three crews."

"Do you remember how big those crews were?""

"As I recall, the night shift was the smallest, maybe twenty men. It could have been less."

"Who was the foreman?"

"I think it was Martin Witt. He had been here a long time and had seniority."

Murphy was dismissed, leaving Artemus and Inspector Dawes silent, mulling over the possibilities. Artemus put his log book back on its shelf and turned to face Dawes.

"Inspector, I think this matter is really in your hands now. I don't have any doubt that we are dealing with drugs here, that shipments have been arriving on these rehab ships for years. You need to get your drug people and probably the feds involved. No one except the two of us is aware of the information you found about those two ships. Let's keep it that way."

LINDA

"That one dinner at Locke Ober," Linda laughed as she talked to her mother on the phone, "changed everything for Artemus and me."

"Did you tell him you are pregnant?" her mother asked.

"I did," over a bottle of Dom Perignon, no less.

"And how did he react? Was he happy about it?"

"He was so cute, I wanted to just hug him," Linda said. "He told me he didn't know how to be a father, because his father had never even talked to him as a boy."

"Has life changed at home, sweetheart?"

"Not completely, but it has changed, Mom," Linda responded. "We are now discussing a few things. He tells me when he likes a certain dish and asks if I need money for anything. He still doesn't talk about his business at all. The only thing I know about that is from talking to his assistant, Sydney Phelps. He's a very nice man."

Her mother changed the subject.

"I read that he just sold his company for an estimated $150 million. Is that true?"

"I think it is, but nothing is going to change for months, maybe even a year because the deal is so complicated."

Mrs. Allenby was silent for some time.

"Linda," she finally asked with some hesitation, "do you get any part of that money?"

"Mother!" Linda exclaimed. "You know I signed a pre-marriage agreement that I have no part of the company. I get what I consider an enormous monthly check, more in a month than I make at the Plantation in a year. I am saving a lot. That's enough for me. I don't care about Artemus' company. I only care about him."

"Is he as mean as all of the stories say he is, Linda?"

"Artemus is a brilliant man who was raised to be a machine, with not a hint of social training as a boy. Because of his parents' murders he was forced as a teenager to become a grown man. He doesn't even know the basics of interaction with others, and he is just beginning to learn it with me."

Her mother coughed, turning away from the phone.

"Sweetheart, are you happy?"

"I am happier than I have ever been. And I am going to see my man grow to become a loving husband and a caring father. I will."

For his part, Artemus found himself in a strange position at home. Since Linda's announcement to him that he was going to become a father, he was completely adrift as to how he was supposed to act. Linda was always so cheerful at home, bubbling on about her day and her plans for the future, and he had seldom responded. But he could feel his aloofness slowly peeling away, as he found himself drawn into her plans and dreams. The adamantine shell he had built around his feelings was beginning to crack. He literally didn't know how to act, didn't know what to do, so he let her guide him. He began to talk, haltingly to be sure, but Linda was overjoyed with the shortest conversation.

"Why did you marry me?' he asked her one evening after dinner.

"Because you were so gruff and shy… besides, you're awfully good looking, Artemus."

"Oh, please, Linda. Don't be ridiculous. You couldn't possibly have been attracted to me, since even I know I have no social graces of any sort. Were you after my money?"

"Don't 'oh, please' me, Artemus. I could care less about your money. Do you care about it?"

"I have lots of it. I don't think of it at all."

"What do you think about, Artemus?" she asked quietly.

"My father told me the only thing that was important was to make money. He said that's why you go to school, why you don't waste your time with games and sports or anything that takes you away from your goal."

It was the longest statement that Linda had ever heard him utter.

"And yet you don't think about the money you have made?"

"No, only the process."

In early April they were invited to Plymouth to celebrate Easter with the Allenbys. Artemus had only met them once, when they had shown up unannounced in Hingham. It was a short meeting, as he had walked out of the house shortly after the introductions.

"Do you want to go, Linda?" he asked.

"I would like you to actually meet my parents. Not like the last time."

"I'll try," he promised, then added, "since they will be the only grandparents our child will know."

Linda and her parents were Catholics, so they attended Mass at St. Peter's in Plymouth, followed by a very short tour of the historic town, with the mandatory stop at Plymouth Rock and Town Brook. Linda insisted that they drive past Plimoth Plantation, where she worked, the outdoor museum that took the spelling of its name from the book, *Of Plimoth Plantation*, written by William Bradford, the first governor of the colony.

"Why are you studying the old dialects?" Rupert Allenby, Linda's father, asked.

"Because," Linda responded, "we are going to try to make the place as authentic as we can, with role players impersonating the actual Mayflower people."

"They came from all over England," she added.

By any normal standards, the Sunday was a minimal success, but to Linda, it was obvious that her husband was at least trying to be civil. On the way back to their home, she took his hand and squeezed it."

"Thank you," she said very quietly.

New England weather never follows any rules. Two weeks after a reasonably warm Easter, it was snowing, a wet, heavy snow that was miserable to shovel and harder to drive in. Linda, trying to get to work, slid her car into one of the trees along the driveway. She slogged back to the house where Artemus was also preparing to leave.

"Artemus, I just slid my car into a tree. I have an important meeting today at the Plantation or I would just stay home. Can you give me a ride, or let me take your car?"

"Take mine. I'll have Sydney get a tow truck over here and send one of the company trucks for me. Be careful driving. 3A gets really slippery."

He walked over and gave her a kiss and watched from the kitchen as she walked to the garage.

He had just picked up the phone to call Sydney when the explosion rocked the entire house. He raced back to the window to see the entire three-car garage engulfed in flames.

"Noooo!!!" he screamed and raced for the back door but was forced back by the heat as soon as he opened it.

"No! No! No!"

He slumped to the floor in tears, his head in his hands. Firemen responding immediately to the huge explosion, found him in that position when they arrived and pulled him from the house, which was just beginning to catch fire. They took him to his office where Sydney tried unsuccessfully to console him. Inspector Dawes arrived half an hour later, took one look at Artemus, shook his head and asked Sydney to use the phone in his office.

"I need to warn Rebecca Walton," he said and left the room.

"Find me a bed for my office," Artemus moaned. "I'll stay here."

"Mr. Webb, would you like to stay at my house?" Sydney asked, a bit uncertain.

"You heard me, Sydney. I'll stay here."

Sydney left him sitting blindly behind his desk. He found Dawes on the phone with Rebecca Walton.

"I'll order a guard for you," he was saying. "And you better have them check your car."

He was about to hang up, but added, "And Rebecca, stay out of sight. Go to a friend's or a relative's house, after the guard gets there."

He hung up the phone, looked at Sydney and shook his head sadly.

"They had just begun to form a marriage, Inspector," Sydney said. "Mr. Webb had finally let his guard down and begun caring for his wife. Did you know she was pregnant?"

"We have to get him out of here," Dawes said, picking up the phone again to call his headquarters. "They'll make another attempt."

"He'll never leave. Where would he go? Other than you and me, he knows nobody. Just as he was starting to find a life, Mr. Webb is now again completely alone, and I doubt he will ever again let someone in. Certainly, he will accept no help."

A week later the funeral was held at St. Peter's in Plymouth. This time Artemus did attend, sitting in the front pew alone, head down, stone-faced. He nodded as Linda's family, colleagues and friends offered their condolences. He remained sitting during the Mass oblivious to the rest of the congregation standing, kneeling or sitting during various parts of the liturgy. When it was over, he stiffly hugged Rupert and Missy Allenby."

"I'm sorry," he whispered. "It should have been me in that car."

ARTEMUS

Artemus had never been so alone. Even as a virtual outcast at Deerfield, he had found a sort of companionship with Sydney Phelps, and briefly with Allison Fielding. But now at twenty-four, he was utterly, completely alone. Sydney was an employee, with whom he had no social interaction at all. He had lost his wife, just as he was learning how to become a husband, and in the future, a father. There was no one else, no one to speak with in his personal despair. He couldn't even go to Boston at night because Scollay Square was being closed down, even though Joe and Nemo's was still operating, and Jeffrey Belcher, the hot dog expert, was probably going there every weekend. For several nights he sat in the dark in his living room, physically unable to move, almost unable to breathe in the social vacuum he had created with his isolation. Until the moment he had heard that awful blast that took Linda's life, he had not realized the incredible depth of his loneliness. More than once he considered suicide. Help came from a completely unexpected source.

Artemus had moved back to the house after the carpenters finished removing the debris from the garage area and restored the main house from any damage that had been done by the fire. He was rummaging around in the kitchen when he heard a knock at the back door. It was Rupert Allenby.

"I'm sorry I came without any warning," the man said, "but I wonder if I could speak with you for a few minutes, Artemus."

Artemus wasn't sure how to respond. Other than Inspector Dawes this was the first visitor he had ever had at his house in more than five years. He held out his hand to Linda's father and motioned him to come into the living room.

"You don't have to give me notice, Sir," he said to his father-in-law. "I am happy to have you in our house."

Rupert noticed the plural that was used in "our house," and felt a small jolt of emotion.

"I don't know how to put this, Artemus," he said, "but it occurred to me that you must be feeling very much alone. I wondered if I could help in any way."

There was an uneasy silence for some time before Artemus looked into the eyes of his visitor.

"Mr. Allenby," he said softly, "that is one of the nicest things that has ever been said to me. I thank you. I am sure that Linda has told you that speaking is not one of my strong points. The fact is, at this moment, I don't have anyone in the world I can speak with. She was just beginning to succeed in teaching me."

He took a very deep breath and looked away.

Rupert Allenby hesitated a moment.

"Artemus, you have lost a wife and a future child. We have lost a daughter and a future grandchild. All of us are grieving. I would like to offer you our house any time you want. We have a small apartment separate from the main house, and we would be honored if you would come to visit as often as you want. I think it would be good for you."

He got up and draped his sweater over Artemus' shoulders.

"Like it or not, you are our son."

Perhaps for the first time in his life, Artemus was unable to speak because he was overcome by an emotion other than anger or scorn. He got to his feet a bit unsteadily and held out his hand to this man who was offering the one thing he knew he needed.

"Thank you, Mr. Allenby. I don't deserve your kindness."

"But you do, Artemus. And from now on, please call me Rupert."

He handed Artemus a paper that contained his address and phone number.

"There are to be no rules, Artemus. You won't have to speak a word if you don't want to. But we both know that being with someone is the most important thing there is for you right now. And your presence, silent or not, would be very good for Missy and me in our grief."

The following weekend, Artemus took them up on their offer. The Allenbys had a lovely home on Bay View Avenue in Plymouth, with a widow's walk on the roof from which one could look out on Cape Cod Bay. A mile from the house, Plymouth Beach stretched across the shallow bay almost touching a neighboring beach that sprouted from Duxbury. Rupert Allenby took him down to the beach the first hour he was there.

"I go for long walks," he told Artemus. "It really helps to clear my mind and ease my tensions."

"That sounds good to me, Rupert," he responded. "I haven't been running for months. I'll take your suggestion right now."

Rupert watched this enigmatic man stride off along the beach, surprisingly limber for such a large person. As he considered the problems that Artemus was facing, he felt his own tensions ease.

It was Rebecca Walton on the phone.

"Mr. Webb, are you all right?" she asked. "I was horrified when I heard about your wife."

"I'm fine, Miss Walton. And how about you? This must be frightening for you as well. It appears that note was no idle threat."

"I am with my parents in New London," she answered. "To be honest, I don't know what to do. Frankly, I don't like running away from anything."

"I would stay out of sight for now," Artemus said. "This is more than serious. We are now counting seven murders, possibly nine with Francobaldi and Martin Witt. Let's let Inspector Dawes and his police resources handle this for now. You might even consider getting completely out of New England while they do, if you have any friends elsewhere. I would hate to see your parents endangered as my wife was."

Rebecca noted the subtle change in the man, actually considering other people.

"I think that is probably good advice, Mr. Webb. I do have friends in the San Francisco area that I could visit. I'll phone them right away.

"Will you keep me informed?" she continued.

"I will," Artemus replied. "Call me with your phone number when you get settled."

"Sydney, I need a gun and a permit to carry," Artemus said laconically as he entered his office. "Can you arrange that, or do I have to go myself?"

"I can get that done. There will be papers to sign, and a background check to endure."

The paperwork was all finished in two weeks. Sydney presented Artemus with a Colt Commander pistol, engraved with his initials in the handle. Artemus had never held a gun of any kind before, not even a play one, which would never have been allowed by his father, who considered any toy a useless plaything.

"I will need lessons in using this properly," Artemus told his assistant.

"I arranged for that at the Boston Firearms Training Center in Everett," Sydney responded, handing him a card with the address. You start next Monday at 10 A.M."

That Monday, after Artemus returned to his office following the gun instruction, there was a letter waiting for him on his desk. He ripped it open and scanned the single sheet inside. In a woman's handwriting it read:

"Dear Artemus, I have been so unhappy because they wouldn't let me see you again. I don't care about them anymore. My address is 3518 C Oakhurst Lane in Brighton. I need you. Allison."

Artemus simply stared at the letter, his mind unable to focus. The image of Allison had somehow become indelibly etched in his consciousness and he had no defenses to resist the memory. Finally, he balled up the paper and threw it in the direction of the wastebasket, determining to confront the woman if she was actually at that address and drive her out of his life permanently.

❧

Just after dark, Artemus pulled up to the curb in a quiet apartment district of Brighton. Just as he was getting out of his car, he heard a loud pop from the address Allison had given him. He wasn't sure if it was a gunshot, but he walked quickly to the stairs that led to apartment C, catching a fleeting glimpse of a large man running down the stairwell on the far side of the building. With a feeling of dread, he approached the door of Allison's apartment. It was half open. He entered the room and saw her on the floor, lying in a pool of blood. She turned her head slightly and tried to speak. Artemus rushed over to her and gazed down at the face that was so incredibly familiar.

Her eyes focused on him and she tried to smile, uttering a single word before she died, "…love."

He looked around and spotted a pistol, lying just under the bed. It looked strangely familiar to him, so he reached over and picked it up. The letters "A.W." were etched in the handle. It was an exact copy of the pistol he had just purchased.

Realizing that he was holding the murder weapon, he hurled it against the wall where it slid down behind the bed. He looked down at this dead woman who had somehow become so important in his life and he began to cry. In a state of mental shock, all thought of self-preservation drained away and he fell to the floor beside Allison's dead body, not even registering the scream of the sirens that were fast approaching the apartment.

He knelt there, blood-soaked, cradling her head on his lap, with broken spirit and numb mind, tears flowing freely down his cheeks. That was how the police found him. They had been alerted by an anonymous phone call that a gunshot had been heard at Allison's address. Inspector Dawes was in the first car to arrive at the scene.

Without resisting, Artemus was taken away in a police ambulance and placed under hospital arrest.

REBECCA

"MILLIONAIRE MURDERS GIRLFRIEND!"

The headline blared across the front page of every newspaper in America. Three hours after the *Boston Globe* hit the streets, Rebecca picked up the *San Francisco Chronicle.* The article featured a two-column picture of Artemus Webb in full glare, a picture that would convict him immediately in the minds of most readers. The article outlined the story in lurid details, emphasizing the anti-social nature of the purported killer. It even hinted at a connection with the death of his wife in a car explosion and the murders of his parents years before. In the press Artemus was cast as a possible serial killer.

Rebecca showed the article to her friend when they met at breakfast, remaining silent until the woman had finished reading.

"Is that the man you were working for?" her friend asked with a shocked look on her face.

"He didn't commit the murder, or any others," Rebecca said with conviction. "He couldn't have. He isn't capable of such a thing. I'm flying back to Boston. He needs all the help he can get."

"Rebecca, the man is a serial killer. Are you crazy?"

Rebecca blew up.

"He's a serial killer in this rag of a newspaper. Not in real life. I respect Artemus Webb. He is gruff, I'll admit, but he is honest, and if you get past that wonderful glare, he is fair."

She went to the phone and booked a ticket with TWA, a night-flight, non-stop to Boston.

The following morning, having nodded off to sleep on the plane for brief naps, Rebecca rented a car and drove south to Quincy. She burst into the office at Webb Shipyards finding Sidney at his desk.

"Miss Walton, what are you doing here?" a surprised Sydney exclaimed.

"I've come to renew my services with Mr. Webb. Has he been arraigned yet?"

Sydney assumed a sad face and shook his head.

"I'm afraid that Mr. Webb won't be needing your services at the moment. He is in a state of shock and unable or unwilling to communicate with anyone. I will contact you if he changes."

"Mr. Phelps, I have no intention of leaving. I will see Mr. Webb whether you recommend it or not. He is not only in grave danger with the law, he is in grave danger period. He needs a lawyer now."

"With all due respect, Miss Walton, you are hardly qualified to be his lawyer, now of all times."

"I have a verbal contract with Mr. Webb, called a 'full-time retainer.' I will take a dismissal from him, not you. Good day."

She stormed out of the office, she drove to a pay phone and called Inspector Dawes.

"I thought you were in California, Rebecca," Dawes said.

"I was until last night, Inspector. But I am here to help Mr. Webb. Can you get me in to see him? I have a contract from him that he calls a 'full-time retainer.'"

"He is currently under hospital confinement at Mass General. I think I can get you in there. Can you meet me at the main entrance of the hospital at 1:00 this afternoon?"

"I'll be there."

She was horrified when she saw him sitting there. His body was slumped, completely lacking in muscle tension. His eyes were glazed, moving constantly around the room, seeing nothing. His hands were clasped on his lap, thumbs moving constantly. Artemus Webb was not in the room.

"Good afternoon, Artemus," she said softly, using his first name to see if he would react. He didn't.

"It's Rebecca, your lawyer. I came as soon as I could."

His eyes focused on her.

"Hello, Rebecca. I thought you would be here before long."

He forced a small smile.

"I'm afraid you have come for a losing cause."

"What losing cause?" she demanded. "You have been framed. Without even hearing the details I know that. And I'm going to help you prove that."

"You're wasting your time, Rebecca. It was my gun that killed her. I was holding her when the police got there."

"Did you shoot her?"

"No."

"Then damn it, Artemus, stop talking like that."

She looked over to Inspector Dawes.

"How long are they keeping him here?"

"Until they feel he is capable of being moved."

"He hasn't been arraigned yet, has he?"

"No."

"Can I speak with him alone, Inspector?" she asked politely.

Dawes got up, patted Artemus on the arm, and left the room.

Rebecca took off her coat and got out a legal pad and pen.

"Now Artemus, tell me what happened, as fully as you are able."

"I got a letter from Allison two days ago," he said weakly. "It said she wanted to see me, but they wouldn't let her. It said she had to see me."

"Did she say who 'they' were?"

"No, I just told you what it said," he almost snapped.

She smiled at this tiny vestige of the old Artemus.

"And you drove there that night?"

"Yes. As I got out of the car, I heard a gunshot, and saw a man run away at the far end of the building."

"Can you describe him?"

"Just that he was bulky, almost my size but not quite."

Rebecca made a note and put a star next to it.

"Did you have your gun with you?

"No. It was at home in my safe."

"But you said it was your gun that killed her."

"It was. It had my initials on the handle."

"There must have been two guns made, or they broke into your safe," she said, writing feverishly. "Can you give me the combination to the safe?"

"It's written on a label under the bottom left drawer of my desk."

"Do you have a house key hidden somewhere?"

"Under a large rock beneath the window to the right of the door."

"Did you keep the letter from Allison?"

"No, I just threw it away on the floor. The cleaning people probably threw it in the garbage."

A nurse knocked and entered the room.

"I'm afraid you will have to finish, Miss Walton. Mr. Webb needs his rest."

Rebecca rose and put on her coat.

"Artemus, I'll be back tomorrow, hopefully with good news."

She met Inspector Dawes in the hallway.

"Has he told you what his story is, Inspector?"

"Not really. He was so dysfunctional when he was arrested, he wasn't clear on anything. You seem to have awakened him. Did you find out why he went to that girl's apartment?"

"Yes. He wanted to get her out of his life. And I can tell you, Inspector, this was all timed and staged by the same people who killed his wife."

She paused for a second.

"Inspector, I need to get into his house. Will you come with me in the morning?"

"Yes. Do you have a key?"

"I know where he keeps one."

"Where are you staying?"

"I'll book a room at the HoJo's in Hingham. I'll meet you at the house at 9:00. Or for breakfast at Friendly's in Hingham at 8:00."

"I'll see you at the restaurant."

The key was under the large rock under the window, just as Artemus had told her. Rebecca and Inspector Dawes entered the home to find it surprisingly in order.

"I expected everything to be turned upside down," she told Dawes. "Maybe there's nothing they are looking for."

She found the safe combination taped under the drawer and then realized that she had never asked Artemus where the safe was. It took them over an hour to find it, well-hidden in a closet filled with blankets, pillows and other bed things.

Rebecca had told Dawes about the gun, and she held her breath as she opened the safe. There, in a walnut box, with a document that allowed him to carry a gun, was the very Colt Commander pistol that Dawes had examined in Brighton at the murder scene, with A.W. incised in the handle.

"Keep this our secret," Dawes told her. "Now we have to find out who bought these guns. And it would be important to find out if Artemus had the receipt for one, or two pistols."

"Are there police records to tell us who sold the gun?" Rebecca asked him.

"Absolutely, especially since he has a license to carry. That has to go through the police department. I'll look it up and we'll pay that gun shop a visit."

"Will you keep this gun as evidence, Inspector? I don't like leaving it here, in case these creeps decide they want to ransack the house."

Dawes put the gun in his case, promising to register it as evidence for the trial.

Rebecca linked her arm in his as they left the house.

"Inspector," she said, smiling, "We're going to solve a whole bunch of crimes before we finish here. And that is exactly what Artemus told me when I took his little minor assault case. He said that this was going to become one of New England's biggest law cases."

❧

It was two weeks before Artemus was judged well enough to be transferred from Mass General Hospital, to the city jail. Rebecca was there to greet him. She noticed a significant change in him. He was once again standing tall, showing definite signs of renewed energy. He was aloof, and while he still hadn't found his glare, as she called it, he was once again almost intimidating.

Because of his position as a major New England businessman and a first-time offender, he was given a single cell at the jail. Rebecca was his first visitor.

"The arraignment is in two days," she told him. "That's where the judge tells you what the crimes are that you are accused of. He may ask you to plead guilty or not guilty, but that is usually held off until the preliminary hearing."

She paused to let him think about it.

"Of course, you are pleading not guilty. I don't want any more of this crap that you killed Allison. You did not!"

"There is a lot of evidence against me, Rebecca," he said. "I don't have much optimism about anything right now."

"Listen, Artemus, you big jerk, I was raped as a teenager and I fought against the whole system and won, and I sent that asshole to prison. We are going to do the same thing now. But there are a whole bunch of assholes who are going to prison, and some to the death chamber."

Artemus was silent, sitting there on his cot, his mind far away in Deerfield. He had rejected Allison when he first saw her and came to regret it. Now he was faced with another very strong woman and he mentally told himself not to make the same mistake again.

"Okay, Rebecca, let's go for it. Tell me what to do and I'll try to do it."

She smiled at him and patted his hand.

"We're going to win this thing. I'll be back in two days for the arraignment. Don't worry about it."

He smiled wanly from his prison cot.

"Thanks, Rebecca."

She got up to leave the cell, and he called after her.

"And I no longer object to being called Artemus."

❧

For two days, Rebecca was a whirling dervish, running between Quincy, Brighton and the state offices in Boston. By the time of the arraignment she was more confident than ever. The proceedings took less than a half hour. Judge Jason Mallory reviewed the police reports and spoke directly to Artemus.

"You are charged with first degree murder in what appears to be a very concise case. I will hold this over for a preliminary hearing to be held within the next thirty days. Do you understand the charges?"

"I do, your honor."

"Do you have anything to add?"

"We would like to request bail, your honor," Rebecca said.

"This is a first-degree murder case, Miss Walton. Bail is denied."

"There are many precedents where bail was allowed in first degree murder cases, your honor. Mr. Webb is an upstanding member of the community and has never been in court before."

"He has enough money, Miss Walton," to run to anywhere in the world and lead a life of luxury.

"You honor, Mr. Webb has never left New England. It isn't possible for a New Englander to live anywhere else in the world."

The judge positively smiled and considered her statement.

"Would you consider bail with the stipulation of house confinement, Miss Walton?"

"I would your honor. Mr. Webb leads a very sedentary life. That would be perfectly acceptable."

"Very well, Miss Walton. Bail is set at $2 million dollars with confinement to Mr. Webb's house excepting travel to and from the court."

Artemus was free that afternoon. The pre-trial hearing was set for August 10.

The pre-trial hearing was a formality. The District Attorney presented the prosecution's case with a minimum of details. That Artemus was found at the murder scene and his gun was the apparent weapon, the judge almost immediately held the case over for trial. Artemus pled not guilty and the trial was set for September 18. Since he was confined to his house, he had Sydney transfer his desk there, putting in an intercom system so that they could communicate on business matters. He brought back his old housekeeper and cook and settled in with his maps and city plats to work out his plans for land development in New England. Rebecca appeared several times on most days, peppering him with questions on every possible subject. He finally stopped asking her why she wanted such information.

Rebecca spent several days interviewing the families of the three workers known to have been murdered, as well as the wife of Martin Witt who was presumed dead. Her interviews resulted in road trips to various parts of New England to visit with other members of the men's families. One day, when the trial was only a week away, she stopped at Artemus' house for a meeting.

"I went back into your father's logs," she told him, "and looked up the shipyard dates for the rehabs on all of those ships on Francobaldi's list. I compared those dates to the bank statements of Francobaldi and the four men you fired. In every case, there was a significant deposit that corresponds to the ship arrivals. They are spread over nearly a ten-year period. Prior to that first ship on the list there are no unusual deposits in any of those accounts."

"Why are you telling me all of this?" Artemus asked almost without interest.

"Because tonight the second to last ship on that list, the *Dartmouth*, is arriving at your docks."

"I know that," he said with sarcasm. "I do run this business you know."

"I am telling you that because I don't want you to do anything unusual except check it in. That ship is the centerpiece of a very large FBI operation."

Artemus almost snorted with anger.

"Why wasn't I informed of this?"

"Because you are about to go on trial for murder. And the FBI doesn't want that complicating matters in any way."

"That's bullshit, Rebecca," he said sharply, picking up the intercom.

"Artemus, don't do that. Don't call Sydney into this. Please."

He put the phone down, looking closely at her.

"There is something else involved here, that you're not telling me."

Rebecca considered her words carefully.

"I believe that that ship and the people involved with it, are going to allow you to walk away as a free man."

THE TRIAL

It took almost two weeks before the jury was empaneled, and the trial was set to begin. It proved nearly impossible to find twelve jurors who were unaware of the case, because it involved a young man who was fabulously wealthy and who filled the newspapers with massive amounts of wild gossip. Artemus was portrayed as a loner, a tyrant, a braggart, a sociopath, even a psychopath. The story of his "lurid love affair" with the murdered woman, who turned out in real life to be Angela Maywood, was filled in with minute detail, even though the relationship had lasted barely two weeks some six years before. In fact, only Artemus, Sydney, Rebecca and Inspector Dawes knew anything about Allison Fielding.

Finally Judge Hiram Bigelow empaneled a jury of seven women and five men. On October 4, the trial began.

"Ladies and Gentlemen of the jury," Assistant District Attorney William Amalfi, the prosecutor began, "this is a very simple case. Artemus Webb, in a fit of anger, for which he is quite famous, shot his lover in cold blood. The murder weapon with his fingerprints on it was a pistol he had just purchased, with his initials, "A.W." etched in the handle. He was found crying, holding his lost lover. The state is seeking murder in the first degree."

He went on for more than a half hour, painting a lurid picture of sex and violence. Artemus, his head down, his eyes vacant, forced himself not to listen.

Rebecca, trying mightily not to appear nervous on her first criminal case, informed the court that she was postponing her address to the jury until she began her case for the defense.

The prosecution's first witness was the police sergeant who first arrived at the scene of the murdered woman's apartment. He described the scene with Artemus holding the woman's head in his lap, covered in blood. He described finding the murder weapon near the wall beneath the bed.

"Why were you at that scene in the first place, Sergeant?" the prosecutor asked.

"We received a phone call that there had been a gun shot at her address."

"Did the caller identify himself?"

"No, it was a man. He hung up immediately."

"At the murder scene, Sergeant, did the defendant resist the arrest?"

"No," the officer replied, "I would say he was in a state of shock, almost unable to speak."

Attorney Amalfi went to his desk and retrieved a manila envelope.

"Will the court mark this as material item 1?" he asked the judge.

He withdrew a pistol from the envelope.

"Sergeant is this the weapon you described as the murder weapon?"

Sergeant McAfee turned the gun over in his hands.

"Yes," he responded. "I marked it. That is the weapon we found. You can see the initials here in the handle— 'A.W.'"

"And sergeant, did you find any fingerprints on the murder weapon?"

"Yes, one set, those of the defendant."

Amalfi retuned the pistol to the envelope and handed it to the judge.

"No further questions, your honor."

Rebecca rose and walked quickly to the witness stand.

"Sergeant McAfee, how long have you been a police officer?"

"27 years," the officer answered with pride.

"And in those 27 years have you been at other murder scenes?"

"Yes, several times."

"In this instance, Sergeant, when you found Mr. Webb holding the woman, would you say that he looked like a man who just committed murder?"

"Objection," said the prosecutor, standing up. "That is asking the officer for an opinion."

"Your Honor," Rebecca responded, "I am asking a long-standing officer about his reaction to this crime scene in relation to others in his experience. I am not seeking an opinion; I am seeking an observation."

"You can answer the question, Sergeant McAfee."

The officer hesitated for a moment, considering his response.

"No," he said, a bit hesitantly, "Mr. Webb looked more like a man who has just lost a family member."

"Sergeant, you say that you were responding to a phone call that reported a gun shot. Can you tell me the time of that phone call?"

Sergeant McAfee looked at his notebook.

"It came in at 20:11,"

"Is that 8:11 P.M. in our laymen's terms?" Rebecca asked with a smile that was returned.

"Yes, Ma'am."

"And what time did you arrive at the murder scene?"

"At 20:24, uh 8:24."

"So it took you thirteen minutes to respond. Thank you, Sergeant McAfee."

Rebecca dismissed him.

Mr. Amalfi next called a succession of witnesses to testify to the extreme anti-social behavior of the defendant. He began with a young man named Ricky Malfusi.

"Mr. Malfusi, can you testify to an encounter you had with the defendant during your grammar school days."

"I was coming home from school when Artemus Webb stopped me. He beat the shit out of me and left me laying in the street."

"Was this something unusual," the attorney asked.

"He did the same thing to five of my friends. We were all afraid of him."

"Thank you, Mr. Malfusi. No more questions."

Rebecca almost ran to the witness box.

"Mr. Malfusi, how old were you when this supposed beating occurred?"

"I was in the seventh grade."

"Was there a reason that Artemus Webb confronted you?"

"Not that I remember."

"I will remind you, Mr. Malfusi, that you are under oath. Let me ask that question again. Was there a reason that Artemus Webb confronted you?"

"Well, we had beat him up before."

"We? Who are 'we'?"

"My friends and me. We considered him a snitch who was telling stories about our fathers not doing their jobs at the shipyard."

"And you beat him up? Six of you?"

"Yes."

"And you destroyed his bike?"

"Yes."

"Were the others whom you say Mr. Webb beat up, the rest of the gang that attacked him?"

"Yes."

"Did Artemus Webb ever fight you again after that?"

"No. He left all of us alone after he had beat us up."

"To your knowledge, was Artemus Webb ever in a fight with anyone?"

"No. He never talked to anyone. He just came to school and went home. He never spoke to anyone. He was weird."

"Did he ever get in trouble in school?"

"Not that I remember. He was the best student in the class."

"Thank you, Mr. Malfusi. No more questions."

The next witness was Jason Burr, Artemus' roommate at the Deerfield Academy.

"Mr. Burr," the prosecutor began, "you were the roommate of Artemus Webb at the Deerfield Academy, is that true?"

"Yes."

"Can you describe your experience?"

"Artemus never took part in anything at Deerfield, except the classes. He hardly spoke to anyone, didn't play sports, didn't come to the games."

"Did that bother you?"

"Hell yes, it bothered me. He hardly ever spoke to me either and I was his roommate. I got out of there after one semester."

"Thank you, Mr. Burr."

Rebecca smiled as she slowly approached the witness.

"Mr. Burr, did Artemus Webb ever fight with anyone at Deerfield?

"No, not that I know of."

"Did he get into shouting matches or arguments?"

"No."

"How was he in class?"

"He was an "A" student, except in art and P.E., which he refused to take."

"So he was not an athlete?"

"He was the best athlete in the academy. He ran all the time and lifted weights. But he refused to go out for football or anything for that matter."

"Did you ever ask him why?"

"I did. He said he wasn't in school to waste his time. He was there to learn how to make money."

"And you resented that?"

"Hell yes. He could have been a star in football. He would have been if he wasn't so unfriendly all the time."

"Thank you, Mr. Burr."

The next two state witnesses simply repeated what Malfusi and Burr had reported, that Artemus Webb was an unsocial man. They added that he was very intimidating because of his size, his intelligence and his eyes.

"His eyes stop you before you even start to talk to him," one of his workers at the shipyard stated, careful not to look at Artemus.

Rebecca didn't bother to question the last two witnesses. The following morning, she would begin her defense.

❧

The old cruiser *Dartmouth* had initially been mothballed in the Philippines before being moved, first to San Pablo Bay near San Francisco and then to Norfolk, Virginia. The ship drew a great deal of unseen attention, staked out by the FBI as well as a team of dock workers specially selected by Inspector Dawes. The ship sat untouched for almost two weeks before a crew from the shipyard boarded to begin the process of rehabilitation. It was the day that Artemus' trial began. Two days later, three men from the night shift boarded the ship, dragging a pair of cutting torches into the hull. Hours later a black van pulled up to the ship and the workers began loading boxes until the van was nearly filled. The vehicle departed, and the three men returned to the drydock area to resume their work there.

The activity around the ship was filmed and all participants photographed. FBI agents followed the loaded van into the city. It pulled up to a large warehouse near the waterfront in South Boston, met there by three men who emerged from a pair of black sedans parked in the shadows. Two occupants of a third car remained in it. The van backed through a large door which was quickly closed, remaining there for more than an hour before emerging to the parking lot. As it left the lot, the car with the two men pulled out behind it. Agents followed the two vehicles to a deserted parking lot in Quincy, where the van driver carried a duffle bag to the car and deposited it in the trunk. From all directions FBI agents descended on the two vehicles and took the three men into custody. More agents tracked the other two cars as they left the warehouse parking lot, photographing the occupants and staking out their houses.

The following morning Frank Murphy led a crew aboard the *Dartmouth*, ostensibly to evaluate the work that was necessary to bring the ship back to standards. They photographed the interior of the hull, including an area where there was evidence of a false wall having been removed from the port side of the bow.

A permanent watch was placed on the ship as well as the warehouse where the truck had delivered its cargo.

❧

"Ladies and Gentlemen of the jury," Rebecca began, walking from her desk to the jury box. I would like to summarize the prosecution's arguments you have just heard, because by the time we are finished, those arguments will have melted away. Artemus Webb did not commit murder; Artemus Webb is incapable of such violence, regardless of how people see him as a non-social man. In our testimonies we will prove that he did not commit the murder of Angela Maywood, whom Mr. Webb knew as Allison Fielding. You will learn that it was not Mr. Webb's gun that was used in the murder, and that the police were informed of the murder before the fatal shot was even fired.

"I call as my first witness, Inspector William Dawes."

Dawes smiled at Artemus as he took the witness stand and received a black stare in return. Artemus had not spoken ten words since the trial began and remained in a mental zone that nothing seemed able to penetrate.

"Inspector Dawes," Rebecca began, "you have been involved in the case of the murder of Darius and Melinda Webb for many years now, isn't that true?"

"Yes, I was involved from the very beginning."

"And you are familiar with the story of Artemus Webb and the woman he knew as Allison Fielding?"

"Yes."

"Can you tell the court the nature of that story?"

"I can. It is very odd, to say the least. Miss Fielding, whom we now know as Angela Maywood, intruded herself into Artemus Webb's running schedule when he was a student at Deerfield Academy. It led to a single afternoon of love making promoted by Miss Fielding. The woman then disappeared. A few years ago, Mr. Webb received a letter saying he could find her at Maddie's Sail Loft in Marblehead. He caught a glimpse of her and then she disappeared again. That is the extent of their relationship, until Mr. Webb received another letter from the woman."

Rebecca handed the inspector a letter and asked him to read it.

There was a definite rustle in the jury box when Inspector Dawes finished reading the short letter. Even Artemus looked up in interest, wondering how on earth Rebecca had found the letter.

Rebecca entered the letter as defense evidence and turned back to Inspector Dawes.

"The murders of Darius and Melinda Webb weren't the only crimes you have been investigating. Isn't that correct, Inspector?"

"Yes, there are several more murders related to the Webb Shipyards," the inspector answered.

"Can you be specific?"

"A few days after Mr. Webb took over his parents' shipyards, he fired his attorney, Winston Haverill. Mr. Haverill was found dead the following day. It appeared to be a suicide but that was later changed to murder."

"Inspector, can you tell the court the reason for Mr. Haverill's firing?"

"When he took over the company, Mr. Webb discovered that Haverill had been stealing from Darius Webb's company for years. It was a large amount, more than a million dollars. Artemus Webb demanded the money be repaid and Haverill's contract abrogated."

"Have there been more murders since then?"

"There were four workers among some fifty who were laid off. Three of them have been murdered and the fourth is missing."

"And what progress have you made in solving those crimes?"

"Until very recently, none."

"What has happened recently, inspector?"

"To be honest, the murder of Angela Maywood."

Rebecca went to her desk and returned with a manila envelope similar to the one the prosecution had entered as evidence. She handed it to Inspector Dawes, who opened it and withdrew a pistol.

"Inspector, will you tell the court what you are holding?"

Webb looked directly at the jury.

"Miss Walton and I found this pistol in the safe of Artemus Webb. Along with it we found the bill of sale for the pistol. The serial number on the bill of sale matches that on the gun."

"Thank you, Inspector. That will be all for now. The defense calls Sergeant McAfee back to the stand."

After McAfee had been reminded that he was still under oath, Rebecca handed him the pistol that had just been identified by Inspector Dawes.

"Sergeant, can you describe this pistol?"

Sergeant McAfee registered surprise in his face as he took the gun from Rebecca. He turned it over several times, and then looked up at her.

"This is the exact same gun as the murder weapon. It has the identical initials. They are twins."

"Did you, or anyone else check the serial number on the murder weapon and trace it to the purchase?"

The sergeant fidgeted noticeably in his chair, embarrassed at this obvious omission.

"No."

Rebecca turned to face the jury, holding up the pistol.

"This is the gun that Mr. Webb purchased three weeks ago, not the weapon that was found at the murder scene. Mr. Webb kept his gun in the safe in his home because he had not yet completed instructions, he was taking at the Boston Firearms Training Center in Everett. The murder weapon was purchased by someone else."

She turned back to face the police officer.

"Before I end your testimony, Sergeant, I would like to recall your testimony earlier about the timing involved. You testified that the call received by the police came in at 8:11 and that you arrived at Miss Maywood's apartment at 8:24. Is that correct?"

"Yes."

"Thank you, Sergeant. That will be all for now. Your witness, Mr. Prosecutor."

"The State has no questions at this time."

Rebecca surveyed some papers at her desk.

"The defense calls Mrs. Earlene Blackwood."

An elderly lady, walking with the aid of a cane, walked to the witness stand.

"Mrs. Blackwood," Rebecca began, "thank you for coming this morning. You live a floor below the apartment where the murder occurred. Is that right?"

"I do. I used to see that lovely young woman come and go all the time."

"On the night of the murder, did you hear a gunshot?"

"Yes. It was very loud, even with my hearing aid."

"Do you know the approximate time when you heard it, Mrs. Blackwood?"

"I know the exact time. It was 8:15, because it was the commercial break for 'I Love Lucy.' I never miss that show. I always get up to take my medicine during the commercials."

Rebecca withdrew a paper from her briefcase.

"Your honor, I would like to present as evidence a program log for that 'I Love Lucy' show which was provided by Channel 3. It shows the commercial break at exactly 8:15."

She turned to the prosecutor.

"Your witness."

Prosecutor Amalfi stalked over to the stand.

"Mrs. Blackwood, you admit that you wear a hearing aid. How are you so sure that what you heard was a gunshot and not a car backfiring, for instance?"

"Oh, it was a gunshot. It was almost right over my head. It was more like a pop than a big bang a car might make. It was a shot, because right after it, a man came running up the stairs to Miss Maywood's apartment. I think it must have been that man who is on trial,"

She pointed over at Artemus Webb.

"So you heard a man running up to the room, after you heard the gunshot. Is that correct?"

"Yes, that is correct. It might have been a couple of minutes after I heard the shot."

"No more questions, your honor," a very deflated prosecutor declared.

Rebecca returned to the witness.

"Thank you, Mrs. Blackwood. It seems your testimony places the murder four minutes after the police were warned it was going to happen. We are deeply in your debt."

"The defense calls Billy Francobaldi."

Artemus snapped to attention, making eye contact with Rebecca, a look that asked a simple question—how did you find him?'

Billy Francobaldi entered from outside the courtroom, escorted by a police officer. He shambled slowly to the witness stand, his eyes on the floor.

Rebecca wasted no time.

"Mr. Francobaldi, did you purchase a Colt Commander pistol from Mid Cape Firearms in Hyannis in the last month?"

"I…I don't recall. I got a gun a while ago, but it wasn't on the Cape."

Rebecca handed him a paper.

"Is this your signature on this bill of sale?"

He hardly glanced at it, then looked away and down.

"I guess so."

Rebecca turned to Judge Bigelow.

"Your Honor, this is a copy of a bill of sale from Mid Cape Firearms. It is signed by Mr. Francobaldi. If you compare the serial number with the murder weapon, I believe you will find they match."

"So, Mr. Francobaldi, you purchased the firearm that murdered Miss Maywood. Did you pull the trigger?"

"No! I didn't murder that woman."

"But your gun did, Mr. Francobaldi. If you didn't, who did you give the gun to?"

"I don't know. I didn't give it to anyone. It must have been stolen."

"Mr. Francobaldi, both of us know that this murder ties in with at least six other murders in the last five years. Are you going to take the rap for all of them?"

"Objection, Your Honor," Attorney Amalfi roared. "That statement is completely reckless and without foundation."

"Your Honor," Rebecca retorted, "my statement, as Mr. Francobaldi well knows, is true. This murder, which by now everyone including the prosecutor should realize, was a plot to set up my client, Mr. Webb. In the past five years, both of his parents were murdered, as was his lawyer, Mr. Haverill, three of his workers, his wife and now Miss Maywood, alias Allison Fielding. And Mr. Francobaldi is connected to all of them."

She spun around and glared at him.

"Isn't that true, Mr. Francobaldi?"

"I'm...I'm not going to answer that," he said, barely audibly.

"I believe you came here under police custody," Rebecca said. "I will reserve the right to call you back, Mr. Francobaldi."

Once again lawyer Amalfi had no questions.

"The defense calls Martin Witt."

This time Artemus gasped and came fully to attention. For the first time in the trial, he was almost his old self, his eyes beginning to take on the defiant look he once maintained naturally. Rebecca had managed to resurrect two men whom Artemus had thought to be dead.

A rough-hewn man entered through the rear door. He was wearing jeans, work boots and a plaid shirt. He hadn't shaved in several weeks and had made no attempt to trim his beard.

"Mr. Witt, will you identify yourself to the court?"

"I am Martin Witt. I worked at Webb Shipyards for almost thirty years. I and three of my fellow workers were fired when Artemus Webb took over the company from his parents, who had been murdered."

"Is it true that you have been in hiding?" Rebecca asked softly.

"Yeah, it's true. I watched those three fellow workers get murdered. I would have been too, but I ran when I saw this big guy coming after me and Ralphy Menicotti. Ralphy's dead. I'm still breathing."

"Are you, like Mr. Francobaldi, in police custody at this time, Mr. Witt?"

"Yeah, that's right. I got involved in some stuff at the shipyard."

"Do you know who that big guy is?" Rebecca asked.

"The police showed me his picture."

Rebecca drew a photograph out of an envelope.

"Is this the man?"

"Yeah, that's him. That's the guy who killed Ralphy, and probably Joey and Billy too."

The prosecutor started to rise and object, then slowly sat back down.

Rebecca handed the photo to the judge.

"Let the record show that Mr. Witt identified this man, who goes by the present name of George Knowland. He is currently being sought by the police in connection with the several murders I just mentioned."

She turned back to Martin Witt.

"Mr. Witt, you say that you were involved with a problem back at the shipyard. Can you tell us what that problem was?"

He fidgeted in his seat, avoiding eye contact with anyone in the courtroom.

"Me and the three guys I mentioned were hired to take some boxes out of the holds of ships that were coming in for rehab. We torched open some false walls in the hull where the stuff was concealed. We guessed it was probably drugs since most of those ships were coming out of Asia, but we never knew. We got five hundred bucks for each ship we opened."

"Who paid you?"

"We never knew. All I know is that I got an envelope in the mail with $500 cash in it a couple of days after we done the work. All of us did. That was a lot of money for an hour's work."

"That is all the questions I have for you, Mr. Witt."

"The prosecution has no questions, your Honor. But may I request a meeting in your chambers?"

The judge and two attorneys left the courtroom through a rear door.

Once seated, Judge Bigelow, turned to William Amalfi.

"Mr. Amalfi, you called for this meeting."

"I did your Honor, because I think it best that the state withdraws the complaint against Mr. Webb. Miss Walton's defense has been superb, and very clear."

He made a nervous bow in Rebecca's direction.

"Miss Walton, are you in favor of that? Somehow I think you have much more to say before this case is closed."

"I do, Judge Bigelow. I gratefully accept the admission of Mr. Webb's innocence. But Mr. Webb will understand if I delay the news for a day or perhaps two because I believe, in the course of questioning more people in the context of this trial, we can bring closure to all of those other crimes that have circled around him."

"It is Thursday, Miss Walton. I would be willing to adjourn until Monday at 9:00."

"Thank you, your Honor."

Artemus was driven home in a police car, since he was still under house arrest. Rebecca drove to her motel in Hingham with Inspector Dawes.

"Rebecca, I am not comfortable with you staying at the motel," Dawes said as they drove onto the Southeast Expressway. "You are getting very close to exposing a major drug ring and a bunch of murderers. After today in court, you could be in real danger."

"What do you propose, inspector?" she replied, a bit testy. "I'm really not afraid, but I'll listen to your suggestions."

"The HoJo where you are staying has interior corridors," Dawes said. "I am going to drop you off in front. We have a couple of agents inside. I want you to go into the lobby and then come to the end of the hall. I'll meet you in back and we'll move you to another place. Our agents will turn on the light in your room and If nothing happens right away, one of our men will turn your light out half an hour or so later and wait in the hall."

"I don't think they are stupid enough to try something as simple as that," Rebecca objected. "If they are coming after me, they'll hit me on the road or with a sniper at the courthouse.

"We have a safe house for you for the weekend. And I'll have an escort for you to the courthouse on Monday morning."

Rebecca looked over at Inspector Dawes.

"Do you really think they will try to kill me?" she asked quietly.

"When you hear the information, I have for you tonight, you will think so too, Rebecca. We have one of the men involved in the drug ring and he has been singing like a canary."

Rebecca entered the lobby as instructed and walked quickly down the corridor to a door at the back. She opened it to find two men waiting, who roughly grabbed her arms and pushed her into a waiting car. She was blindfolded, and a hand closed on her mouth. She smelled something acrid before she passed out.

Inspector Dawes awoke with a terrible headache. He had just gotten out of his car when he was struck by something very hard. He remembered nothing after that. Groggily, he got to his feet and staggered into the hotel, climbing the stairs to the second floor and Rebecca's room. Two men sat in chairs outside the door.

"They have her," he mumbled to the two officers, who jumped up to steady him on his feet. "They hit me and must have taken Rebecca. Let's get downtown."

Artemus answered the bell from the front door to find Rupert Allenby standing there, the morning newspapers in his arm.

"I thought you might like to see what they are saying about your trial, Artemus. Linda told me months ago that you didn't get any of the papers."

"I've never been interested in what they had to say, Rupert. But come in. It was nice of you to think of me."

Rupert gave Artemus the papers, and went back to his car, returning with two large coffees and a bag from Dunkin' Donuts.

Artemus looked at the *Boston Globe*.

"Webb trial all but over," read the headline.

He looked quizzically at Rupert.

"This is one article you should read, Artemus," his visitor said, sitting down and taking a sip of his coffee.

Artemus read the lead article. It reported the events of his trial in some detail, pointing out how each of the prosecution's arguments had not only been deflected by the defense lawyer, a neophyte at that, but shockingly shattered. The article was almost an editorial because its conclusion was that Artemus Webb should be released immediately.

"She has done a remarkable job for you, Artemus," Rupert said.

Artemus nodded and put the paper down.

"I sat there amazed," he admitted. "How on earth did she find Martin Witt? And Billy Francobaldi? And she came up with the letter I received from Allison. That had been thrown away in the garbage. And she found the receipt for the second gun that Francobaldi bought."

It was Allenby's time to nod in agreement.

"And the old lady who watches "I Love Lucy."

Artemus would have laughed if he had been able, but it was something he had seldom done.

"I think the prosecutor wants to drop the case against you, Artemus. He was all slumped over when he asked the judge for a meeting. I think that's why the judge adjourned the trial until Monday. The *Globe* certainly thinks so, and so does the *Herald*."

"I thought I was finished," Artemus admitted sadly. "I was mentally set to go to prison. She has saved me, and I don't deserve it. I gave up."

"That's one of the reasons I came this morning, to tell you that you have your whole life ahead of you. Just let a few people into that life, Artemus. I think you were ready to give up because you had nothing going in your life. And no one."

Artemus was silent for some time, looked around and picked up his coffee.

"Do you know something, Rupert, I have never thanked, or complimented anyone in my life. I laid awake last night thinking about that. Actually, I think I thanked Sidney once."

"From what my daughter told me, you were trained not to."

"I am beginning to realize that," Artemus admitted. "But you…and Rebecca…are beginning to undo that training."

He got up and held out his hand to the older man.

"Thank you."

The two men talked for more than an hour, mostly about the details of the trial. Rupert was about to leave when there was a knock at the back door.

"That'll be Dawes," Artemus said with a smile. "He never uses the front door."

They admitted a very dour and tired inspector.

"What's the matter, Inspector?" Artemus asked. "You look like you just lost your best friend."

"Even worse, Artemus," Dawes said sadly. "They have kidnapped Rebecca, and right from under my nose."

Artemus felt a rock sink in his stomach.

"Kidnapped? Who?"

"I assume it was the mob," Dawes said. "Someone knocked me out just before I was to meet her and take her to a safe house. When I awoke, she was gone. There is not a trace of her, and no chatter at all on the streets."

"What action, if any, is being taken, Inspector," Rupert asked.

"I have a meeting with Judge Bigelow this afternoon," Dawes said. "The trial can't continue without a defense lawyer, and there is no one ready to take over."

Dawes looked over at Artemus.

"Everyone believes the trial is about to be conceded, Artemus. I see you have the papers here. But Rebecca has introduced a whole set of other crimes, and I fully believe she was about to unravel the entire mess on Monday."

Artemus agreed.

"In about a month," he said, "that woman has solved what we have been unable to do in five years."

"I have most of the details she had," Dawes observed. "We have a jail filled with suspects for these crimes, but Rebecca was going to give us the main guy."

"Do you think she's dead, Inspector?" Artemus asked, dreading the answer.

"Probably," he answered after a pause, then added, "But I thought Witt and Francobaldi were dead too."

"I've already given up once during this thing," Artemus said. "I'm not giving up again. She's alive. I know it."

Dawes and Allenby looked at each other, then laughed.

"Is that the Artemus Webb we have all come to know and love?" Dawes asked.

Artemus laughed too.

VINCENT SCALABRESE

Rebecca was vaguely aware of voices in the room as she slowly came out of her stupor. She couldn't make out words, only that some were being spoken. Her head throbbed; her body ached. But slowly the fog around her began dissipating, and she forced her left eye to open slightly. She was lying on a sofa, a soft one and the blurs of two people were standing about ten feet away conversing. She moaned, and both blurs moved at the same time. There were no details. One of the blurs she assumed was a big man left the room, the other moved over toward her.

"Welcome back, Miss Walton. We have been waiting for you. You already missed breakfast and lunch. I feared you would also miss dinner."

The voice sounded hollow, almost like the ones you hear in a horror movie.

She opened her eye fully. A man came slowly into focus. He is old, she thought. He has hair that is pure white, a lot of hair, she thought, for an old man. He is dressed in a gray suit with a blue tie. His shoes are highly polished. I never look at shoes, she told herself.

She attempted to lift herself up on her elbow and failed, sinking back to the couch with a groan.

"Don't try to get up yet," the man said in that hollow voice. "It takes a while for the chemicals to wear off. Just lie there, Miss. Walton."

Slowly she came back to life. After what seemed an eternity, she was able to sit up, though her head was still splitting.

"Drink this," the man said, handing her a glass of water. "Take your time. Drink it all."

She noted that there was something bitter in the water, but she drank it anyway, handed him the glass and sat back in the soft couch, her head pressed against the back.

"Where am I?" she asked weakly. Then a little stronger, "Who are you?"

"Where and who doesn't matter, Miss Walton. You are alive. That is all that is important."

Her head still throbbing, she looked around the room. They were in a large, very elegant hall, paneled in dark walnut, with a grand piano in one corner and luxurious leather couches and chairs grouped in several areas. One side of the room was almost filled with large windows that looked out on a pond surrounded by forest, perhaps a quarter mile away. There was a wet bar along the interior wall.

She turned to face the man. He was sitting in one of the leather lounge chairs smiling.

"Why did you kidnap me?" she demanded sharply. "And what are you going to do with me now that you have."

"Oh, you are quite mistaken, Miss Walton," the man said. "We didn't kidnap you. We kept you from getting murdered. And we intend to keep you alive."

Rebecca's eyes shot fire at the man.

"If you didn't kidnap me, why did you blindfold and drug me?"

"Because we have our own identity and whereabouts to protect. You don't need to know any more about us than is necessary."

Rebecca's mind was racing. I know this man, she thought, but she just couldn't quite recall why she knew him. His identity was right on the edge of her memory, so she stalled until it clicked in.

"If you don't want to kill me," she asked, "who does?"

"You know the answer to that very well, my dear," the man said in a fatherly fashion. "Those you were about to expose in court."

"Could I have another glass of water?" she asked, changing the subject, still trying to identify her captor.

"Of course."

He walked to the bar, filled a glass with ice and put it under the tap.

With the first sip, Rebecca knew who the man was and where they were. She walked to the windows.

"If you want to hide your location from me, why did you allow me to look out on Farm Pond?" she asked turning to look at him.

"The man's eyes showed the slightest trace of surprise and she knew she was right.

"There are a thousand ponds in this part of New England," he said, a bit amused. "Why do you suppose this one is Farm Pond?"

"Because I know you live in Sherborn, on Farm Pond, Mr. Scalabrese."

The look of amusement became a broad smile.

"Very good, Miss Walton. Very good. I don't know how you came up with that, but I congratulate you, and I apologize for having taken those unpleasant and obviously unnecessary precautions. I should have known better."

He walked to the door.

"I'll have Robert show you to your room," he said. "You can freshen up for dinner if you wish. We have a great deal to discuss."

❧

Inspector Dawes was admitted into the chambers of Judge Bigelow bearing the news that they had lost the defense attorney in the Artemus Webb trial.

"What do you mean you lost her?"

"She's been kidnapped, Your Honor," Dawes replied. He outlined the events of the night before when Rebecca Walton had disappeared.

"Do the police have any suspects in this kidnapping?"

"Miss Walton was about to expose at least a dozen major crimes," Dawes said. "I assume that those about to be named are behind her disappearance. I was trying to get her into a safe house until the trial continues on Monday."

"Inspector Dawes, this is most curious," the judge said, sitting back in his chair and staring at the ceiling. "I'm not sure I have encountered anything similar. The prosecutor wants to drop all charges against Mr. Webb. But Mr. Webb's attorney asked that the trial continue at least one more day. We have a case that clearly has the wrong man accused of murder and any number of other crimes are about to be exposed if the trial continues."

He stopped, considering another angle in the matter.

"Has the press been informed about Miss Walton's disappearance?"

"No. Outside of the police, only Mr. Webb and his father-in-law are aware of it."

"Keep it that way, Inspector," the judge commanded. "We will convene on Monday as if nothing has happened. Perhaps over the weekend you will find her, or she will find you."

Dawes laughed.

"Your Honor, I would put my money on the latter."

"One more thing, Inspector Dawes. I would make every effort to protect Mr. Webb."

"He is now residing in the safe house we had set aside for Miss Walton."

⁂

"Miss Walton, do you mind if I ask you how you know my name?"

"I saw your picture in a newspaper article. You were attending a dedication for a baseball field in Sherborn."

Scalabrese shook his head, looking intently at the young woman sitting across from him at dinner.

"That's incredible," he exclaimed. "Why on earth would you remember me?"

"I was more interested in the man next to you in the picture."

"To be honest, I don't even remember the dedication, much less who was there with me."

"It was your next-door neighbor's son."

"Saltonstall?"

Rebecca nodded.

Scalabrese registered the information and quickly changed the subject.

"Miss Walton, I am very impressed by the abilities you have shown in Webb's trial. Not only as a lawyer, and on your first case at that. But especially on your investigation prowess. I was looking for Billy Francobaldi myself and couldn't find him. How did you?"

"Mr. Scalabrese, you just kidnapped me. Why on earth would I disclose what I know about this trial to you?"

"I told you, I didn't kidnap you. I put you under my protection."

"So I am free to leave?"

Scalabrese smiled and picked up his knife.

"Enjoy your dinner, Miss Walton. This is excellent veal. Would you like some wine? I have a very nice Masi Amarone."

"Thank you," Rebecca said with defiance in her voice, holding out her glass. "I *would* like some of your wine."

Rebecca looked at the man who was now her captor. He's actually very charming, she thought. Could he really be as ruthless as the police reports say he is?

"Mr. Scalabrese," she said, looking him directly in the eye. "You say you are protecting me. From whom? And why?"

Scalabrese maintained her eye contact.

"You appear to have solved a whole string of murders and are about to expose a rather elaborate drug ring, Miss Walton. It is in my interests that you are successful. I can't afford to have you killed."

Rebecca looked away, deep in thought. Then she turned back to him.

"You seem to know everything that I have discovered. Why don't you just take what you know to the police?"

Scalabrese let out a gentle laugh.

"I do like you, Miss Walton. When you are finished with this Webb trial, would you consider working for me?"

"I doubt it," she responded seriously. "But my question still stands. You certainly have contacts in the police department who could act on your information."

"Miss Walton," he countered, "of course I have such contacts, but I maintain what you would call an 'adversarial relationship' with the police department in Boston. I like the way you are acting on the information that we both have.

"Besides," he added, "you seem to know more about it than I do and that is why you are here. As I told you, I value your abilities. Are you sure you won't tell me how you found Francobaldi and Witt? I need to train my people better."

Rebecca sighed.

"That was a very fine dinner, Mr. Scalabrese. Perhaps the best I can ever remember. I suppose it deserves something in payment. I found Francobaldi by tracing his habits back more than fifteen years. It seems he was an orphan and his foster parents finally threw him out as a good-for-nothing. But he has several cousins. They had him hidden in one of those three-level houses in New Bedford. As for Witt, I just badgered his wife until she got sick of me and told me where to find him. He was hidden away at his uncle's house in Boxboro."

"Just hard work," Scalabrese marveled. "My boys are just going to have to start doing more digging."

"Not graves, I hope," Rebecca said, getting up.

Scalabrese let out a hearty laugh.

"Touché, Miss Walton. Very good."

"Thank you for your hospitality, Mr. Scalabrese, and I suppose for your protection."

"I think you will find everything you need in your room, Miss Walton," he said. "I look forward to more conversations in the morning."

Rebecca not only found a complete set of toiletries in her bathroom, but a closet full of night clothes, dresses, shoes and coats, all in her size.

"Girl, your quality of living just took a major leap forward," she exclaimed out loud, holding up a pair of silk pajamas and stepping into some fur-lined slippers.

❧

Vincent Scalabrese was, if nothing else, an exceedingly gracious host. A lavish breakfast buffet had been laid out when Rebecca descended to the dining room after a surprisingly restful night. Fully recovered from her nausea of the day before, she found she was ravenously hungry and dove into the buffet table immediately. She was halfway through breakfast when Scalabrese appeared.

"Good, I see you have helped yourself, Miss Walton. I trust you slept well."

Rebecca, holding a piece of bacon in her hand, smiled.

"I have never slept better, Mr. Scalabrese. I think that silk pajamas must inspire a good night's sleep. For that I thank you."

"We have some business to attend to this morning," he replied. "When you are finished, please come into the den."

With that he left.

She downed a final cup of coffee and followed him.

"Undoubtedly you have wondered what my role is in all of this," Scalabrese began. "Since you probably have figured it out already, I will come straight to the point. These people you are after in clearing your client have given my profession a very bad name. They are amateurs and have begun to make life very difficult for me and my organization."

"How is that possible, Mr. Scalabrese?" Rebecca asked with an edge in tone.

"They are killing people all over the place," he replied, "which always makes my organization a prime suspect. I assure you, Miss Walton, we have played no role in this entire matter."

Rebecca looked directly at him.

"You seem to know everything that has taken place. Why don't you deal with it yourself?"

"And cause more headline bloodshed? Please, Miss Walton, I abhor headlines."

Rebecca was silent for some time, doodling with a pen and pad that she had found on the desk.

"So you want me to do your dirty work?"

Scalabrese laughed, not looking at her.

"If you do it, it won't be dirty," he said. "And I know you are capable of handling the entire thing. I can give you the one piece of evidence you need—the killer."

He handed her a piece of paper with a name and address written on it.

"If you would be so kind as to make a phone call..."

He pointed to a phone on the desk next to her. Rebecca read the name and lifted the phone handle.

She was unable to reach Artemus who had been taken to the safe house the day before by Inspector Dawes. She dialed the Boston Police, asking for Inspector Dawes.

"The Inspector is not on duty," the operator told her. "It's Sunday, you know."

"Can I have his home phone?" Rebecca asked politely. "It's very important, about the Webb murder case."

"I can't give you his home phone, but if you will give me yours, I'll have him phone you."

"I can't give you my number either," Rebecca answered. "Tell the inspector that Rebecca Walton is calling and that I'll call back at 10:00 this morning if he can get to the station by that time."

Precisely at 10:00 Dawes picked up the phone on the first ring.

"Rebecca, where are you? Are you all right?"

"Yes, on the second question, Inspector. I have an urgent task for you to do today. You will need support. Go to 112 Water Street in Salem. You will find George Knowland there."

The phone clicked, and Dawes was left staring at the receiver.

With a team of special agents, Dawes sped toward Salem, only about twenty miles north of Boston. Being Sunday, traffic was light but on the tortured, winding roads that New England is famous for, it still took them almost an hour to reach the famous seaport town. The address was an old nineteenth century ramshackle house not far from the famous House of Seven Gables. The squad pulled up a block away and agents spread out to encircle the house. Heavily armed, a pair of officers crept toward the front door. One gave a signal and the other kicked in the old door, which shattered on impact. They rushed into the room, weapons ready, to find George Knowland, tied to a chair and gagged. There was no one else in the house.

"Your source could have saved us a lot of heart beats, Dawes," the agent laughed when the rest of the team entered the room. This guy has been handed to us wrapped like a Christmas present."

"The mob has to be involved in this," Dawes said quietly. "The real mob. Let's take him downtown and see what he has to say."

❧

Following her phone call to Dawes, Rebecca was left on her own for the rest of the morning, Scalabrese telling her he had personal business to attend to. She walked through the exquisite grounds, filled with plants she couldn't identify. The lawns were manicured like one of the finest golf courses. A large greenhouse occupied a secluded space in the garden. It was filled with hundreds of orchids. She marveled at the enigma presented by Vincent Scalabrese—apparently ruthless in his underworld dealings but refined in every sense of the word in his private life. Now that she understood that she wasn't in the least bit of danger, she found that she was beginning to like the man.

Finding a pair of binoculars in the den, she went back to her room on the second floor and focused on Farm Pond in the distance. A pair of loons floated easily at the far edge, while Canada geese communed in several of the coves. The famous New England fall foliage was nearing what the locals called "the peak," a time when in a good year, the golds and reds of maples and birch simply shimmer in the cool sunlight. This is a good year, Rebecca thought, marveling at the glorious fall mirror presented in the pond's waters. The color was particularly beautiful because of the dark contrast of the pines mixed in among the hardwoods.

She heard a knock at her door. It was Robert announcing that lunch was to be served in the parlor. She found Scalabrese already seated there when she came down from her room.

"Well, Miss Walton," he said with a warm smile, "I trust that you had an enjoyable morning."

"It was a beautiful morning. That is a fantastic view of the pond you have, and the foliage is spectacular."

"I agree. It is one of the reasons I built this place back when I was young. I enjoy it much more now than I did then."

Rebecca looked long at the old man, keeping his eye contact until it was clear he wasn't going to back down.

"Mr. Scalabrese…"

"Can't you call me Vincent, Miss Walton?"

"No, I can't," she retorted. "Then you will start calling me Rebecca and I don't want to get that close."

She continued.

"Mr. Scalabrese, this morning I walked around your estate, amazed at the beauty, the artistry, the imagination that is evident, not only there, but in this magnificent house. I can't reconcile it with what you do."

"What you are asking," he suggested, "is how can a man, with as scabrous a history as I have, be capable of esthetic values?"

Rebecca laughed out loud.

"Will you just listen to yourself! No mobster in the movies could get a grip on 'scabrous' and 'aesthetic' in his speech. And in the same sentence!"

"I did go to school, Miss Walton," he said flirting a bit with a twinkle in his eye. "At least you could give me credit for that."

Rebecca got serious.

"I'm sorry. That was unfair. Those are wonderful words. They just don't go with the usual movieland Italian accent. But seriously, how can you balance your two sides? I was raised a skeptic. I would like to know."

Scalabrese was silent for some time, considering the question.

"I don't balance them," he said. "I live two lives."

"Do you have a family, Mr. Scalabrese?" she asked softly.

"I did. My wife died thirteen years ago. I have three children, but they won't visit me."

He stopped and laughed.

"They do accept my checks."

It was Rebecca's turn to be silent.

"So you live alone, in this elegant place, with everything that a human could dream of? Are you able to make a decision for your other life in these surroundings?"

"Of course. Do you think I have an office in town and work 9:00 to 5:00? Really, Miss Walton. Life isn't constructed that way."

"Are you sorry for the decisions you have made?"

Once again there was pause, this time a very long one.

"When I am talking to a vibrant young person like you are, Miss Walton, I am sorry. But when I was your age, the option wasn't offered to lead a life such as you will hopefully lead. I was raised to the profession I am in, and while I am sorry, I am also a very proud man."

Rebecca leaned over and took the old man's hand.

"Mr. Scalabrese...Vincent, if I get out of whatever thing I'm in, I would like to visit you in your beautiful home. But I would never accept your checks."

She rose and left the room, not seeing the single tear that trickled down the old man's cheek.

THE TRIAL

At 9 A.M., order was called, and Judge Bigelow entered his courtroom. Once settled behind his desk he looked up and scanned the room. Prosecutor Amalfi was in place. On the defense side, Artemus Webb sat at the table alone. Behind him on the other side of the rail were Rupert and Missy Allenby, who had joined Sydney Phelps, the only three friends that Artemus could count in his life of isolation.

"Is there no lawyer for the defense?" Judge Bigelow asked.

From the rear of the courtroom, Inspector Dawes rose.

"If it please, Your Honor, I would request a conference to bring you up to date on what has occurred with the defense attorney."

There was a loud buzz in the courtroom. The jury cast uneasy glances back and forth among themselves. The prosecutor, William Amalfi, looked confused. Judge Bigelow immediately stood.

"I will meet with you, Inspector and the prosecutor in my chambers."

Once inside, the judge turned first to attorney Amalfi.

"On Thursday you said you wanted to withdraw charges in this case. Is that still the case?"

"Yes, Your Honor. Mr. Webb is undoubtedly not the murderer."

"Okay. Now Inspector, what has happened with Attorney Walton?"

"As I told you on Saturday, Your Honor, Miss Walton has been abducted. We do not think it was a kidnapping. It now appears that she was taken for her own good, to prevent others from doing her harm."

The judge sat back in his chair, now fully interested.

"For her own good? By whom?"

"We think she was taken by the local mafia."

"Oh, come now, Inspector," Amalfi protested. "That's ridiculous. The mafia is protecting her, from whom?"

"If my guess is accurate, Your Honor, we are about to find out. I am certain that Miss Walton will be in this courtroom this morning. She wants the trial to continue to expose the actual killers."

Judge Bigelow exhaled loudly.

"Alright, Inspector. I will recess this trial until 1 P.M. this afternoon. If Miss Walton hasn't appeared by that time, I will accept Mr. Amalfi's withdrawal from the case and the trial will end."

When the three men returned to the courtroom, Rebecca was sitting next to Artemus, deep in conversation. A few minutes earlier, a long white limousine had pulled up to the courthouse. A squad of armed men had jumped from two vans to protect her as she entered the courthouse. They escorted her literally to her seat.

Judge Bigelow almost smiled as he sat down.

"Miss Walton," he said, "you are late."

"I'm sorry Your Honor," she responded with a smile. "I was unavoidably detained."

"You may continue with your defense."

"Thank you, Your Honor, the defense recalls Billy Francobaldi."

Once again, Francobaldi was led into the courtroom by a police officer, since he was still being held as a suspect in the murder of Angela Maywood.

"Mr. Francobaldi, do you now admit that you purchased a gun that was identical to that of the defendant, Artemus Webb?

After a nervous pause, Francobaldi nodded, then said "Yes."

"Why would you want a pistol with the initials 'A.W' on the handle?

"I don't know."

"Mr. Francobaldi, the fact that you purchased the actual murder weapon in this case makes you the prime subject for premeditated murder. Are you willing to take that rap for someone else? Who told you to buy the gun?"

Perspiring heavily, he looked nervously around the courtroom as though asking for help. Then his shoulders slumped, and he looked up at Rebecca.

"Lodge."

"Lodge? Does he have a first name, Mr. Francobaldi?"

"Jacob."

"Why did he want you to buy that gun?"

"I don't know. He just told me to go to Hyannis and pick it up. He didn't say anything else. I took it to his office in Sandwich. That's all I know. I didn't kill that girl."

"Mr. Francobaldi, did you do other things for this Jacob Lodge?"

"No."

"Who told you to hang out at the Webb Shipyards?"

"I did that on my own."

"Mr. Francobaldi, may I remind you that you are under oath and still a key suspect in a murder trial? I will repeat the question. Think carefully before you answer. Who told you to go to the Webb Shipyards?"

"Lodge."

"What did you do when you were there?"

"I just looked around. I really was interested in the old ships."

"Mr. Francobaldi…"

Rebecca droned out his name, as a threat.

"Okay, I recruited some of the workers."

"To do what?"

"I don't know what they were supposed to do. They were just supposed to look for certain ships that were coming in for rehab. That's all I know."

"Did Lodge also tell you to institute the civil law suit against the Webb Industries?"

"No."

"Did you do that on your own?"

Francobaldi hesitated for a long time.

"No."

"Who told you to bring that suit, Mr. Francobaldi?"

"I don't know. I just know they were part of the family. And when they get involved, you do what you're told."

"What do you mean, 'part of the family'?"

"I mean the mafia. I don't know how they got involved in this, but I just did as I was told."

"Did you want to sue the Webb Shipyards?"

"Hell, no, I didn't. Do you think I'm crazy? I wanted to just disappear."

"What did Mr. Lodge think of all of that?"

"He was really pissed. He threatened to kill me, and he cancelled the suit. He told me to disappear. I did. Until you found me."

Rebecca turned and walked back to her desk.

"Thank you, Mr. Francobaldi. That will be all for now."

"Your Honor, the defense calls Jacob Lodge."

Once again, a police officer escorted the witness into the courtroom. Artemus studied the man intently, trying to bring him up to the image of the man he had met at the Harvard Club. Lodge seemed to have aged overnight, so gaunt and pale was he, with disheveled hair and a three-day beard. Even Francobaldi, whom Artemus regarded as a wimp, looked more alive.

"Mr. Lodge," Rebecca began, "what business are you in?"

"I'm an investor."

"What kind of investments?"

"Mostly stock, but I do a fair number of commodities as well."

"Are you successful?"

"I would say yes. My portfolio speaks for itself."

"Where do you bank, Mr. Lodge?"

"The First Bank of Boston. I have been there exclusively for several decades and my family before me."

"Is that your only bank relationship?"

"Yes."

"Have you ever had an account in the Shawmut Bank, Mr. Lodge?"

"No."

"Are you sure? I will remind you that you are under oath."

Fear crept over Lodge's face, and he visibly trembled.

"Perhaps I had a small account there years ago," he said, almost whispering.

"What do you consider 'a small account'?"

"I think it was just a savings account."

Rebecca went to her desk and returned with a thick folder.

"Your honor I would like to enter this as defense exhibit 10."

She turned to Lodge.

"Mr. Lodge, would you review these documents and tell the court what they are?"

Lodge opened the folder, took a quick look, and sighed, his head drooping.

"Tell us what they are, Mr. Lodge," Rebecca prodded forcefully.

"They are my bank accounts at Shawmut Bank in Pembroke."

"And, Mr. Lodge, what is the date of the top statement?"

"September, this year."

"And now, Mr. Lodge, would you tell the court what the balance amount is as of last month?"

There was a long silence.

"$743,453."

There was a loud buzz around the courtroom and Judge Bigelow called for order.

"Mr. Lodge, would you call that a 'savings account?'"

The witness looked to be in a state of shock.

"No," he mumbled.

Rebecca returned to her desk and pulled out another sheet of paper which she handed to Lodge.

"Mr. Lodge, can you tell me what this is?"

He scanned the page.

"I don't know what it is."

"Oh, I think you do. What does it look like?"

"It looks like a list of ships of some sort."

"Precisely, Mr. Lodge, and what is written next to each ship?

"A date."

"How far back do the dates go?"

He looked closer at the list.

"About ten years."

"Ten years. How long ago, Mr. Lodge, did you open your account at Shawmut Bank?"

"I don't remember."

"Well check the folder on your lap, what is the date of the first statement? How many years ago?"

He wilted completely.

"I don't want to answer any more questions."

"Just one more, Mr. Lodge. Is that first statement ten years old?"

He nodded, then quietly said "Yes."

"Thank you, Mr. Lodge. That is all for now."

The officer had to assist Lodge in leaving the courtroom.

"The defense calls Malcolm Saltonstall."

The man was the epitome of the Boston Brahman as he strode to the witness stand—confident, aloof, and arrogant. He was wearing docksiders, denims and a Harris Tweed sport coat, with elbow patches.

"Mr. Saltonstall are you familiar with an attorney, Winston Haverill?"

Saltonstall hesitated for effect.

"No, no I don't think that name is familiar."

"He was an attorney, found hanged, in Hingham. Does that ring any bells with you?"

"Oh, I think I remember reading that story. Tragic.

"It's strange you don't remember Mr. Haverill. Your name appears in his log several times before he died."

The faintest glimmer of alarm appeared briefly in Saltonstall's eyes, something Rebecca immediately noticed.

"In fact, it appears that you and he were investment partners in a Springfield firm—Murdock and Bridges."

She handed him another thick folder.

"Would you tell the court what this is?"

Saltonstall took the folder with evident disdain in his attitude. He glanced briefly at the first couple of pages.

"These are monthly investment summaries."

"Would you read the names on the top please."

"Winston Haverill."

"And?"

"Malcolm Saltonstall."

"And what is the balance on that statement, Mr. Saltonstall?"

The arrogance was now completely gone from the man.

"A million and a half dollars."

"Would you like to rethink your answer about knowing Winston Haverill?"

Saltonstall's voice was now half an octave lower than when he first took the stand.

"Yes, I knew him, as a partner in those investments. But I didn't want to get involved somehow in suspicions about his murder. I know how you lawyers work."

"Murder, Mr. Saltonstall? Did I say he was murdered? I don't think it was reported as anything but a suicide at the time. Are you saying he was murdered, Mr. Saltonstall?"

"You see, Your Honor," he said turning to the judge. "She is putting words in my mouth."

"I think you did a very good job of putting them there yourself," Judge Bigelow responded with sarcasm. Answer the question."

"I just assumed that it was a murder. That's all I intend to say about the matter."

"Mr. Saltonstall, looking through these investment reports, it appears that there are almost identical, rather substantial amounts being entered on a regular basis for more than ten years. I drew up a list of the entry dates. Can you corroborate the accuracy of this list? You can compare them with the statements if you wish."

"He simply glanced at the list and nodded."

"I'll take your word for it. The list looks reasonable."

"Can you tell the court the source of these large entries? They are around $30,000 each."

"I was constantly moving securities around. It was natural to move money into a safer investment account."

"And Haverill did the same? His investment entries are almost identical. That's rather curious wouldn't you say?"

"We were in friendly competition. We didn't want to be outdone by each other, so we always invested the same amount."

Rebecca produced the same list of ships that she had shown to Lodge.

"Mr. Saltonstall, can you tell me what this is?"

He looked at the list and gave it back to her.

"It appears to be a list of ships."

"Will you look at the dates beside each ship?"

"Why. Is it important? What in the hell am I supposed to be looking at, or for?"

"I want you to compare the dates of the ships with the investment dates I just handed you. Do you see anything peculiar about them?"

"They are almost the same dates. Just a few days off. Big deal."

"A few days off in what way, Mr. Saltonstall?"

"The investment dates are a couple of days after the ship dates."

"All of them?"

Saltonstall looked more closely this time.

"Yes."

"Now isn't that peculiar," Rebecca said with high sarcasm.

"What the hell are you getting at?" the witnessed almost screamed, turning again to the judge for help.

"Do you know Jacob Lodge?" Rebecca asked without letting up.

"Yes, of course I do. I have lunch with him practically every day."

"And do you know Michael Winslow?"

"You obviously know I do!"

"Wouldn't you say it is even more peculiar that both of those friends of yours have almost identical investment deposits on the same days as you and Haverill?"

Rebecca fixed Saltonstall with a combative stare.

"That will be all for now Mr. Saltonstall. But I will see you again on the stand shortly."

She turned to Judge Bigelow.

The defense calls Michael Winslow.

Winslow had been sitting in the back of the courtroom, placed there at Rebecca' s request by Inspector Dawes so he would be sure to hear the testimony of his two friends. He was a beaten man before he was sworn in.

"Mr. Winslow, were you in the gallery for the last two witnesses?"

"Yes," he responded weakly.

"Do I need to bring out your investment records or are you ready to testify that you had similar deposits to those of your friends, Mr. Lodge and Mr. Saltonstall?"

"You don't need to bring them out. My records are about the same."

She handed him the list of ships.

"Do you know what these ships are?"

"No."

"Are you sure? Look at them again."

He shook his head.

"Your Honor," Rebecca said, entering the list as evidence, "this is a list of ships that arrived for rehab at Webb Shipyards and the dates of their arrival. I am entering the list as evidence along with the investment dates of all three of the men just questioned."

She turned back to Winslow.

"Now, sir, you, Lodge, Saltonstall and Haverill were all paid $30,000 every time one of these ships entered Webb Shipyards. Why?"

"I refuse to answer that question. It might incriminate me."

"Those ships were carrying drugs. Isn't that right?"

"I refuse to answer that question."

"And you turned those drugs over to dealers, didn't you?"

"I refuse to answer that question."

"Darius Webb found out about it, didn't he? And you had him and his wife murdered."

"I refuse to answer any more questions."

"Oh, it's not just one murder you are facing, Mr. Winslow. It is also the murders of Haverill, and three of the shipyard workers, and Linda Webb and now Angela Maywood. Are you willing to take the blame for eight murders, Mr. Winslow?"

Winslow sat in the stand, stolid and mute. Finally he looked up at Rebecca.

"I didn't kill anyone."

It was almost a plea for help.

Rebecca recognized it for exactly that.

"No more questions."

Judge Bigelow slammed his gavel down.

"This court is recessed until 1:00 this afternoon. I will see the attorneys in my chambers now."

"Miss Walton," the judge began, "it is obvious to everyone in Boston by now that Mr. Webb is the most forgotten man in this trial. The prosecutor has been wanting to free him for three days. As have I. When are you going to bring this to a conclusion?"

"This afternoon, Your Honor. I have two more witnesses to call."

"You have been piling up felons for several days now. Is there any room left in our jails for any more of your witnesses?"

"You need cells for two more, Your Honor."

"The defense calls George Knowland."

He was a large man, 6'4" and weighing more than 260 pounds, a size that would be intimidating even if he didn't have a permanent scowl on a visage that was designed to be scary. His hair was a random scramble above an unkempt full beard. Dark eyes stared defiantly as they scanned the courtroom.

Knowland was escorted to the witness stand by two officers. He was in handcuffs, anchored to a foot manacle. Once seated the officers remained on both sides of him, while he was sworn in as a witness.

Rebecca remained standing at her desk for some time while a continuing buzz filled the courtroom. Finally, she picked up some papers and approached her witness.

"Mr. Knowland, will you tell the court the conditions of your testimony today?"

"I won't tell the court shit," he hissed.

"Then I will, whether you like it or not. Is it true that you are testifying to limit the sentence for the crimes you have confessed to?"

"I didn't do all of those murders," he mumbled.

"All of them? Did you murder Darius and Melinda Webb?"

"No."

"Did you murder Winston Haverill?"

"I hung him up, but he was already dead. I didn't kill him."

"Did you murder the three workers from Webb Shipyards?"

The witness sat there staring down.

"Yes."

"Did you murder Linda Webb?"

"I didn't blow up her car. I don't even know how to make a bomb like that."

"Did you murder Angela Maywood?"

"Yes."

Rebecca turned and faced the jury.

"So Mr. Knowland, you admit to four murders, including the one that my client Artemus Webb is accused of. Is that correct?"

"Yes."

Rebecca spun around.

"Were you present when Darius and Melinda Webb were murdered?"

"Yes."

"And Winston Haverill?"

"Yes."

"You know who killed them?"

"Yes."

"Who?"

Knowland looked up at Rebecca and sneered. Then he pointed toward the gallery.

"That man killed them."

The courtroom erupted with noise. Judge Bigelow banged his gavel several times, calling for order.

Knowland was pointing at Sydney Phelps.

SYDNEY

He didn't even move. He sat there, just a few feet behind Artemus, with a face devoid of expression.

"The defense calls Sydney Phelps to the stand."

Slowly Sydney rose, adjusted his necktie, smoothed out his suit coat, and walked casually to the stand. Artemus, his face frozen, watched as his trusted advisor calmly sat down and placed his hand on the bible and made his oath.

"Mr. Phelps," Rebecca began, "that's not really your name is it?"

"Sydney Phelps is my name," he replied.

"Let me rephrase that," Rebecca responded. "Sydney Phelps is only one of your names, isn't that true?"

He remained silent for several moments, then nodded.

"The court can't hear a nod, Mr. Phelps."

"Yes, I have used other names," he said.

"What name were you born with?" Rebecca asked.

"Sydney Phelps."

"Now, both of us know that is not true, and I will remind you only once that you are under oath. I will repeat the question. What was your birth name?"

There was a major pause before the man answered.

"I was born Samuel Maywood."

There was a loud gasp from everywhere in the courtroom.

"You are Angela Maywood's brother?"

"Cousin."

"Your cousin? And yet you had her murdered?"

"I did nothing of the kind. That idiot who just testified is crazy. I have murdered no one."

Rebecca changed the subject.

"Where were you born, Mr. Maywood?"

"I am now known as Sydney Phelps and prefer to be addressed by that name."

"But that name was stolen from someone else, Mr. Maywood. It isn't your rightful name."

"I stole it from no one. I made it up."

Rebecca went to her desk and returned with an inch-thick book.

"This is the yearbook from Amherst College in 1950. I enter it as evidence in this case. I refer you, Mr. Maywood to page 34, which is marked. Will you read the name of the student in the top left corner of the page?"

"He looked at the yearbook, and quietly answered, 'Sydney Phelps.'"

"And what is his major field? It is printed below his name."

"History."

"Sydney Phelps was hired by the Deerfield Academy the following September. Isn't that right, Mr. Maywood?"

"Yes."

"But that Sydney Phelps was you. Isn't that right? Or shall I enter the Deerfield Academy yearbook as evidence as well? Your picture is in it."

"That won't be necessary," he said flatly. "Yes, that was me who was hired by Deerfield."

"What happened to the real Sydney Phelps?"

"I have no idea. I just took his name to get the job."

Rebecca produced a newspaper article from 1953.

"Sydney Phelps' body was dug up in a tobacco field in Northampton when they were ripping the soil for a new crop. He had been shot in the head. The murder was never solved."

"That has nothing to do with me," Maywood spat.

Rebecca laughed sarcastically.

"That remains to be seen. But we are interested in other matters at the moment."

"Where did your family live, Mr. Maywood?"

"In Amherst."

"Near the college?"

"Yes, as I recall."

"At 270 Main Street, Mr. Maywood?"

"I think that was the address."

"That is the house next to the Emily Dickenson home, isn't that right?"

"I think it was."

Artemus, who had followed the questioning closely, let out a groan. That was the house where he had made love to Allison."

"Did you arrange for your cousin to seduce Mr. Webb in that house, Mr. Maywood?"

"I haven't the faintest idea what you are talking about."

"You were stalking Mr. Webb way back then, weren't you? He was only a high school student, but you were stalking him. Why?"

"Once again, your imagination is running away with you, young woman. I have no idea what you are talking about. I was Artemus Webb's history teacher, nothing more."

"Nothing more, Mr. Maywood? Nothing more? I would say you wanted his father's company and devised this incredible scheme to get it."

"You are crazy!" the man almost screamed, losing his habitual composure. He turned to Judge Bigelow. "She can't keep making accusations like this out of thin air."

The judge scowled from his bench.

"A far worse accusation has already been heard in this courtroom, Mr. Maywood. Don't look to me for support. Answer the defense's questions."

Rebecca went on.

"In Artemus Webb you had an introverted, almost completely antisocial teenager who stood to inherit his father's company if his parents should somehow die. You killed them to make that happen, didn't you?"

"I was the man's employee," Maywood stammered. "How could I possibly take over his company?"

Rebecca went back to her desk, fingered through some papers and returned to the witness stand.

"Can you tell me what this is, Mr. Maywood?'

He took the paper and glanced at it.

"It's a Power of Attorney."

"Signed by whom?"

Maywood paged through the document to the end.

"Artemus Webb."

"Can you tell the court what a Power of Attorney Is?"

"It gives a person legal power over the assets of a person or company."

"Who is the person in this Power of Attorney who gets control of Artemus Webb's company?"

"Sydney Phelps."

"So, in the instance of the death of Artemus Webb, Sydney Phelps, now known to us as Samuel Maywood, would take over the control of Webb Shipyards. Is that true?

"There is no need for you to answer that, Mr. Maywood," Rebecca stated, turning back to the jury. Then she spun back to him.

"Did Artemus Webb realize he had signed this Power of Attorney?"

"Of course he did. He wouldn't have signed it if he didn't want to. He did nothing that he didn't want to do."

Artemus jumped to his feet.

"That's a lie!" he shouted, trying to get around the table to rush at the man he knew as Sydney Phelps. "That's a goddamned lie. You must have hidden that paper in a bunch of other documents to get me to sign it."

"That will be enough, Mr. Webb, the judge yelled, banging his gavel over and over. "Sit down or I'll have you restrained."

Rebecca hurried over to Artemus.

"Artemus, please," she whispered. "Let me deal with this. You have already been cleared of this crime. Please sit down."

Reluctantly, Artemus stood there, staring arrows at the man sitting in the witness stand. Then slowly he returned to his chair where silently he continued to fume.

He nodded his head and looked up at her.

"I'm okay now, Rebecca. This is impossible to tolerate."

"I know. We're almost finished here."

She returned to Maywood.

"What is the date on this spurious Power of Attorney, Mr. Maywood?"

"You find it. I'm finished talking."

Rebecca took the document and turned to Judge Bigelow.

"May the court record the date of April 10, 1958. That is one week before the car explosion that took the life of Linda Webb. Her death was a mistake. That bomb was placed in Artemus Webb's car. It was meant for him."

Rebecca turned to Judge Bigelow.

"Your Honor, we have already heard sworn testimony from George Knowland that this man, Samuel Maywood, was the murderer of both Darius and Melinda Webb. He was also named as the murderer of Winston Haverill, and probably Linda Webb and the real Sydney Phelps. He also ordered the murders of Joey Giambo, William Brodsky, Ralph Menicotti and Angela Maywood. I ask the Court to order him into immediate police custody, and to drop all charges against my client, Artemus Webb."

"Mr. Prosecutor, what say you?" Judge Bigelow asked.

"If it please the court, the Prosecution wishes to drop all charges against the defendant, Artemus Webb."

"So ordered!" gaveled the judge with a wry smile. "Mr. Webb, you are free to go."

He turned to the bailiff.

"I assume that the halls outside are filled with police officers. Will you ask that they take this man into custody?"

Maywood, the quiet, and quite brilliant Sydney Phelps, was handcuffed and taken away by two officers.

Artemus sat at the table stunned, staring at nothing in particular. The major support in his life had just collapsed and he was in danger of being buried alive. There wasn't the slightest joy at being exonerated for the murder of Allison.

Rebecca was also without the joy that was to be expected from a major legal triumph. She knew well the damage that had been done to her client, a man who had lived literally in a social vacuum, supported only by his own brilliance and the aid of an assistant who had secretly wanted him dead.

She sat down next to Artemus and put her hand on his arm.

"I'm sorry, Artemus," she said quietly. "I know what he meant to you."

"How long have you known about Sydney?" he asked without looking at her.

"Since before that ship came in with the drugs. That's why I didn't want you to call him and tell him about the police action."

He was silent, trying to make some sense out of the impossible.

Inspector Dawes walked up to the desk and held out his hand to Rebecca.

"Miss Walton, that was a masterpiece! In one trial you have managed to just about fill the entire Boston city jail."

He turned to Artemus.

"Artemus, come on, I'm taking all of you to dinner to celebrate your release."

He beckoned to Linda and Rupert Allenby to join them. Slowly Artemus rose, straightened himself to his full height, took a deep breath. And he smiled. He took two steps toward Rebecca, held out his arms, and hugged her.

"Thank you," he murmured. "Thank you."

AFTERMATH

It was a strange emotion radiating around the table at Durgin Park, the legendary Boston restaurant. While everyone at the table was thrilled that Artemus' trial had gone so well and that he was fully exonerated from the horrible murder of Allison Fielding, as Artemus insisted on calling her, the sheer magnitude of the string of deaths that had occurred was a weight on their feelings that couldn't be ignored. Of everyone at the table, Rebecca was probably the best equipped to put everything into perspective because she was relatively new on the scene. Her remarkable discovery ability had tied all the loose ends together in a coherent package. Inspector Dawes and Artemus were having a difficult time putting those disparate elements together, especially the shocking duplicity of Sydney Phelps. The Allenbys, of course, were connected mainly by the tragic death of their daughter and weren't very much aware of all the other events involved.

Eventually the talk all came to focus on Sydney Phelps. No one at the table could persuade their mind to accept the name Samuel Maywood.

"I have known him for almost a decade," Artemus observed, shaking his head. "How can anyone maintain a role that long, and right to the very end? I trusted him with everything I had, and he worked hard to increase our success."

"Come on, Artemus," Rebecca protested, "he was letting you do the work in a business you were quadrupling in size and value. He thought that in the end, it was his wealth."

"But how could he have planned it all so far in advance? I mean, with Allison, and all of the assignments he gave me?"

"We have to admit it," Inspector Dawes broke in, "the man is probably a genius. He certainly had you and me fooled Artemus. He was a logical suspect at first in your parents' deaths, but he was so convincing I put him completely on the back burner."

"What about the real Sydney Phelps, Rebecca?" Inspector Dawes asked. "Didn't anyone around Amherst miss him? And when his body was found, wasn't anyone aware that another man had been using his name?"

Rebecca considered the question for a while.

"Apparently, the real Sydney Phelps had no close family. As for the body that they discovered, it was never actually identified because there was no missing person report."

Artemus was astounded.

"You mean you made up that whole thing about Phelps' body being found?"

Rebecca smiled sweetly at him.

"It was only logical, don't you think?"

"But how did you figure out that our Sydney Phelps was a phony?"

"Yearbooks."

"What about Haverill?" Rebecca asked Inspector Dawes, changing the subject. "Why kill him?"

It was the one thing in the case that she hadn't figured out with her investigations.

Dawes had an opinion.

"I think that when Haverill was fired, the others figured that somehow Artemus had found out about the drug ring. It might have scared them. I'm still not convinced that the three 'Harvard Club men' as Artemus calls them are not involved in some of these murders. They were certainly tied to Haverill."

"They were also as stupid as I told them they were," Artemus said. "Why would they leave such a paper trail with their cash? All of them."

"Mr. Scalabrese told me that they were amateurs," Rebecca said. "Their actions certainly back up that statement. You remember that they each got $30,000 per shipment. Mr. Scalabrese told me the heroin was worth a hundred times that amount."

Dawes laughed out loud.

"Mr. Scalabrese, is it, Rebecca? Someday you'll have to tell us about your life as a mafia kidnap victim."

"He is probably the most charming man I ever met," Rebecca said, also laughing. "And I don't often use those two words together."

"Well, he is in for a rough shock," Dawes said in a serious tone. "We netted his son in the drug roundup. He was in competition with his own father, and on his father's turf."

"Oh, he knew all about his son's involvement," Rebecca said quite seriously. "He told me it would be one less check he had to write for his kids."

The evening wore on. For more than three hours they rehashed every aspect of the trial and the events surrounding Sydney Phelps. When they had pretty much exhausted the story, Artemus raised a glass of wine for a final toast.

"Sitting in this room are just about every living person that has been important in my life. I want to thank each of you. I have been a fool to think that I could live as I have. I discovered that the morning that Linda was killed."

He nodded toward Rupert and Missy Allenby.

"When she died, I realized that I didn't have a single person in the world whom I could turn to. No one. Sydney had never been part of my private life. No one was. At that time, Inspector, I regarded you as a pain in the ass. And I had not yet met you, Rebecca."

He looked intently at each of them.

"It was the loneliest moment of my life and I was petrified."

He turned to the Allenbys.

"Rupert and Missy, you actually adopted me when I had been a complete jerk to your daughter and to you. You saved me. Thank you."

"And William," he said, using the inspector's given name for the very first time, "Out of sheer arrogance, I insulted you from the moment I met you, and it was only your persistence that has brought us to this moment. Thank you."

"Lastly, Rebecca, I have a thousand questions for you about how you compiled all that information, found all those witnesses, and unraveled a mystery that didn't seem to have a solution. You were amazing. Thank you.

"I thank each of you because individually and as a group, you have given me a rebirth, and I intend to make the most of it if I can.

SYDNEY

It was a raucous crowd of prisoners who welcomed Artemus to the jail in Boston. He had come seeking a few answers, though he didn't have any confidence that he would find them. Sydney was to be arraigned in two days and Artemus wanted to speak with him before he was either released on bail or sent to a different prison to await trial.

He found his former assistant shockingly composed, the same man he had known since high school, with the same calm demeanor that never seemed to change.

"Artemus," Sydney said as he was admitted into the conference cell, "I was hoping I would see you. With all my heart, I want to apologize to you for all I have done."

"Do you actually have a heart, Sydney?" Artemus asked gruffly. He refused to call the man Samuel. "Were you actually after my money, or were you playing some sort of game? If it was a game, you had me beat."

"I was actually living in that little house in Amherst when the idea came to me. A friend mentioned you, a bright, aloof freshman at Deerfield Academy, who wanted nothing but to learn how to make money and who was already the probable heir to a sizeable fortune. He told me that this kid, you, would socialize with nobody at the school, and would participate in nothing. I asked myself, what if I could get onto the faculty at Deerfield? Maybe I could work my way into his trust. My first crime, the one I am most ashamed of, was to assume the identity of Sydney Phelps, a young man who had just graduated from Amherst. He was quite brilliant, and I robbed him of a wonderful life. But he was perfect for my plans because he had no family and few friends from the college."

It was the most words that Artemus had ever heard Sydney speak, the most words, he mused, that he had ever allowed him to speak.

"How did you get tied up with Saltonstall and that bunch?"

"They found me," Sydney answered. "They had been working their scheme at Webb Shipyards for several years. I had ingratiated myself with your father's attorney, Winston Haverill, by using my influence over you as an introduction. He eventually put me together with Saltonstall, Winslow and Lodge who saw me as a way of insuring their drug smuggling scheme. I proposed that we get rid of your parents and bring you in, a teenager, as the head of the company. I assured them that you could easily be maneuvered."

"Did you kill my parents?" Artemus asked reluctantly, not really wanting to hear the answer.

"I did not. Your father had discovered the drug shipments and had taken his discovery to Haverill, whom he trusted. Haverill introduced me to George Knowland, who was supposed to take care of it, but Knowland said he wouldn't do it if I didn't get him into the house. I had been in contact with your father all the time that you were visiting factories and I reported to him almost daily. He was very proud of you, I might say."

"He never told me," Artemus responded bitterly.

"He didn't know how. He had raised you to be a robot and he didn't know how to change the relationship."

"I phoned your father several times the day he died and told him I was coming to Hingham and asked to meet with him. That got me and Knowland into the house. Although he denied it at the trial, he was the killer of your parents. I watched with guilt and horror."

"And Haverill?"

"That was Winslow and Knowland. When you fired Haverill, the three of them thought that Haverill was exposed and they called Knowland, whom Haverill had paid to do your parents' murders. Winslow gave Haverill a drug that killed him and Knowland set it up to look like a suicide. Winslow wrote the note blaming you."

"And Allison?"

"I'm not sure who ordered Knowland to kill her. I certainly wouldn't have done that to my own cousin. I feel great guilt in using her the way I did. I set up your seduction in Amherst and wrote that letter telling you to find her at Maddie's, but I didn't know she had written you that last letter. She was as much taken with you as you were with her."

"Why, Sydney? Why did you even get Allison involved with me and then make her disappear?"

"You said it yourself, Artemus, after you had missed her at Maddie's. Control. I could keep you dangling anytime I wanted just by bringing her back for a moment or two."

"And lastly, Linda. Who put that bomb in my car?"

Sydney who had been looking at the floor the entire time, raised his eyes to meet Artemus'.

"I did."

Artemus controlled himself with great difficulty, his body tensing. He closed his eyes and took a deep breath, then looked at his would-be killer.

"Why?"

Sydney held his gaze.

"It was the final act in my play. With you dead, I would have access to more than $150 million. It was pure greed, Artemus. Pure greed."

Artemus regarded the man with disgust.

"Do you have a wife, Sydney? A family?"

"No. In all these years you never asked to meet them. You never asked me about anything in my private life."

Artemus got up from his chair.

"One last question, Sydney. Why didn't you run? You knew that Rebecca had all the details. You even let me get involved with Saltonstall and his cronies. And you kept coming to the trial and sitting there calmly. Why?"

"It was the role I had learned to play. I suppose once you know that the game is lost, it isn't important anymore. I wanted to maintain my assumed identity to the very end. I suppose I liked Sydney Phelps better than I liked Samuel Maywood."

Artemus walked slowly out of the room, turning at the door.

"Goodbye, Sydney."

FUTURE

"I'm so proud of you, sweetheart," Sandra Walton gushed, rushing up to her daughter when Rebecca finally arrived at home following the trial. She embraced her in a long hug.

"You made quite a name for yourself, Becky," Simon Walton said. "They are saying you are the new all-star in the legal world."

"*They* don't know what they are talking about, Dad," Rebecca responded sarcastically. "That trial was over before it even began. I can't believe the District Attorney even brought it to court. The fact is, he didn't begin to do his job. He thought he had such a cut-and-dried murder; he didn't even bother to check out the murder weapon correctly."

"What are your plans now?" he asked.

"I've been offered a junior partner position with a big law firm in Boston. It's flattering, but I think I'm going to wait a while before I commit to anything. Of course, I have my 'standing position' with Artemus Webb. He is closing the sale of his shipyards for $150 million and wants to go into the land development business. He's really a little child in many ways.

It's going to be rough for him for a while since his assistant is in jail. But I think I prefer criminal law and don't want to get bogged down in commercial suits."

"Is it true that you were kidnapped by the mafia?" her mother asked, once again growing serious. "The papers made a big deal out of that."

Rebecca laughed.

"I think the correct version is that I was taken into protective custody by the mob. There is a definite story there, but it's not one that is going to get published. To be honest, I really think I am going to have a new friendship with Vincent Scalabrese."

"Rebecca!" her mother exclaimed, as usual shocked by the utterances of her daughter. "How can you? That man is a known killer. He doesn't have a moral bone in his body."

"But Mom, he really is a beautiful man. My God, he raises orchids!"

She saw her mother recoil, almost in fear.

"Relax, Mom" Rebecca said. "He's over 80. And I'm not going after him. But he is intelligent, refined, interesting, and very lonely."

"Well, he deserves the last of those qualities. I really don't want you socializing with such a man."

Rebecca laughed out loud.

"And you want me socializing with all of the rapists, cheaters, liars and thieves who are my own age?"

Simon Walton interceded.

"Now please, you two. You have been fighting battles like this since you were a pre-teen, Rebecca. Give your mother a moment's peace. Please. Tell her you have no romantic interest in Vincent Scalabrese."

"Oh, Dad, you always understood me, as nobody else has. Of course I have no interest in him, except that he is an amazing man who has lessons to teach...."

She turned to her mother, holding up her hand, palm out.

"...except in sexual things, Mom."

Then she added, quite seriously, "And he did probably save my life."

❧

Robert answered the intercom when she rang it at the massive wrought-iron gate.

"Robert, it's Rebecca Walton. I've come to pay a visit with Mr. Scalabrese."

"Of course, Miss Walton. He will be delighted to see you."

It had been more than a month since the end of the Webb trial, and Rebecca had debated whether she wanted to see the man again. Everything in her upbringing urged her to simply forget Vincent Scalabrese but she had been battling her upbringing as long as she could remember, and finally she decided to follow her instincts as she always had done.

"Miss Walton, I can't tell you how delighted I am to see you," the mafia leader said, his face aglow in his broadest smile. "I was hoping somehow that I would meet you again. I want to congratulate you on a masterful job in that trial."

"You gave me the key piece, Mr. Scalabrese. I just followed a train of logic."

"Can you call me Vincent," he asked simply. "Then I can call you Rebecca."

"It's a deal, Vincent," she said with her warmest smile. "Here I brought you a Christmas gift. I noticed when I was here on 'vacation' that you raise orchids in that conservatory outside. I think this one is called *Cymbidium angelica*, the angel orchid, perfect for Christmas."

He took the vase and plant, carefully scrutinizing it.

"It is indeed! I have only a single such species in my collection. Thank you. Now please, come and have a coffee and let us talk."

They spent the afternoon in non-stop conversation, covering every issue of the day, every subject except the law and their relative positions on either side of it. The sun was going down when Rebecca took her leave.

"This has been a wonderful afternoon, Vincent," she said, holding out her hand. "I hope we can repeat it often."

The old man grew very serious.

"That was the first time in my memory that I have talked to a young person who didn't seem to care about my past, Rebecca. My children, including the son who was exposed in your investigation, wanted to speak to me only about power or money. In one day you have become a better daughter than I deserve. Please come back."

He held out his arms and she accepted his warm embrace.

❧

Artemus was ensconced in his new office on the Hingham waterfront. When his trial was finished, he found that he couldn't bear to enter the office at the shipyard, because he had to walk past the desk that Sydney Phelps had occupied. He decided on a complete change, even before the final papers were signed on his sale of Webb Shipyards. He had rented a small building and purchased property to build a major office complex on the South Shore in Marshfield. He soon discovered that he didn't have the slightest idea of how to fill out a new staff because he had never been willing to become involved in matters of interviewing and hiring. He had called in Frank Murphy and told him he was putting him in charge of the routine business of the shipyard until he had a staff capable of taking over. And then he sat alone in his new office amazed at his complete inability to formulate a plan of action. He needed Sydney, something he had never consciously considered. Until the last couple of months, he thought that he had no need for anyone.

Finally, he picked up the phone and dialed Rebecca Walton, who had taken that position as a junior partner in the prominent law firm of Shirley, Buxton and Meschery in Boston.

"Rebecca, this is Artemus…. Oh, I'm fine. I've moved into my new offices in Hingham. I was wondering if you could come down for a meeting. I have a bunch of things to discuss with you."

They agreed to meet the following Monday morning.

Rebecca found Artemus behind an old oak desk that was cluttered high with file folders of various thicknesses. Other than his desk and chair and one additional oak arm chair, the room was empty. She stood in the doorway, mouth agape, her eyes circling the room.

"Artemus, what the hell is this? It's certainly not an office. What, if anything, are you doing?"

Artemus looked up sheepishly.

"I don't know what the hell I'm doing, and I'm even failing at doing nothing," he said trying to make a joke of it. "The fact is, I am completely unprepared for my new role in life and I badly need help."

Without a word, she walked over to the desk, pushed Artemus out of his chair and picked up the phone. She dialed 411 for information and got the number of the Dorchester Office Furniture Company. After a few preliminary questions, she said.

"Send a crew out here and furnish the office of Artemus Webb, Inc., 43774 Ocean Ave., Hingham. I want nothing cheap. I want it furnished for a man of substance. When? Well, tomorrow morning at 8:00. Any later and I'll find another company to do the work. Of course you can come by this afternoon. Thank you."

She turned to Artemus who was regarding her with complete astonishment.

"Now," she said, "let's get out of here. If you don't have anything but a desk, I assume you can't serve a cup of coffee. For Christ's sake, Artemus, you are a rich man. What the hell are you doing?"

He ignored her outburst.

"Let's go over to the East India Coffee House," he suggested. "As I say, I have lots of things to talk about."

Fortified by cappuccinos and scones, Artemus bared his soul to the young woman he still regarded as his lawyer. He had been so amazed by her defense of him that he had tripled the fee she had billed him. And he had gotten a tentative extension of her agreement to handle his legal matters on an ongoing basis.

He went straight to the major item on his list.

"Rebecca, I was raised to have nothing to do with people, to concentrate on business and let others do the mundane work. The fact is, I have almost no friends and I don't know how to do anything but make money. I need help on just about everything."

"I suppose Sydney did everything for you," she said, marveling at the naivety of this strange man.

"He even found me a wife. How would I be able to do something like that?"

"He found you Linda Allenby?" she said incredulously.

"He placed an ad in the *Harvard Crimson*."

"I don't believe it," Rebecca said, shaking her head. "Who fed you and cleaned your house?"

"Sydney found me a housekeeper and a chef."

"Do you belong to any clubs or organizations?"

"I work out in a health club."

"Doing what?"

"Lifting weights. Running."

"Do you play any sports there?"

"No."

"Do you go to church?"

"No."

"Do you have any hobbies?"

"No, my father insisted they were a waste of time."

Rebecca sat back in her chair and regarded Artemus with amusement.

"What on earth do you do with your spare time, Artemus?"

"I don't have any. I work."

"Who do you actually know by name… who's not in jail."

"You, Inspector Dawes, Rupert and Missy Allenby."

He paused, his mind stalling.

"I think that's all."

Rebecca was now astounded.

"That's ridiculous."

"I need another Sydney. Would you consider taking that job?"

"Are you kidding me, Artemus? Hell no, I wouldn't take that job. And no to the first thing too. You absolutely don't need another Sydney. You need a life. I am going to draw up a plan of attack to get you that life, Artemus. And if you say no to anything I suggest, I'll fire you. Is that clear?"

He nodded, smiling.

"Do you know that I just learned how to smile about three months ago?" he said. "Linda taught me that, just before she died, and her parents are helping now."

"You are going to start going to church. Do you have a church?"

"I was baptized at the Old Ship Church."

"Fine, and you're going to become their chief contributor. Open up that wallet of yours. Become known to the pastor. I want you to introduce yourself next Sunday."

"He already knows me. He buried my parents, but I didn't attend the funerals."

"You didn't go to your own parents' funerals? Jesus Christ!"

"Do you know any of your neighbors?"

"No."

"I want to you meet at least one neighbor a week."

"How?"

"Walk over to their house. Knock, and introduce yourself. Tell them you would like to get to know them. I will want the names of those you meet, so concentrate when they tell you their names. Write them down if you have to."

"Did you ever graduate from Deerfield Academy?"

"No, my parents were murdered so I left and began working at the shipyard."

"Call the headmaster tomorrow and make an appointment. Go back and graduate. And when you do graduate, you are going to college. We have dozens of them in the Boston area."

"I don't have time for college."

She burst out laughing.

"Artemus, you are about to close a deal for $150 million. You are already worth more than $100 million. You have time."

He changed the subject completely.

"Rebecca, I need your help in closing that deal for the shipyard. I really do."

"I can't help you with that. I'm in criminal law, but I'm with a law firm now that has more than 120 lawyers and CPAs in every imaginable area of expertise. I'll get you a contract lawyer and I'll get you a private lawyer/CPA for your business dealings. I'll set up a meeting later this week to introduce you to the partners."

They talked until early afternoon, when Artemus realized that he had not even thought about lunch.

"Have you ever had a hot dog at Joe and Nemo's?" he asked suddenly. "Could I take you to lunch?"

He paused, then continued.

"And maybe tonight we could go to Anthony's Pier Four for dinner."

Rebecca sat back in her chair, a curious look on her face.

"Artemus, have you ever asked a girl out on a date?"

He hesitated, positively blushing, and then shook his head.

"Are you asking me for a date?"

He held her gaze for a long time. Then nodded.

Rebecca jumped to her feet.

"Artemus Webb is asking me out on a date!" she exclaimed to the entire coffee house. Then she smiled at Artemus.

"Hell yes, Artemus. Let's go get a hot dog at Joe and Nemo's."

Lightning Source UK Ltd.
Milton Keynes UK
UKHW012020051119
352968UK00001B/26/P